# Dale Mayer

## SIMON SAYS...
# THINK

A KATE MORGAN NOVEL

SIMON SAYS… THINK (KATE MORGAN, BOOK 10)
Beverly Dale Mayer
Valley Publishing Ltd.



ISBN-13: 978-1-778866-20-3
Print Edition

# Books in This Series

### The Kate Morgan Series

Simon Says… Hide, Book 1

Simon Says… Jump, Book 2

Simon Says… Ride, Book 3

Simon Says… Scream, Book 4

Simon Says… Run, Book 5

Simon Says… Walk, Book 6

Simon Says… Forgive, Book 7

Simon Says… Swim, Book 8

Simon Says… Die, Book 9

Simon Says… Think, Book 10

Simon Says… Fight, Book 11

# About This Book

Vancouver Detective Kate Morgan has had bad days before, but getting a message about her long-lost brother hit her hard. She couldn't trust some anonymous source, yet neither could she let any tip slide. What if it was the one tidbit that gave her information as to what happened to Timothy, now missing some twenty-six years and counting? She would do anything for those answers.

Simon St. Laurant, the reluctant psychic and her steadfast boyfriend, knows Kate is hurting on a level he has never seen before. He understands and would do everything possible to help her, even if it pushes him out of his comfort zone with his *gift*. When a little boy contacts Simon from the other side, he's trying to be hopeful …

However, as the case unravels, it doesn't go in the direction either of them thought—or had hoped it would.

# CHAPTER 1

*Mid-December*

SEVERAL DAYS LATER Detective Kate Morgan walked into the office at ten o'clock in the morning.

Rodney looked up and smiled. "Wow, a late start for the day, *huh?*"

She groaned. "I had to stop in and see the dentist this morning." She tapped her mouth. "When Doug tackled me in the interview room, I took a blow on this side and had some cyst form," she muttered, as she headed straight for the coffee machine.

"That sounds disgusting."

"Yeah, right?" She gingerly sipped her hot coffee and winced as it washed over her mouth. "Anyway, it's all fine now." She sat down at her desk, sighed loudly, let her eyelids drop, and just relaxed. "Besides, I needed a couple days off."

"You sure did." Rodney chuckled. "The good news is, we finished the rest of the open cases. Of course the bad news is that we have more new ones to take their place."

She nodded. "There is always another case." She sighed and asked, "Anything important?"

"They're all important."

"Don't give me that," she said. "Anything major, anything different, anything unique?"

At that, Reese walked in and put a parcel on Kate's desk.

"This just came in for you."

Kate frowned at it, then opened it up. It seemed to be a wooden puzzle box. She shook her head. "I don't know why I have this."

"I don't know either," Reese confirmed, "but it's obviously addressed to you."

She frowned at the intricate box. "I hate these damn things. I hate anything that makes me feel stupid, and puzzle boxes always make me feel stupid."

"Why?" Rodney asked, as he walked over, looking at her gift. "Who's it from? How come nothing identifies the sender?"

She frowned, picked up the packaging, and nodded. "Good point."

Rodney added, "We should also have some system in place where we don't let people open parcels like these, unless we know for sure it's safe."

"I don't know that it *is* safe," she murmured, "but it's, for sure, a wooden puzzle box."

Rodney nodded, examining the gift. "I think you take out one of those pieces, and the whole thing comes apart somehow."

"You think so?" she asked. She frowned at it and tugged on one random piece. Sure enough, it came right out, and the whole thing fell apart. Inside was a small piece of paper. She picked it up, thinking it must have been some note from Simon. As she read the words, she froze. "*Uh-oh.*"

"What's the matter, Kate?" Rodney asked.

She looked over at him, the color draining from her face as she tried to speak.

He came around and snatched the note from her hand and read it. "What the hell?"

She looked at it again and frowned at Rodney.

Lilliana came over and asked, "What's going on, you two?"

"Look at the message that was inside the puzzle box." Rodney pointed at it.

"Read it," Kate muttered. "Read it out loud." Kate waited, squeezing her eyelids closed, waiting to hear the words that were now indelibly burned into her brain.

Lilliana read it out loud, as requested. "*Kate, if you want to see your brother again, time to start looking. You know what happened. You just have to think. Or maybe get Simon to help.*"

Kate swore, as her thoughts mixed and churned in her head. She stared up at the two of them. "Oh my God."

"Easy, Kate," Rodney told her. "You don't know that your brother's alive. You don't know that this isn't just some sick joke."

She stared up at him, tears in the back of her eyes, and she nodded. "I know that. … I know all of that, and yet it doesn't make a damn bit of difference. If there's any chance that my brother is alive—"

"I know. We understand," Rodney stated firmly. "We'll get to the bottom of this, honest."

She swallowed hard, even now as tears welled up in her eyes, and nodded. "Maybe, but who the hell would even know I was back to work today? Who the hell would know that my brother had gone missing all those years ago? Who the hell knows about Simon?"

Rodney and Lilliana shared a glance, then faced Kate. Lilliana said, with no mercy in her tone, "Those are questions we'll have to ask you."

# CHAPTER 2

KATE STOOD OUTSIDE her department, completely numb. She stared up at the sky, blind to the world around her, until somebody took her arm. Startled, she turned to see Simon standing there, looking at her with one of the most tender expressions she ever could have imagined. She pulled herself together and asked, "Who called you?"

He shrugged. "Lilliana."

She sighed and then nodded. "Yeah, it would be her."

"Rodney called too," he added, with a smile. "I half expected Owen to call as well, but I guess he's off on Christmas holidays, albeit a bit early. That really cuts down your team, what with Andy still on medical leave." He studied her for a long moment, obviously worried.

She groaned. "I am capable of looking after myself, you know?"

"Of course you are," he replied, as he guided her to his vehicle.

When she saw it, she said, "My car is here."

"No, it's not," he countered. "I dropped you off at the dentist, waited for you, and then drove you to work this morning."

"Oh." Confused, she looked around and realized that's probably why she had been standing here, staring at the parking lot in confusion, because she couldn't locate her car.

"I completely forgot that."

"I think you had other things on your mind." He urged her into his car and closed the passenger door for her. He got in the driver's seat, turned to her, and asked, "Do you want to go straight home, or do you want to get food?"

"Straight home."

"No," he argued, "food first."

She glared at him. "Then why did you even ask?"

He chuckled. "I wanted to see how cognizant you were of your own needs."

"I'm fine," she snapped.

"*Uh-huh.*" He didn't say anything else but headed for one of the places she absolutely loved.

They arrived quickly. As she stared up at the parking lot of the restaurant, she muttered, "I don't think I can be social."

"You don't have to be social," he stated. "We can pick it up and bring it home, but you will be surrounded by people who understand your need for silence today."

"Would she allow me back though?" she asked, looking at him. "You know what she's like. She's a force, who races through your world, fattens you up, and then leaves again, all with a satisfied chortle."

He burst out laughing at that description and nodded. "That's pretty close. Yet she does it out of love."

"Does she? I wonder sometimes," Kate shared, as she groaned, staring up at the mom-and-pop Italian restaurant.

"You haven't eaten, and, if I don't force you to eat, you won't," he pointed out, eyeing her. "At least here, I know you'll get a decent meal."

"Or I'll take it home," she muttered.

"Either way," he said, undoing his seat belt, "let's go in

and get a meal. Then we'll take some home too, so we don't have to worry about food."

"It's a weekend, but it's not a weekend," she muttered.

"I know. I've already put our plans on hold."

Her shoulders sagged, as she remembered that they had planned to take the weekend to go sailing. She didn't even know what to say. When he opened the passenger door and helped her out, she realized just how disconnected she was from the world around her.

"We'll park sailing for the moment," he said. "Right now we'll go inside, we'll eat, and then we'll go back to my place and talk."

"I don't think there's anything to talk about," she replied, as she walked in front of him.

"Good, which would imply that you ... found out who was behind this."

"How much did Lilliana say?"

"Nothing," he told her, facing her. "She just told me that it was rough and very personal. So, when I saw you standing there in the parking lot, looking lost, I realized that she was correct. I know you'll get around to telling me when you feel like it."

She groaned as he opened the double doors to the restaurant, then muttered, "You should probably find somebody who's easier to live with." At that, he turned her to him, and she caught the glint of anger in his expression.

"Don't say that," he declared in a harsh whisper. "Nobody knows the pain we have both gone through. In many ways, we are perfect for each other, because we both understand how much the other has been through."

Mama barreled out to welcome them. She scolded Simon immediately, saying he should have called ahead.

Simon smiled and explained, "If I don't get Kate to eat today, she won't eat at all. So, I brought her here. Then we'll take home some leftovers with us."

Mama immediately nodded. "Good, good, good. It's always best fresh, but, if you can't always have fresh, at least you should have leftovers."

He laughed. "Nothing quite like your leftovers, Mama."

"No, there isn't," she confirmed immediately. He burst out laughing, and she grinned at him. "Come, come," she said, as she raced him to the table farthest back, which had somehow become their table.

He seated Kate on the side where she couldn't look out. She stared at him, and he nodded. "Maybe for just this moment, you could turn it off, or at least postpone it until we get home."

She nodded, but, even then, her brain wasn't fully functioning. It rolled over with all the things she had shared with her team, to all the million questions they'd asked, and to all the things she was afraid she hadn't told them that needed to be said.

Simon immediately pulled out a small notebook and handed it to her. She looked at it, dazed. "Anything you need to write down, put it down, and try to forget it for now," he suggested.

She stared at him. "You really do know me, don't you?"

"Inside and out," he stated, with the gentlest of smiles. "And that's why I'm here right now. We can handle this. Whatever it is, we'll get there, but we'll talk about it when we get home. First, I want you to unwind and to get some food."

Her lips twitched. "You and Mama Rosa."

At that, Mama reappeared, and she had a small bottle of

wine that she immediately uncorked for them.

Kate tried to say no, but even Simon pointed out, "It would help you relax."

She sank deeper into her chair. "I'm not sure I will ever relax again."

"You will," he stated. "It may take a bit, but you will."

Under his watchful gaze, she had several sips. Before she even had a chance to do much more, Mama had returned with a basket of fresh bread and a bowl of garlic butter.

Her stomach growled immediately. Simon nodded. "And that's why we're here."

She didn't say anything, just picked up some bread, dipped it in the rich garlic butter, and popped a big bite into her mouth. If nothing else, he was right about that. She needed energy. She needed fuel for what was to come, because whatever it was, it would be painful as hell. It already was. Her heart had been ripped apart by simply reading the note, and the thought that somebody was playing games over her brother was enough to torment her for a very long time.

As much as she didn't like people as a whole, most of the time it wasn't personal. She just thought that the world was full of assholes. Simon was helping her to rebalance some of that, but every case that got nastier and crazier only reaffirmed her belief.

When she looked up at him, she shared, "Colby wants me to see the shrink on staff."

His eyebrows shot up. "And did you tell him where to go?"

"No," she whispered. "In this case, I think ... he might be right." Simon sat back.

She read the surprise in his gaze and knew that he needed an explanation, but she wasn't up for it yet.

When Mama returned a few minutes later with her little notepad, ready to take down their orders, Simon looked at Mama and smiled. "Why don't you just give us whatever the special is?"

She beamed and nodded. "And I'll get you something different to take home," she offered, with a smile. Happily, she took off at the same speed she had arrived at.

She was a force to contend with when she was on the move, and, even for the size of her, she could move. She was always happy and appeared to be very healthy, regardless of the extra weight, which was not slowing her down at all. And, wherever she was in terms of fitness, her heart was the healthiest thing about her. It was always full of love, full of caring.

Ever since her husband's nephew had drowned, they were even more interested in helping Kate out every time she showed up. Yet not a whole lot anybody could do to help her out on this one. She wasn't even sure she had anything to offer as a break in the case of her long-lost missing brother.

She'd always known that something would pop to the surface at some point, but she hadn't expected it right now. Yet here it was, right in her face. She munched away on bread, until a huge plate was set before her, filled with long pasta tubes stuffed with cheese and meat and all kinds of good things. It smelled like heaven itself.

She didn't say a word, just tucked into the food. Both Simon and Mama looked on with joy. Kate stopped eating, glared at the both of them, and grumbled, "I do eat, you know?"

Mama gave a sniff, then turned and walked away, as if that revealed everything as far as she was concerned.

Kate glared at Simon, and he smiled at her. "You're doing just fine. Keep it up."

Because the food here was just so wonderful, she didn't mind the order to eat. Mama's food was just that good. As a matter of fact, it was beyond good. "It's a great thing she opened up a restaurant. It would be a sad day for all of us if this place ever closed."

"Right," Simon agreed, "and thankfully they're doing pretty well."

"Have they ever asked you for any business advice?" He smiled over at her, and she nodded. "Of course they have. Did you bail them out?"

"Nope," he stated cheerfully. "I showed them another way to make it all work. We had to restructure a few things, but, since then, they're doing just fine."

"Of course you did," she said, with a nod. "That's so you." When he looked at her inquisitively, she shrugged. "Don't mind me, Simon. I'm just in a weird mood."

"Oh, I see it, and believe me that I can't wait to hear what this is all about."

At that, she winced and stared down at her plate again.

He added, "After you've eaten."

Not even wanting to get into the discussion of what was to come, she immediately buried herself into eating her food, hoping that maybe it would hold off his interest for now. He was right. She did need food. She didn't even remember if she'd eaten all day. The entire day had been a scramble the minute that puzzle box had arrived. She'd been a little late coming into work this morning, but that was nothing compared to what had happened once she'd gotten there.

When she couldn't fit anything else into her stomach, she groaned and sat back. Looking over at him, she noted he was doing a decent job on his meal too. "I don't know how they ever dreamed up this recipe," she muttered, as she stared down at the huge stuffed noodles on her plate, "but they're excellent."

"It's what they do," Simon stated, "and, luckily for us, they're very good at it."

She couldn't argue with that. When Mama came back again, she looked at the amount of food on her plate and frowned. Yet Kate held up a hand. "If I hadn't eaten so much bread, I might have gotten down more pasta," she admitted. "However, both are divine." Instantly Mama's face beamed, and Kate knew she'd said the right thing.

"I'll pack this up for leftovers," she said, and she turned and looked at Simon. "Do you still want to take more food home?"

He nodded. "Yes. If nothing else, neither one of us wants to worry about food tomorrow."

"Or the next day," Kate muttered.

"In that case," Mama declared, "I'll send you home with enough." Then she bustled away, only to return a little later with a huge bag. "Make sure Kate eats," was her final word, and Mama was off again.

Kate stared at the bag, then frowned at Simon. "Somehow I must not have noticed that six of us are living at your place," she muttered. "This has got to be enough to feed my entire team."

"And, if need be," he suggested, "we can always bring in the team, and you can feed them too."

"Hell no," she argued. "That would start something that would never end. Most of them don't eat half the time either." Instantly Simon frowned, and she waved her hand. "It's fine. We're used to it."

"Being *used to it* doesn't make it right."

She sighed. "Whatever. I'm good to go home, whenever you're ready."

He immediately stood up and helped her out to the vehicle. She wasn't an invalid, yet he was treating her as if she were delicate. Not so much that she would blow up about it, not when he knew that something had hurt her so deeply that she wasn't sure if recovery was even possible—or, if it was, how to take even the tiniest step toward it.

He drove straight home and once again helped her to the penthouse elevator, holding the big bag of leftovers and extra food in his arms. Harry saw them and raced over to help, taking the food bag.

Only then did Kate realize that Simon was half supporting her.

Simon smiled his thanks to Harry and noted, "She had a pretty rough day at work."

Harry nodded immediately. "I can't imagine many good days in her job," he muttered. And, with that, he followed them up to Simon's penthouse apartment to leave the bag and then stepped back out again.

As soon as he left, she looked over at Simon. "I don't know why I'm so affected."

"Yes, you do. You just expect to be stronger."

She winced at that. "I should be stronger."

"No," he said, with a smile. "Being strong sometimes is normal. Being strong all the time, particularly when some personal blow is happening, is not. At times you must bend a bit to maintain resilience. Then other times you must bend before you break, and that is today."

SIMON SETTLED KATE on the couch, popped open another bottle of wine, and brought her a glass. She reached for the glass and took a sip without even arguing this time, as he watched from the sidelines.

When he retrieved his glass and rejoined her, he said, "Now give me the gist of it."

Simon sat close enough to touch but not in her space, trying to give her enough room to get out whatever it was that had gone on. He'd heard a little bit of it from Lilliana, but she had also mentioned how it was best for Kate to tell him herself. The way Lilliana had prepared Simon like that suggested that Kate needed him right now, more than ever.

And finding her standing in the parking lot—staring around, completely lost, as if whatever happened had affected her on so many levels that she was incapable of functioning—meant that it was something huge. As he looked at her right now, he realized it really was true. Whatever had hit her was personal, and that could only mean something about her brother. He reached out a hand and laced his fingers with hers. "Anytime," he urged.

She looked at him, and then tears filled her eyes.

Good, that was one of the things she needed to do. Then he just waited and waited.

Finally she took a deep breath and rubbed her face. "A parcel was delivered to my desk this morning," she began. "A little wooden puzzle box was inside. And honestly, I hate puzzles because …"

"Because if you don't solve it, you feel stupid," he added.

Her gaze flashed up to his. Then she slowly nodded. "Exactly. I rarely, if ever, solve them. They're just not my thing, and I feel completely intimidated by them."

"Okay, so somebody delivered you a puzzle."

"Yes, but it wasn't hard to open. At my first try, it just fell apart in my hands. Maybe it was supposed to. ... I don't know. Forensics has it right now. A note was in it." She repeated the message in the note, her tone almost devoid of emotion, so cold, so empty, as if to feel anything would be so heartbreakingly painful that it would cause her to shatter.

When he heard the words in the note and understood the meaning behind it, his own heart squeezed hard, and he realized what a shock this had been for her.

She took a deep breath and continued. "Then, after that, came a million questions from my team. They had to interview me for absolutely everything they possibly could think of. Questions I didn't want to answer, questions that I'm not sure I answered correctly," she admitted, with a wave of her hand. "How does one answer correctly after so many years? It's been so long, yet not long at all. I keep that file on my desk as a daily reminder."

"And do you have it at home?"

She blinked several times at him. "I have a digital copy, so I can access it anytime."

"Good," he replied. "You mentioned sending it to me at one point in time, but I don't think you ever did."

"I will now." She scrubbed her face again. "I just hurt on levels I didn't even know I could hurt from."

"Tell me why you hurt," he prompted her, eyeing her curiously. "That would help me understand just what's going on."

Surprised, she shook her head. "I don't understand."

"Are you hurt that somebody is playing games with news of your brother? Are you hurt that potentially you've missed something on your brother's case? Or is it just the fact that this has brought it all back up again?"

"Any and all of the above," she declared. "Nothing is easy about this, and I could do nothing to even prepare myself for it. What if somebody is using my brother as a game? I don't know if that's the biggest thing for me. I can't help but wonder whether he really does know something, or there's something else involved here."

She took a moment and then sighed. "And, if he knows something, damn it all, … I want him in my interrogation room, and I want him in there now. If he doesn't have information, what's his purpose for doing this?"

"To hurt you," Simon stated, "to send you off balance, to take you off your game, to stop you from looking into something else."

That set her back in shock.

Simon nodded. "At the moment you're still caught up in whatever this asshole wants you caught up in mentally. That is the one thing you must consider, at least in the sender's mind. Maybe he knows nothing, and, by keeping you fully occupied on this, he's doing something else and trying to get away with it."

Her breath let out with a hard *whoosh*. "Good God." She stared at him in shock. "I was so hung up on it being about my brother and somebody knowing something that it never even occurred to me that it could be just a diversion, a distraction."

"So then, a distraction from what? And what kind of a diversion would be a good strategy to get you off your game? So who would know enough about what's going on in your world, or the work that you do, to realize that this would be a good strategy?"

"Those are the questions I need answered," she replied immediately. "Other things too, such as, does he know about

Timmy being missing, and how would he have gotten that information?"

Simon shook his head. "So much is available on public files, newspapers, and missing person's databases, it probably wouldn't have taken very long to get it. Honestly, if they were looking for something to pin you with or to put you off balance, they found it. Whether he realizes it or not, it was the absolutely perfect thing to do to you. On the other hand, you aren't alone, and you have people around to help you get through it."

Her breath let out once again in a hard *whoosh* as she stared at him. "But what's wrong with me that I never even considered that?" she cried out.

"Nothing is wrong with you," he snapped, his tone hardening. "Don't even go down that pathway. You would have thought of it eventually. I just brought it up sooner. You needed time to absorb everything. Then bringing back all the heartbreaking memories with your team asking you a million questions, of course that set you off further, sending you down the pathway that would have terrorized you. It would have terrorized anybody."

He patted her hand, and she looked at him, misery in her expression. He asked her, "The thing is, ... why he did it is part of it, but does he know anything about Timmy? Or is it literally somebody just playing games?"

"I don't know," she muttered, freeing her hands to rub her temples.

He could see that she was starting to get angry, but Kate being Kate, it wouldn't be at anyone except herself. "You don't get to trash yourself over this." Her hands dropped, and she glared at him. "That's bound to be your immediate response."

"Of course it is," she muttered. "I mean, if it's something major going on that they want to hide, then they're using me as a decoy. ... Now that we have so much of the team's attention on this, it makes sense in a really sad way."

"And everybody jumped in to help you," he noted, "so that should make you feel better."

"Feel better?" she muttered. "I don't know if that's quite the right wording."

"Another thing you also need to remember is that you're not alone this time, and that you're not a child anymore. You are not responsible for what happened, and you now have skills and resources behind you."

She took a deep breath, giving him half a smile. "That is exactly what I needed to be reminded of."

"Park that child from the past," he suggested. "She can come out and cry whenever she needs to, but she also needs to know that she isn't alone and that people are there for her now."

"It also means," she added, "that I'll have to speak to my mother."

He felt his own insides twisting at that one. "Or," he offered with a smile, "you send Rodney to do that job."

"My mother's always been kind of a charmer with men," Kate pointed out, "so I'm thinking that would be a bad idea."

"Then send Lilliana," he suggested. "She doesn't take shit from anybody, and, if truth be told, she would see through your mother very quickly."

"Honestly ... maybe I'm doing Rodney a disservice by thinking he wouldn't. ... I'm just—"

"You're afraid," he said immediately. "You're afraid of what your mother would say and how they would view you, after spouting off all her poison."

Kate shuddered, closed her eyes, and then nodded. "God, we're so ..." But she couldn't come up with the word, so he supplied it for her.

"We're vulnerable," he muttered. "That's all. We're vulnerable, and the people who want to hurt us will strike out to catch us at the very lowest times in our lives." He hesitated, then added, "Like now."

# CHAPTER 3

KATE WOKE UP the next morning, feeling a little bit more like herself. Lying in bed, she did a quick evaluation. She was upset that she'd been so easily thrown, yet Simon had been correct. Anything to do with her brother, particularly in this way, would have sent anyone in her situation into a spiral.

She was back to herself now, at least she hoped she was, and needed to get back to work. She had to get to a place in her head where she understood the job that needed to be done. She also had to gear up for a fight, as she knew Colby would try to take her off the case. That wouldn't work. She would walk. She suspected they already knew that, but it wouldn't change anything for the moment.

She got out of the shower and quickly dressed and headed to the kitchen, Simon was already there waiting for her. He looked up, assessed her closely, and then smiled. "There she is."

"I'm back," she stated with a nod, only to pause to open her mouth to thank him.

Simon immediately shook his head. "No."

"No what?" she grumbled. "Why can't I thank you?"

"Because it's not necessary between us," he murmured. "I was just doing what any decent human being would do."

She snorted at that. "Including the lovemaking afterward?"

His grin flashed in her direction. "I just thought that might help take your mind off of life."

"Yeah, it sure did," she muttered, with a wave of her hand. "Just make sure that's not a remedy you're passing out to everybody else you're trying to help." He burst out laughing, and she grinned. "It does feel better to be back. It was a pretty-rough night, but, waking up, I feel ..." She stopped, considering the right word for how she felt. "*Centered*, if that makes sense."

"Centered is good," he agreed. "Centered is very good."

She smiled. "I have no idea what today will bring," she warned.

"Nope, I get it," he noted, with a smile. "I do want you to send me a copy of the digital file you have."

"Oh, right." She frowned at him and asked, "Any particular reason?"

"Yeah, if I can do anything, I want to help."

She had to think about that because it was so hard for her to let anybody in, but, if he could help, well ...

"And, yes," he added. "I know you don't really want my help, if you don't have to, yet ..."

"Yet," she interrupted, choking up as she walked closer, taking the chair across from him, "I would do an awful lot to get this case solved. I *need* this solved."

"And I hear you," he murmured. "Let's just keep it to that."

She smiled and nodded and went through her phone, then quickly emailed him a copy of her file on Timmy. "That should be all you need," she said.

"Good, and I will stay in touch throughout the day, just to ensure that all is well."

"You'll have to," she shared, standing and walking to the coffee machine, where she programmed a cup, "because I'll probably get so busy that I won't even think to update you."

"I know," he said. "And, considering that this is as tender of a topic as it is, any updating that you can do on your mental health would make me much less of a basket case, should you be thinking of ignoring me."

Picking up her cup, she turned and stared at him.

He nodded. "Hey, it's what happens when you start caring for people," he noted.

Her shoulders sagged, and she nodded. "I do owe you that."

"No," he declared, immediately bristling at her tone. "You don't owe me anything."

She raised both hands in frustration. "Look. You know I suck at relationships. And now, dealing with this Timmy note, obviously everything I say will set off alarms for somebody right now," she muttered. "So let's just forget that I'm even talking. If I could go back to bed, I would, but obviously that won't happen for a very long time. Thus, I would very much appreciate a little bit of ... leeway."

"Leeway works," he agreed. "I'm not here to make your life difficult."

"So far," she groaned, rolling her eyes, before taking a sip of coffee, "you've been the one person instrumental in making my life move in ways I hadn't thought possible. I just need you to understand that I appreciate it all."

He nodded. "Fair enough. Do you want me to drop you off at work?"

She immediately shook her head. "No." She sipped her coffee again before wincing, as it didn't hit the spot. "I believe my wheels are here. I can head out on my own."

He nodded. "They are."

"Okay, I want them at work with me," she replied. "I have no idea where today will take me, but I want to be prepared, just in case." Walking over to him, she wrapped her arms around him, and they shared a quiet hug. "And thank you again." Making sure she didn't stay in the hug too long or put too much emphasis on the *thank you* part, she immediately walked into the elevator, ignoring his call for her to have breakfast. "I'll grab something later," she called back.

And, with that, she raced to her vehicle and headed to the office. As she walked in, most of her team was already assembled. Rodney immediately looked at her and frowned, so she frowned right back. "I am not leaving this to you guys," she declared.

"I'm not sure you should be anywhere close to it though," Colby replied, coming out from his office.

"Maybe not, but Simon made a very good point last night," she noted, as she looked around at her team. "He wondered, and I think it's valid, if this could merely be a distraction to pull away our attention from something else."

All three of her team members looked at each other and then back at her. Their boss Colby nodded as well.

"It's possible," she stated, with a nod. "I don't have any way to know that obviously, but somebody is yanking my chain. He potentially knows just enough from the public records to pull that information together, and I guess it wouldn't have taken all that much for a phone call to be made to the department to see whether I was here or on days off, and when I would be back in," she explained. "So, yes, this could be all about my brother, and it could be something completely different."

"That's an interesting concept." Colby looked around at the team. "Thoughts?"

Rodney immediately shook his head. "No idea," he replied, "but, if this came from Simon, I would say that would be very valid. I don't know why anybody would try to do something like that to Kate though."

"Other than to hurt me, then deception works," Kate pointed out, "but it's something we need to keep an open mind about. It is a possibility though. And, for that open mind part, we definitely need to be on the lookout for this being something completely twisted and bizarre."

Colby shook his head and sighed. "It seems as if everything nowadays with you is twisted and bizarre."

"And here," she replied, with half a smile, "I thought only Simon's cases were that way."

"Maybe," Colby conceded. "It's definitely a consideration right now."

"I'm not trying to get in anybody's way," she added, "but I do worry that this isn't what we are really looking at. Yesterday I wasn't thinking straight," she admitted, as she looked around the room. "And I gave you as much information as I could. However, I'm quite sure I missed a bunch, so I will spend some time this morning, getting some of that down on paper. I think the bottom line right now is that we can't rule out that something else is brewing, and, for whatever reason, either they want me off the case, or completely out of the office," she suggested, turning to look at Colby, "or just looking elsewhere."

Colby nodded. "I'll take that up with the brass. Of course I had to update them this morning, and there have been calls for you to take some time off and to let us as a team go through this."

"Of course there has, and I get that," she said, "and, if you do that, I'll hand in my resignation right now."

He winced. "Somehow I figured you would say that."

"No way this is going on around me without my being involved," she declared, staring him down. "I get it. We have liabilities, and we have things that need to be sorted in terms of making sure the case sticks, if it goes to court. But it's also very important that whoever is playing these games doesn't get a free pass, just in case it is simply a diversion."

"You won't make it easy, will you?" Colby asked, staring at her glumly.

She gave him a brilliant smile. "You wouldn't want me to either. That same tenaciousness I use on these cases is exactly what I'll apply to this one. This asshole, whoever it is, doesn't get to get away with this," she announced. "No way, not now. This asshole is mine."

"Yet we can really do nothing if that is what the person who delivered the puzzle box is after," Lilliana pointed out. "It's just something that we must keep in mind on the side."

"Exactly," Kate agreed. "So, did you guys get anywhere with any of the research overnight?"

Rodney smiled and spoke up. "We checked the cameras around the department, and it was delivered by a young teenager. He doesn't seem to have anything to do with it, but we are working to track down his identity, as it was dropped off for you personally. Reese has her assistants tracking the kid on the street cams and hopefully we'll see where he goes. Forensics has the box, and they haven't found anything as of yet, but we have pulled all the files in regard to your brother's case. Plus, I have a list of people to contact over Timmy's disappearance." When she winced at that, Rodney nodded. "It'll be painful, but no other way to make it happen."

"Agreed," she muttered. "I know it'll be painful, and, with any luck, maybe it will finally bring in some info. Living with the constant lack of closure, the constant not knowing what's going on and who could possibly have done this, is heartbreaking," she murmured.

"And you really have no idea who would be involved?" Lilliana asked.

Kate shook her head. "No, I really have no idea. I was seven. Timmy was five. We went to the same school that he was taken from. I've thought of this case for years. Who could it be? Who could have done this? Whose MO was to steal children from schoolyards? And I've gone through everything I could find, everything I could remember, over and over, looking for a link."

"A complete stranger could be involved," Rodney suggested.

"Yes, of course."

They all nodded.

"That would be the hardest to solve," Lilliana noted.

"Especially after all this time," Colby added.

"Exactly," Kate replied, "so anything that you guys can do would be absolutely wonderful, and, if it turns out some asshole is just yanking my chain for some reason, I would really like a few minutes alone with him," she shared, her jaw firming up.

Colby snorted. "Now *that* you won't get."

"But you could let me have just two minutes," she repeated, looking at him with a serious expression, but still a twinkle was in her eye.

He shook his head. "No, not happening, and Simon doesn't get a few minutes either."

"I'm kind of hoping that"—she rolled her eyes—"he can help us out."

Rodney turned to her. "Will he try?"

"I think so," she said, carefully watching Colby and gauging his temperature. "I know Simon was pretty upset for my sake."

"Of course," Rodney agreed, with a smile. "Yet we also know that he can't always connect."

"No, he can't always connect, and often you don't want him anywhere close," Colby noted, "because the last thing we want is to disclose the fact that a psychic helped us out."

"Yeah, especially this psychic," Kate muttered, with half a smile, "because he really doesn't want anything to do with that part of his world. He's getting a little bit better at controlling it, so maybe that's all good. Still, it's not easy on him."

"Of course not," Rodney added, "but he does a hell of a job."

"When he has information, whatever that information is," she noted, "I have certainly come to listen to it now. I don't like the questions about it. I don't like being asked whether it's valid, not valid, or anything else. All I can tell you is that, when he says, *Move*, well, … I tend to move."

"Yeah, you mean like when that house blew up?"

"Right," she agreed, "like the house that blew up."

"There is a method to that psychic madness," Colby confirmed, and, seeing her stare, he raised his hands. "As long as he keeps you guys alive, I'm all for it. Still, he's not an excuse for shoddy detective work. He can give us directions. He can give us concepts and thoughts, maybe things to consider, but no way can we rely on him solely to get the job done." He looked back at Lilliana. "You had a suggestion in terms of Timmy, her brother's case?"

She nodded and turned to Kate. "Do you want to be part of a discussion with your mother?"

Kate winced. "I thought about that the whole way in today. We have nothing to do with each other, but whoever goes will get an earful about me."

"Yeah, I was thinking I could go," Rodney offered.

She stared at him and shook her head. "I understand why you would think that, but she will eat you alive. I would say Lilliana is the best person to talk to her." Kate grimaced when she witnessed the flash of hurt in Rodney's gaze.

"I agree," Lilliana said. "From what I saw in the transcript," she noted, "she's a man-eater, isn't she?"

"Men can do no wrong—well, some men. Yet all women can do no right. Just being female, you'll totally piss her off," Kate shared. "My mother would try to charm Rodney, whereas you? ... You will get information, and it's information we need."

"Good," Lilliana stated, with a knowing smile. Then she laughed. "I think I should take Rodney with me."

"Do that," Kate agreed. "I tell you, if there was ever a good cop, bad cop scenario already preordained, it's this one."

"Is she that bad?" Rodney asked. "She's your mother."

Kate groaned, as she stared at him. "See? You think every woman who gives birth is Mother Theresa. You're a pushover. And that's why Lilliana is going with you." He glared at her, and she nodded. "I get it. You think that I'm just being a hard-ass and that I don't really understand my *poor mother* and all the rest. So you'll have to make your own decisions about this one. I can't help you with that. Yet I spent my entire childhood believing that I was the absolute worst child ever for losing my baby brother and that there was absolutely no hope for me … ever."

"She blamed you, didn't she?" Lilliana asked, with a hard tone.

"Of course she did. There was nobody else. There wasn't anyone we could point a finger at. So, it was all me, as far as she was concerned. I took the blame, and I think for a while there I may have even been a suspect, although that could have just been my traumatized juvenile brain on overdrive," she muttered.

"Yet we see and hear of cases around the country," Colby pointed out, "where all kinds of child kidnappers are loose out there, and their targets get younger and younger every day."

Kate nodded. "And this was what? Twenty-some years ago now?" she noted, with a shake of her head. "God, it's hard to believe it's been that long. Anyway, I'm available for questioning, and please go talk to my mother and see how far you can get."

"Are you sure you don't want to come?" Lilliana asked.

"Not unless she refuses to talk to you," Kate replied, "because any interaction between the two of us would be …" She stopped and added, "No, no, that's not fair either."

"What's not fair?" Colby asked, staring at her.

She looked over at Lilliana. "I might need to go."

"Will it make it easier for your mother to talk?" Lilliana asked.

Kate let out a long sigh. "In my mind, I can see her completely blowing up when she sees me. So, if you can't get her to talk, having me along for the ride is likely to blow it all wide open."

"Perfect," Lilliana declared. "In that case you come and

stay in the car. But it's my investigation and my interview, you got it?"

"Got it," Kate agreed.

# CHAPTER 4

W HEN THEY PULLED up in front of Kate's mother's
address, Lilliana looked over at Kate. "Is this the
house where she lives?"

"No idea," Kate muttered. "Last I heard, she was somewhere on the east side."

"How bad was your life back then?" Lilliana asked.

"Bad, worse. … Nothing quite like a single mom desperate to find a life again, busy off doing other things and
blaming her remaining child for what happened to the other
one," Kate explained calmly. "Foster care was a relief in a
way. Being an adult has helped give me a slightly different
perspective than my childhood version, but not nearly
enough."

"No, of course not," Rodney agreed. "I can't imagine."

"No, especially not if you had two beautiful well-
adjusted parents, with the requisite two kids and white picket
fence around the perfect little house. That's something that I
never even knew existed until I was an adult. And, even then,
really only Simon has made me see that such a scenario really
happens for some people." When Rodney stared at her in
obvious surprise, she shrugged. "I've spent my entire life not
understanding what a family is," she shared, "and Simon is
very much about family."

"Even though he doesn't have any?"

"Yeah, even though he doesn't have any," she confirmed. "At least he has friends, only now unfortunately some aren't friends at all."

"Right," Rodney whispered. "That was tough on him, wasn't it?"

"It's been tough for a long time for both of us," she admitted, "but we made the best of it because that's what we do."

He nodded. Lilliana looked at Kate and added, "Let's go see what the fuss is all about."

"Do you want me to come in with you initially," Kate asked, "or do you want me to come in later?"

Lilliana thought about it and then replied, "Stay in the car for now. We'll go talk to her, and, if she doesn't want anything to do with us, or if she's not forthcoming, I'll send you a text, asking you to come join us."

"Will do." Kate sank back into the car, almost with a sense of relief. As much as she wanted to solve this issue with her brother, the last thing she wanted was to get in contact with her mother. Some people needed to be avoided, and some relationships just needed to not exist. And, for Kate, this was one of them.

Rodney looked at her. "Be prepared. Now that this door is opening, she may want a relationship."

Kate smirked. "Yeah, that's not happening."

He winced. Lilliana pulled his arm and said, "Come on. Let's go see what we can find out."

Kate watched as the two of them walked up to the front door of the big apartment building, hoping to avoid buzzing in. Just then the door opened, and somebody else walked out. They took the opportunity to step in, which was good because, if Kate's mom was at home, they would be one step up in terms of catching her by surprise. It was hard for Kate to even remember her mother in many ways.

When they disappeared from view, Kate stared out at the neighborhood. It wasn't bad. It was a small complex in a poor area of town, but that was okay too. Had her mom married again? That would feel very strange as well. Just the thought of her having remarried, and potentially, God help her, having more kids, was enough to put Kate immediately on the edge of her seat, somehow hoping that her mother wouldn't even be there to answer the door.

It wasn't long before Kate got a text from Lilliana, asking her to come up.

She groaned and muttered, "Here we go, for better or for worse, *Mom*. Let's have a face-to-face meeting for the first time in ..." Kate stopped to think about it and then realized she didn't have an answer for how long it had been. *Forever* worked.

And, with that, she strode up to the apartment, where she found Lilliana and Rodney trying to convince somebody to open the door. Kate walked up to it, stuck her face right into the glass window where she could see inside, and yelled, "Open the fucking door, *Mom*."

With that came a gasp of shock on the other side. The door suddenly opened, and a hand smacked Kate hard, right in the face.

"You bitch, what the hell are you doing back here again?" her mother yelled.

"Look at that." Kate gave a hard smile, ignoring the sting on her cheek and the horror on Rodney's face. "Just think. You wouldn't open it for the police, but you'll open it for me. Your heart is getting bigger."

"I won't open it for you again. What the hell are you

doing, making some complaint against me?"

"No, hardly that," she said, with a forced smile.

"I know that you aren't with the police because no way anybody would have hired you. You're nothing but a loser," she snapped, glaring at her. "So, what the hell do you want from me?"

Kate turned, looked at Lilliana, and said, "Over to you." She smiled at the shock on Rodney's face. "Remember, Rodney, that perfect family with the white picket fence? I didn't even know it was a thing until I became an adult." And, with that, she announced to all of them, "I'll wait out here."

She turned and took a few steps to leave Lilliana and Rodney there to talk to her mother. Kate was still in the hallway, her eyes closed, as she listened to her mother screeching inside. Kate smiled, reassured that nothing had changed. Her mother was still the same, and Kate had nothing to worry about when seeing her after all. In fact, this was way too entertaining. And, damn it, Kate was glad she'd come.

***

SIMON HAD TO admit that he kept one ear tuned to his phone all day. He wasn't sure what was going on in Kate's world, but he kept getting a really weird vibe. He wanted to call her and to demand to know what was going on, why he was getting these weird messages. Yet he also knew it wouldn't be welcomed, and, depending on what she was doing, it could be quite intrusive.

It was damn hard because he wanted answers, but he also knew that she wanted answers too. Of all the people capable of getting answers, Kate was at the top of the list.

The woman was dynamite. She was also a bit of a bull in a china shop right now, but that was hardly the point. She was resilient, and, when she got a hold of something, she just wouldn't let go. And, for all the people who had reasons to be grateful for her, another whole group probably hated her for those same things.

He was all about keeping Kate moving in the right direction, for her own peace of mind. And this case needed to be solved for a very long time. A disappearance from so long ago had all kinds of potential repercussions, and none of them were great. He would do anything he could to help Kate bring this to a peaceful conclusion, regardless of what the outcome was. Having no answers had to be the worst.

With that reminder, he checked his surroundings, closed his eyes, and called out to the ethers, *Timmy, your sister Kate is worried about you and wants to hear from you.* Simon waited to see if that would work. Then he waited a bit more. Sighing, he vowed to try again. His grandmother connected to the spirit world somehow, so he would too—eventually.

He kept working through the day, going from rehab project to rehab project, even stopping to deal with the pending criminal case regarding Bartlett's death, fielding several phone calls. That issue finally neared resolution, though he wasn't looking forward to testifying in the court case against Bartlett's not-so-lovely wife. However, Simon would do it for Bartlett's sake. Nobody deserved to be pushed out a window like that.

As Simon walked into the next rehab project, he looked up to see his foreman Joe arguing with someone Simon didn't recognize. He frowned and walked closer, trying to get the gist of the argument. It very quickly became evident that the quality of the subcontractor's work wasn't up to standard. The subcontractor snarled at Joe, telling him that nobody could deliver what the foreman was fighting for.

At that, Simon strode closer. Joe turned to see him and raised both hands, stating, "The quality of the workers is getting worse every year."

"Maybe," the subcontractor conceded, "and maybe the employers are just bigger and bigger assholes."

"What is the issue?" Simon asked, not sure what they were fighting over.

At that, the subcontractor, a welder, kept snapping that what Joe asked for was impossible. Simon eyed the subcontractor, then walked over to the job needing to be done and immediately picked up the welder and donned a shielded welder's hat and started working. It didn't take him long to complete the job, all as per the code required and as they needed.

He replaced the equipment, then looked over at the welder and stated, "If you don't know how to do this, maybe it's time you went back to school. This is pretty much the standard in our world, and it's all about quality. We don't accept any shoddy work, so either pick up your game or get the hell out." And, with that, Simon turned and walked off. He heard his foreman chortling, but then Joe snapped at the welder.

"That's the boss. He's the one who hires. He's the one who fires. However, in this case, I'll save him the trouble and just throw your ass out of here."

Simon had a smile on his face as he made his way back down to the ground floor, then headed across to the coffee shop. He was damn sorry he and Kate weren't heading out on the boat this weekend. He could really use the time away, especially with Kate. And he knew she could too, but no way she would leave with this Timmy mess going on. If nothing else, she needed some time from the stress and the thought of having to reconnect with her mother. Family could be both good and bad, but, when it came to this shit Kate had for family, the drama was brutal.

Simon kept checking his phone for anything from Kate but found nothing.

When his turn came in the coffee shop line, he quickly ordered, glancing around. How weird that Dr. Burnett was no longer on Simon's radar, no longer here getting coffee. Dr. Burnett would not be an issue in anybody's life anymore. And that just brought more reminders of what people were like, the bad people. Between Dr. Burnett, Kate's mother, Bartlett's murderous wife, and Simon's own childhood, it was amazing Simon and Kate had any compassion for the world at all.

It was a pretty messed-up place out there, a case of making the best of what they had. He had sympathy for those who had experienced something great and wonderful but no longer could find it. Whereas he and Kate had never had anything great at all, and never thought something like that was possible. And yet, having found happiness together now, they both paused and wondered if it was even real. Reality was something both of them dealt with in a patently harsh way.

As he picked up his coffee, hoping to go outside and sit for a few minutes, his phone rang. He glanced down, not recognizing the number, and he didn't answer. When it rang again from a different number, one in his Contacts, he picked up. "What now?" he asked in a brusque tone to the realtor, the obnoxious one who stalked him, trying to get him to work with her.

Ariel snapped, "Why don't you ever answer my calls?"

"I answered this one. However, if you persist in calling me from a number I don't know, I won't answer it," he stated, a bit more snappish than he intended. "Why can't you remember that?"

She groaned. "I did. That's why I called you back."

"Good. Maybe, at some point in the future, I'll get you trained."

Silence came on the other end. Then she snorted. "You're the only one who can get away with saying that shit."

"No," he argued, "it's not shit. It's all about managing what is important to me, which is not to be spammed by people who waste my time," he explained. "I answered this telephone number because I knew who it was. So, if you want to get a hold of me, you'll play by those rules."

"So many rules with you, Simon."

"Maybe. I don't even know why you need a second phone. That always makes me think of a criminal element," he snapped into the phone.

She groaned. "I try not to use this phone very much," she shared. "I'm in the midst of an ugly divorce."

He winced at that. "I'm sorry to hear that, but, if you don't clear your new phone number with me, I'm not answering it."

"The one that you just didn't answer," she replied, with a note of humor in her tone, "is my new phone."

"I'll take that under consideration," he said. "Now, why are you calling?"

She groaned. "Are you always this snappy?"

"No, not always, as you very well know. Sometimes I'm worse." She burst out laughing, which tugged a reluctant grin onto his face.

"Fine," she said, still chortling. "At least you're honest."

"Yes, I am definitely honest," he confirmed. "I presume you have a house you think I might be interested in."

"A house?" she repeated.

Simon frowned at that because a house was not what he'd been thinking of at all. *A property*, he clarified, if only in his head.

"A house?" she muttered.

"No, I'm not talking about a house right now," he stated. "Why did you call?"

"I called because the owners of one of the properties you keep an eye on just dropped the price."

"Yes, but, if they haven't dropped it enough, I'm really not interested."

"You could wait until I tell you what the price is."

"Maybe you should have led with that then," he muttered. "What is it?" She named a price several hundred thousand below what they had been asking.

He paused to consider it. "Why are they dropping the price?"

"Because they haven't gotten any action, just as you predicted."

"When they're ready to drop it the next time, call me back," he said. With that, he ended the call abruptly, a smile on his face for having done so.

It made him feel perverse today, and he would take that. Some days he took his entertainment wherever he could get it. Ariel wasn't likely to call him back at the moment, but he also couldn't be too sure. Still, it was fun to see her angle forward on this because he *was* interested in that building. At least he would be interested in various aspects of the deal. He just wasn't sure that he was prepared to go for anything even close to that current price. He had to get a few things wrapped up first, money being what it was.

Ariel could play all kinds of games with him, but she always knew the bottom line would be profit for some of these buildings, at least enough to keep his habit for rehabbing old properties out of the red.

The minute he ended up losing money, that was a whole different story. He could afford to lose a little bit, but he couldn't afford to continue what he was doing and take huge losses. Nobody could. While he was direct with the realtors he voluntarily did business with, he generally didn't piss them off to the extent that they never called him back. He reserved that for Ariel and other pushy realtors, trying to get his business in all the wrong ways.

After all, they were running a business themselves, and they needed him just as he needed them. Still, Simon tended to keep the unsolicited realtors at arm's length, and that was the way he chose to handle them. Most of the realtors and sellers out there were decent, but Simon had been taken just enough times that he'd definitely learned his lesson.

He wandered off to his next rehab project, stopping to look over the amount of work done before contacting his foreman, Steven, to let him know that Simon was there.

The foreman came down right away, greeted him with a smile, and noted, "Hey, we're picking up the pace again."

"That's good news," Simon said, studying him. "What was the holdup?"

"The usual." Steven shrugged. "Lack of supplies coming in on time, and lack of skilled workers to do the work we need on time."

That was a never-ending issue. Simon paid good wages

to keep good workers, but, with his ever-expanding projects, he was stretching his manpower a little on the thin side. He verbally went through several checks and balances with his foreman, then nodded. "Looks as if you've got things well in hand here. I'll be off then." And he turned to walk out.

He hadn't gotten more than a few feet when he felt a blow to his stomach that bent him over from the waist.

His foreman was right there beside him. "Hey, are you okay?"

Simon gasped for breath and slowly straightened, nodding. "Yeah, I think so."

"Are you sure?" Steven asked. "That looked like somebody sucker punched you a good one."

Simon stared at him and nodded. "Yeah, …. that's what it felt like too." With a grimace, he straightened up more and more, until he stood normally. He took several deep breaths and muttered, "Wow, I haven't even eaten."

"Maybe that's the problem," Steven pointed out. "Man, if I don't eat, my system gets back at me too."

Simon smiled at him. "Time for my lunch then."

"Yeah, I would think so. You take care of yourself because, without you, we ain't got nothing."

Simon laughed. "Thankfully you've still got plenty of things to do."

"For now, but, if you're not at the helm, these projects tend to quickly go down the shit-stream," he shared, with a worried look on his face. "Make sure you look after yourself."

With that, Simon made his way back down to the ground floor, then headed off to a small park around the corner and just out of sight. Once there, he crashed onto the park bench and swore. "What the hell was that?" he muttered to himself. That was one helluva way to get his attention. He blamed some unruly spirit on the other side.

Simon decided to make contact with that angry spirit. He looked around, closed his eyes, and explained, *You can try talking to me first, you know? Violence is not the way to do this.*

When no answer came, he opened his eyes, glanced around, and all he saw was a couple older ladies sitting off to the side, talking, plus two teenagers on skateboards, bouncing back and forth off a set of stairs. In other words, everything looked and appeared normal. Yet whatever the hell that blow was, it was not good, and his foreman was correct. Something came out of left field and literally punched him in the gut.

Reminiscing about those kinds of psychic events was enough to make him reconsider what was going on right now around him. He glanced about again, but there was nothing, nobody, no sign of anything being off. And he liked that even less.

Frowning, he stayed where he was for a few minutes and then decided to head to his office and to get some paperwork done. Just as he went to stand up again, a second blow came out of nowhere and dropped him.

*Damn. I can't reach them, and they obviously can't speak to me either.*

# CHAPTER 5

THE TRIO OF detectives made the trip back to the office in silence. In the back seat, Kate smirked. The discussion with her mother had been much less than satisfactory. Her mother refused to let them inside, so it had all happened outside in the hallway, with her mother screeching about her rights and police harassment all the while. When they got back in their office, Colby happened to be standing there at the main entrance, talking to one of the other detectives. Colby looked up as they walked in, one eyebrow cocked with interest as he raised a hand. "How did that go?"

"Well," Lilliana began, looking a bit embarrassed, "we can expect zero cooperation there."

He shook his head. "I don't understand. How can it be zero cooperation?"

Lilliana explained what had happened initially and how the woman had refused to even talk to them or to let them in. Then, when they brought Kate in, it went from bad to worse, and Kate's mother had literally gone off the wall, screaming at Kate, after striking her. After all that, they asked a few questions of her, but she knew nothing, had heard nothing, had no idea on anything. "Even if she did," Lilliana added, "I definitely got the feeling that she wouldn't cooperate anyway. She wouldn't tell us a thing."

Colby's gaze hardened, and he asked, "Do you think the

issue was compounded by Kate's presence?"

"I don't think Kate's presence would have changed her attitude," she stated. "However, I can tell you, having Kate there completely sent her up the wall."

"So, maybe Kate shouldn't have been there," Colby replied, his gaze studying Lilliana.

"We weren't getting anywhere anyway. After Kate described their relationship, I wanted to see for myself what was going on, so I had Kate come up. You certainly can't blame her for it, since I'm the one who told her to join us."

"And then her mother completely lost it," Rodney interjected. "Completely and totally lost it, screaming at Kate, saying no way she could be a cop because she was nothing but a loser and that this was all just bullshit." Rodney shook his head. "I've seen some pretty shitty people in my life, but wow." He walked over to his desk and dropped into his chair. "It was pretty heartbreaking to listen to."

"As far as the Timmy case goes," Lilliana began, bringing it back around, "Selene has had no updates, knows nothing, and, as far as she's concerned, the reason she knows nothing is because Kate is the one who did something to her brother and hid it from everybody."

Colby turned and looked at Kate.

Kate shrugged. "If you check the files, you'll see that I was seven at the time, so I'm not sure what I was supposed to have done or how I could have completely hidden a body at that age."

Colby frowned at her. "Seven?"

"Yes, seven. Timmy was five." Then she went into a brief discussion of what had happened at the school.

"Good God," Colby muttered, "and she blames you?"

"Yes, but really she's blaming herself, yet can't allow herself to be too blamed, so it's much easier to blame me."

"Right," he murmured. "That's generally the way it happens, isn't it?"

"Yeah, it sure is," she muttered. "Anyway, so after that, life was pretty shitty, as you can imagine, until I became an adult."

Rodney just shook his head. "I don't know how anybody can even grow up in that kind of a scenario."

She smiled at him. "If you mean grow up and be somewhat normal, I'm pretty sure you would say, I'm not normal."

He flushed. "After meeting the woman who birthed you, I regret having thought anything the slightest bit negative about you in all this time we've worked together," he admitted. "The fact that you came from such a disadvantaged start, … and built yourself up into this life? Like wow."

"It was fine, up until we lost my brother," she shared, "and that just finished everything."

"But you couldn't be blamed no matter what, not at seven."

Kate nodded. "I think what my mother's trying to get into everybody's head is that somehow … I must have been working with somebody. In her mind, I was old enough to collude with what? … A pedophile, I guess, and do it knowingly."

"Did you see anybody there at the time?" Colby asked. "I'm sure you've gone over it a million times."

"Ten million times," she muttered, facing him steadily. "I swear to God, if I had a way to freeze that information in my brain, I would have. But I've gone over every person I could even begin to remember who was anywhere around there, not to mention the dozens I assume I've created as possibly being there, … considering I *was* seven. I don't know if anybody looked at school cameras. I don't know if the school even had cameras back then. Even if they did, those films are long gone by now," she noted, frustrated. "I do think that the loss of my brother started some changes in terms of school security, but I don't think anything was in place before that."

"Right," Colby agreed, "and that makes a big difference, doesn't it?"

"It all makes a difference," she declared, "and yet none of it solves the problem. To even think that somebody could just pick up a child and walk away with him is crazy." She shook her head.

"And yet," Colby replied, "chances are, he didn't just walk away with him. Maybe he knew him from some sport or something, or maybe he was a coach or the father of a friend," Colby suggested.

"I don't know," she said. "All of those things are possible. Outside of the case files I have, I don't know if anything else was ever done with the case. I was hoping at some point in time to bring it up to the cold case unit, but you know …"

"Did you ever try?" Colby asked.

"Of course I did," she snapped, raising her hands. "I contacted the detectives back at the time, and they told me that they did everything they could. I contacted all kinds of private investigators, ever since I was old enough to hire anybody. Everybody said that they'd talked to everyone. And maybe they did, but obviously, since my brother hasn't shown up yet, they didn't talk to everybody."

"It is pretty strange to think that somebody could have seen that and yet not realized what they'd seen." Lilliana pointed out.

"And yet it happens all the time," Kate pointed out. "I mean, in this case, what would somebody have seen? A child getting into a vehicle, maybe a man picking up a child, laughing, as the two of them run away, the witness thinking this was great fun, and then what? We don't have any idea whether Timmy knew the person or not."

Kate got up and started pacing around the small space they had. "For the longest time I wondered if somebody, such as a drunk driver, accidentally ran over Timmy in the parking lot, then hopped out and threw him in the back seat and drove off to dispose of his body," she shared. "Every possible scenario that you can think of, ... and plenty more I've already thought of."

Colby scrubbed his face. "I'm sorry to do this to you, but we'll go back over everything again."

"Agreed," she said, a smile on her face. "If nothing else, I guess I can thank this puzzle-box asshole for sending that, just so it brings my brother's case back out into the open and into people's minds. And, if we do another full check, and there's still nothing, it gets parked again for however long until something breaks," she conceded. "And I'll be here when it breaks."

When Colby hesitated, she shook her head. "I'm fine, and, no, ... I had nothing to do with what was going on with my mother. She's just ... *cranky*." Kate looked over at Lilliana, and she agreed immediately.

"Exactly. Kate's right. Having Kate there didn't hurt or help in any way," Lilliana concluded. "What it did do was loosen her tongue so that we saw a clearer picture of her."

Rodney snorted. "And we saw her haymaker, since she took a poke at Kate as soon as she saw her."

"Jesus," Colby muttered.

Rodney nodded. "When she calms down, she may or may not choose to have anything more to do with us. We did tell her to contact us if she hears anything. Yet the words she used as we walked away were similar to the fighting words I heard during hockey in high school," Rodney noted, "when *fuck you* was a pretty popular phrase."

Colby nodded. "So we have some scared witness, or someone up to no good who can't have the cops around her own home, or just an uncooperative suspect."

At the term *suspect*, Kate turned to him. "I guess she could be a suspect. For hell's sake, I want her to be a suspect," she announced, "but only because she's made my life so miserable."

"Where was she at the time of the kidnapping?" Colby asked.

"She was at work," Kate replied, "so, in theory, she has an alibi."

"*In theory*," Lilliana repeated, "but we also know that sometimes you can get to and from work quickly, without ever being missed at work."

"That's true," Kate agreed, "and work was close enough that she could normally walk, and most of the time she walked home. She supposedly was working that day, but I don't have anything other than her own statement to confirm that."

"Did she work most days?"

Kate frowned. "I can confirm that she was away from home most days. Did she work most days? That I'm not sure."

"What do you think she was doing?"

"I know she had an affair with somebody, and having

two kids at home cramped her style, so she used to leave us home alone to go off and be with this guy." Then she winced and added, "Let me be clear that there were always guys. I have no idea how many or who. And, even though I was there, I wasn't old enough to be aware."

"No, of course not," Colby replied, "however ..."

"I know, if there's anything I remember, I'll let you know," she said, with a nod. "I do have some notes that I've never really put much credence into, just because they're the kind of thing that wake you up in the middle of the night, and you don't know whether you're remembering or it was just BS in your head because you're desperate for answers. However, a couple names came up, though I only have first names. They were mostly from phone calls. She talked on the phone a lot."

"What names?"

"Stanley was one," she replied, "and I haven't ever forgotten that name just because I always thought it was some tool—you know, the brand name for tools. As it turned out, he was a tool," she muttered, with an eye roll, "just a different kind." Rodney snorted at that, and Kate laughed. "Believe me, after all the shit I've been through, you find humor where you can, and, if it helps me remember names, I'm all for it."

"Of course," Colby agreed. "Christ, Kate. I can't imagine what you went through. I'm so ..."

"Don't you start now," she warned. "I don't do the whole sympathy thing well, and I sure as hell don't do the pity thing."

"Yeah, no, ... of course not," he muttered, yet staring at her with sympathy.

She sighed. "Look. Just help me find Timmy and also

whoever sent that puzzle box and why, and then we're good," she said. "The fact that somebody brought this up and that nothing else is even happening around town is what bothers me. Because, if this Timmy note was a distraction from the main event, or if it was meant to be something like that, you would think we would know something already, in the way of a crime wave or something."

"You would think." Colby frowned, while nodding.

"Have there been any new cases? Anything at all?" Kate asked.

"Of course," Lilliana replied, "but, outside of several vehicular homicides and two drive-by shootings, which follow the same pattern as the others we've had, I see nothing majorly new to speak of that might fit your crime wave theory."

"Does that surprise you?" Colby asked, eyeing Lilliana oddly.

"No, not really—unless we're looking for something that connects to Kate, then maybe. Yet then it would be completely useless if it did connect to Kate when someone wanted it hidden, remember?"

"True," Kate muttered. "Anyway ... maybe take a look at the files of any cases that came in overnight."

"Do you still think it could be a distraction?" Colby asked.

Kate sighed. "Thinking is one thing. Proving it is another. Considering that somebody is lying about having information on my missing brother, when it's something I rather desperately want, is just cruel and mean," she declared. "If somebody knows me well enough to understand that this would twist me apart and they're having a real old heyday with it, that's pretty upsetting," she noted. "However, if they've been keeping up on the news, seen the number of cases we've solved, and are afraid I'm closing in on their case, then potentially bringing up Timmy now makes sense."

Everybody stared at her for a long moment.

"You have had a ton of news coverage lately," Rodney pointed out, with a nod. "So, in a way, you could be right. It does make a very strange sort of sense."

"And that's part of the problem," she said, "but it also just confuses the issue, which is why I would just as soon not be dragged into all this publicity."

Colby rolled his eyes. "It's not as if any of us have much say in the matter," he noted. "That comes from upstairs, and bigger than that is the fact that we, as a department, need the media."

"Maybe so," she muttered, "but, if it trickled down to having something to do with this, then it's been a bad deal for me."

"Something that we'll keep in mind going forward," Rodney said.

Colby announced, "First off, all of you need to start from the beginning with Kate's brother's case and see if we can come up with anything new. ... Yet still be mindful of any other cases that show up as possibly Kate's kind of cases, such as any strange murders, anything *off*," Colby noted, with another roll of his eyes. "We'll continue to take this on as being a case that does surround your brother."

"Good," Kate declared. "And, for that, I owe this asshole my thanks."

***

SIMON WALKED BACK into his penthouse apartment and organized dinner for the night. He quickly sent Kate a text message, asking if there was any chance she would be coming home, and received a thumbs-up in response. That was good enough for him. If she needed a little extra care tonight, that would be totally okay.

When she walked in, not very much later, and caught sight of him, she immediately frowned.

He swore inside at that. She always knew. No matter what he did to hide these psychic events from her, she always knew.

She glared at him. "What happened?"

He stared at her, then walked over to the nearby mirror and looked to see just what it was that she saw in his facial expression.

"And, no," she stated, "you can't fob me off on this."

"I wouldn't even try," he said, turning to her. "However, I really wish I understood how you always know."

She frowned and repeated, "What happened?"

He sighed. "I don't even know how to explain it, but it was as if I got sucker punched in the gut twice today."

"You got into a fight?"

"No," he countered, "that would be easier to reconcile."

Quickly she hung up her coat and purse, dropping her keys and the small card case she carried on the nearby entry table, as she moved closer to him. "Explain, please."

He gave a shout of laughter. "It would be so much easier if I could."

"Tell me what you can," she murmured. "Did somebody attack you? Did something come out of the blue and hit you?"

"Yes, that one."

She studying him. "So psychically?"

"Something like that," he replied warily. "I was just

walking away from one of my foremen, when, all of a sudden, I was doubled over with pain. I didn't have any idea what it was but thought it could be anything, a bad stomach even. Who knows? So I went to the park across the street to just rest a bit. When I went to stand up again, the same thing basically happened all over again. I got dropped."

"*Dropped*," she repeated, her tone rising in alarm. "As in knocked out?"

"No," he stated immediately. "It dropped me to the ground, much like before. I stumbled back to my feet and sat back down again. I don't think anybody even noticed, but it sure wasn't what I expected."

"Of course not," she agreed, looking at him in concern.

"I'm fine now," he added, with a wave of his hand.

"You're obviously not fine," she stated for the sake of clarity. "Something strange is going on."

"Yes, something strange is always going on. That's my life, remember?"

She winced and nodded. "And I'm sorry about that because there does seem to be a lack of clarity here all the time, even for me."

"How did your day go?" he asked. He was happy that she was okay to pass by the subject of his strange events, and, if he could get her talking about her world, then maybe she would leave him alone, or at least he hoped so.

"I'm not sure that I have a whole lot to say," she replied, "except that we did go to see my mother." She snorted at that. "Poor Rodney, he believes in happy-ever-after, except not when my mother is involved."

He raised one eyebrow. "You do too," he pointed out.

She frowned, shrugged, and sighed. "I won't argue the point right now, but let's just say that meeting my mother was not something Rodney was prepared for."

"How did Lilliana handle it?"

"I think she was half expecting exactly what she saw," Kate shared. "Rodney always has that hope for … people being better than they are."

"Right, so I presume your mother was not friendly."

"Not friendly in any way," Kate agreed cheerfully. "It was kind of funny actually." And she gave him the play-by-play details of what had happened.

He shook his head. "I can just imagine you shoving your face into that door window."

"Yep." Kate grinned. "We sure got her attention fast after that." She laughed, but a bitterness came with it. "She hasn't changed a bit."

He hesitated and then suggested, "Remember that she's been just as affected by what happened to Timmy as you are."

"Has she?" she asked, looking over at him. "I wonder."

"I know, and I'm not surprised that you wonder," he replied. "I would want to understand whether she's really truly unaffected, or this is her defense and guilt for being the one who left you responsible."

"Either way, she was not happy to see anybody."

"Even though it meant potentially reopening your brother's case?"

"I don't think she even thought that was a possibility. She seemed to have a hate on for law enforcement."

"And maybe that's not all that surprising either," he suggested, with a careful look at her. "The whole scenario is upsetting and difficult. They didn't find any answers back then, and, in her eyes, maybe she doesn't want any of it dragged back up to the surface. Maybe she's, I don't know, trying to rebuild her life in some way."

She stared at him and then nodded slowly. "It could be any number of things," she conceded. "Honestly, it was difficult to see her in many ways. Yet there was a childish vindication."

"Of course." He smiled at her. "You are only human."

"Right, but somehow I feel as if I am supposed to be better than that."

"Oh no, no you don't," he argued. "No sitting here chastising yourself for how you reacted to seeing your mother for the first time in what? Ten years?"

She shrugged. "More than that. She didn't believe I was a cop either."

"Did Lilliana explain it to her?"

"No, I don't think so." Kate frowned. "At least not from the part of the conversation that I heard. Lilliana probably considered it personal, so not any of her business. And, if I do have to go back to talk to Selene, well, that's just something I have to do."

"And you'll handle it differently because you're past that first painful meeting now."

"Maybe." She smiled, then nodded. "Yeah, I would. She's obviously got her own issues to deal with."

"Good," he replied. "So now, I suggest that we stay here and have dinner or maybe we should take dinner down to the boat, where we can just sit and relax."

She raised her eyebrows. "You moved the boat close enough where that is an option, isn't it?"

He laughed. "Yes, I would think so. I do have everything ready to go. I just wasn't thinking about where we should have dinner."

"I like the idea about the boat," she said immediately. "A

change of pace, you know?"

He smiled. "In that case, let's go." He walked over to a large takeout bag.

"You knew I would say yes, didn't you?"

"I was hoping you would say yes," he clarified, chuckling. "But just because you did in the past didn't mean that you would this time," he noted, with a smile, "yet I hoped you might."

And, with that, they walked downstairs, and once out on the street, headed to the area where he had the *Running Mate* moored. As she stepped up onto the deck of the boat, she smiled. "It's a beautiful night for it."

"Absolutely stunning," he muttered. "We can sit up here and forget about all the other things in life that piss us off."

She groaned. "If only."

He smiled at her. "We have to allow things to happen. Otherwise, they never will."

And, with that, he walked over to their large table. He set the food off to the side and popped into the galley and quickly brought up some dish towels and wiped down the surface. Within a few minutes, they were seated here, ready for dinner, with a wondrous view of the harbor around them.

"It's absolutely beautiful," she said. "You are truly blessed."

He looked over at her and then nodded. "You're right. I am. That is something I need to remind myself of sometimes."

"You mean, like today, when you got attacked for no reason, by some mystery source that you couldn't even see or remember?" she asked. "And, if you think I'll forget about that, you're wrong." When he winced, she nodded. "Just as you look after me, I look after you."

"What is that? Some relationship rule?"

"God only knows," she muttered, raising both hands. "If there were ever a rule book for such things, I never saw it. And, if there is one, maybe somebody should get me a copy."

"Oh, I don't think so. I think the very best thing for you would be to *not* have a rule book." She frowned at him, so he added, "You're doing just fine on your own."

"Am I though?" she asked, staring at him. "It seems as if you get into more trouble and more issues than any partner should."

"You mean because of you, on behalf of you, or what?" he asked, with a note of amusement. "Still, if you want to turn that around, I could say the exact same thing about you."

"Maybe," she conceded, with a smirk, "but you seem to get into trouble just fine on your own."

He chuckled. "I do seem to know an awful lot of people who don't care to be decent types in this world," he admitted, with a nod. "Yet I was kind of hoping that would all change."

"It might, I suppose," she said, with a shrug, "but I don't know that it'll happen any time soon."

He nudged her plate a little closer. "Eat up. You're always cranky when you're hungry."

She glared at him but immediately started eating. "Gosh, this is really good." She moaned as soon as the first bite went in. Her taste buds came alive.

"I know." He laughed. "That's why we're having it."

She shook her head. "You have an awful lot of takeout. Whatever happened to home-cooked meals?"

"Yeah? And what home-cooked meals do you prepare?"

She winced. "I don't," she muttered.

"So, why am I supposed to have home-cooked meals if you aren't? Besides, most of these restaurants know me by now, and the meals I get are definitely a step above the average takeout."

"They absolutely are," she muttered. "They're gorgeous, delicious, and again … you're very lucky."

He chuckled. "We're both very lucky," he pointed out.

"Yeah." She wouldn't argue with that. When she was done with her plate, she pushed it back, looked over at him, and asked, "So, who hit you?"

He stopped in the act of lifting a bite to his mouth and sighed. "It wasn't physical so …"

She narrowed her gaze at him and nodded. "So, is it connected to my case?"

"I don't know," he said. "I don't have an answer for you on that, even though I asked Timmy and then the angry spirit. Yet no answer from either. So I have no idea how I would even figure it out. At least not yet."

"It's the *not yet* part that's interesting," she murmured. "Because you would think, if it was connected, maybe there would be a little bit more information."

"Not yet," he stated, "and that's one of the things you have to remember. Some of this takes time." She winced, and he had to laugh. "And we know how much you love things that take time," he pointed out, with a note of humor.

"I really don't, do I?" She sagged back into her seat. "Can't these ghosts or spirits or whatnot have another way to communicate without hurting you?" she cried out. "What the hell is that about?"

"I wasn't sure if it was symbolic," he replied.

"Symbolic?" she asked, staring at him. "Meaning?"

"Maybe the *truth* was something that would punch me in the gut."

Her mouth formed a round O as she contemplated that idea. "Wow," she murmured. "Just when I think I've figured out how all this crap with you works, you come up with this. It makes me think of all the layers and layers and how I just don't understand what's going on."

"Not just you," he quipped, with a wry smile. "Often it's the same for me too."

"And that's one of the really horrifying parts about it," she stated, "because, if we thought that we understood this stuff—"

He interrupted her with a chuckle. "If we thought we understood it, life would be easier, but we don't really understand it, so ..."

"So, it's hard," she declared. "I don't want people hurting you like this."

"What do you mean, *like this?*" he asked, with a smile. "If ever people wanted to hurt me over something, let it be this. Let it be something important, something we can get answers to. I can handle that."

"Can't they find another way to communicate?"

"Maybe. I don't know yet," he admitted. "I tried to communicate back, telling them to just talk to me first, before resorting to violence. I figured two blows in the gut were enough for me for the day. If it comes a third time, I might just get angry, and I don't know if that's a good thing either."

"That might be a good thing. Get angry."

"I can't."

"Why not, Simon? You are the one hurting here."

"Because if somebody is deliberately trying to get my

attention, generally it's because they need help," he explained, "and I'm not sure what this is about yet."

"Those gut punches are more like anger, much more like frustration," she pointed out. "Maybe you aren't listening."

"Just like you," he said, with a nod. "What was the message that you got out of the puzzle box note?"

She winced and said, "*Think*. It's always about *think*. And yet I've gone over and over that scenario in my brain so many times. I'm not sure it's even possible for me to do anything differently now."

"Maybe not *differently*," he pointed out, "but maybe you missed something."

"Maybe, but, if I'm missing it, how am I ever supposed to find it?" she muttered. "It happened so long ago."

"And that in itself," he pointed out, "should help you with other cases because, if it's hard for you to remember so long ago, how is it for other people who are in the same boat?"

They went to bed relatively early that night, both of them exhausted.

## CHAPTER 6

**W**HEN KATE WOKE up early in the morning to her ringing phone, she answered it to hear Rodney on the other end.

"We've got an ugly case," he greeted her, and he quickly gave her the address. She stumbled into her clothes, gave Simon a kiss goodbye, and was on her way to her car.

She quickly pulled into a drive-through and picked up strong black coffee to help get through the morning shock. Rodney didn't say much on the phone, but, as she headed toward the address, she realized it was in her old stomping grounds. Her heart clenched as she realized this could be related to Timmy's case. She parked with all the police cars and headed to where Rodney stood, talking to the coroner.

As she walked up, Dr. Smidge glared at her.

She nodded. "I gather it's not fun."

"It's never fun," he barked, "but this one is particularly *un*-fun. You'll have to solve this fast." And, with that, he stomped to his vehicle.

Kate turned to Rodney, one eyebrow raised.

He shook his head. "I can't believe he's even speaking to you that way."

She waved her hand. "He speaks to me like that all the time. I just don't ever take it personally."

"How can you not?" he muttered. "He damn-near tore a

strip off me the minute I arrived."

"Did he get here before you?"

"Yeah, of course he did, hence the strip."

She nodded. "Okay, so what have we got?"

Rodney hesitated, then sighed. "A five-year-old boy."

She winced and nodded. "Okay. Family violence, domestic abuse, drive-by? What is it that got Smidge in a tiff?"

Rodney grimaced. "Seems the boy died at home, but the parents are trying to tell us that it was any number of possible causes. They claim that he was sick for a long time. By the looks of it, this isn't normal *parental* behavior. They're saying that every minute of it they looked after him and checked in on him several times, *blah, blah, blah*."

She listened for what she was not hearing and asked, "You think it's child abuse?"

"Yes," he stated, "and I'm pretty sure that's what Smidge's angry about too."

"So, what do you think happened here?"

"The child didn't go easy into the night," Rodney shared. "He suffered, and that's really upsetting for all of us."

"It's upsetting for any child to die," she murmured, as she walked toward the body. She stopped and wondered how many more little children she would stand over before the world changed. Then she realized that it would be a hell of a lot more than she could ever make peace with.

When Smidge rejoined her, she looked over at him and muttered, "It's always worse when it's a child."

He just nodded and didn't say anything. Then he pulled back the cover so she could see the child's face.

Kate's heart immediately clenched. "Now that is not good," she whispered.

"The family is adamant that they didn't kill him," Rodney shared.

Kate looked back at the family, standing nearby, and the mother had tears in her eyes, but also terror filled her expression. "Maybe didn't *kill* him," Kate suggested, "but what did they do to keep him alive?"

Smidge turned to her. "What do you mean?"

She let out a big sigh. "Let me know on the autopsy as soon as you can."

Smidge's gaze was assessing, as he looked down at the little boy and then back at her. "You think something different is here than what we're seeing?"

"I think what we're seeing is exactly what we're seeing, but definitely something is off about the whole thing." She looked back over at the mom and noted, "I need to talk to her."

"Yeah, you do that," Smidge snapped, his tone laced with bitterness. "I would much rather deal with the dead than the lying living bastards," he snapped.

"This was long-term, wasn't it?" Kate asked.

Smidge hesitated, before he looked down and nodded. "It's been going on a while. I need to do a full rundown to get you more information though."

"I can already see it," she muttered, sadness in her eyes. "The different color bruises, all kinds of evidence of long-term distress for this poor little guy," she murmured. "Do we have a name?"

"Yes," Rodney replied, standing at her side. "Andrew Adam Smith."

In front of her, Smidge straightened, then glared at the two of them. "I'm not sure what you're concocting in those devious little heads of yours," he noted, looking from Kate to Rodney and back. "However, this is the one and only. Do you hear me?" he asked, staring at Kate. "I don't want any more of this on my table."

She smiled at him gently, understanding both the pain in his tone and the reason for it. Speaking softly, she replied, "If you or I could make that happen, we would both be blessed. Yet we know it'll never happen. I'll do my very best to ensure no more cross your desk anytime soon," she noted, "but this kind of thing is almost impossible to stop. As long as hurting, angry people are out there, their loved ones closest to them bear the brunt of it."

Smidge's shoulders sagged, and he nodded. "Fine. Do your best, and I'll get the information for you quickly. I don't know what this is connected to, but it better not be connected to anything I need to hear about."

"Anything I should know before I head over to talk to the parents?" she asked Smidge, pointing to them behind him.

"Those parents, I don't know how guilty they are," he replied, "but no way they get off scot-free." And, with that, he ordered the body to be lifted and loaded. Without another word to either of them, he walked away.

Rodney frowned at her. "Please don't say a connection is here."

"How can I not go there? Timmy was five years old at the time he went missing," she asked. "Consider the reminder to *think* in the puzzle-box message. And look at what we have right now. We have a dead five-year-old child, a child who has been suffering for a long time. I'm just leaving my mind open to this for now. Whether there's a medical reason or not, I'm not sure, but I can tell you that something is very off about this. Smidge will examine that poor little guy with a fine-tooth comb, but you and I will do the same with the family history to figure out what the hell is going on."

"Maybe nothing," he pointed out. "Not everything is always nasty and dark and connected."

"No," she clarified, "but mark my words. This one is. This one definitely is."

With that, he conceded the point with a shrug.

"Names?" she asked him.

"Alana Smith and Adam Smith."

She walked over to talk to the mother, who sat on the doorstep of their home, her face buried in her hands. Kate crouched in front of her, introduced herself, and said, "Mrs. Smith, I need you to tell me what happened." And, with that, the woman raised her tear-stained face.

"He was doing so much better," the young woman whispered. "So much better. He was better, I swear."

Kate narrowed her gaze at her. "And then what?"

Alana shook her head. "I don't even know what to say." She hung her head. "I was gone to a conference for just a few days, and Adam swears he didn't do it. He swears he didn't have anything to do with it, but ..." Then she started bawling.

"Where were you? What conference was that? You need to tell me, so we can check that."

Alana just nodded, beyond able to talk.

At that point, Adam walked over, sat down beside his wife, and pulled her into his arms. "Can't you leave us alone? We've just lost our son," he snapped.

"I am sorry for your loss, Mr. Smith, and I do know that you've just lost your son," she stated, studying him. "That little boy didn't need to die the way he died."

Adam glared at her. "Alana didn't have anything to do with it."

"Maybe not," Kate noted. "So, where were you, and what was your involvement?"

"I wasn't involved at all," he barked.

"If you say so." Rodney glared at him. "We will check your alibi too."

Adam snorted. "We didn't do this."

The woman turned and looked at him, tears in her eyes. "Are you sure?" she asked. "Those bruises are days old."

He stiffened. "Okay, I lost my temper with him once, and I told you that. I called you, and I told you and apologized. I didn't take him to the doctor," he admitted, turning to Kate and Rodney, "because I knew what would happen. But a friend of mine is a doctor, so I brought him over and had him look after my son."

Rodney stared at Adam, his fists clenching and unclenching.

"I've been in anger management training," Adam admitted, "and I've been trying really, really hard, just to ensure that this didn't happen. But I swear, I did not do this."

Kate studied him. "We'll need your friend's name, so we can verify what you've just told us. We also need to know where you're doing your anger management training, though I highly suspect that it's not working that well," she noted, studying him intently. When he flushed with fury, she nodded. "Anger is one thing, but controlling it is a whole different story, Mr. Smith."

"I did not do this," he snapped. With that, he pulled his wife into his arms and held her close. "Honey, I didn't. ... I promise, I didn't do this."

She just sobbed, louder and louder. And, for Kate, who clearly saw the damage done to the little boy, it was obvious what the mother would be thinking. Whether it was the truth or not, Kate didn't know. Yet a ring of truth was in the man's words. However, the evidence in front of her said something else entirely.

She looked over at Rodney, then faced the parents again. "We'll need to get your full statements, and we do need to check out everything you're saying. So, do you want to come down to the station in the morning, or do you just want to do it now?"

"Now," Alana said immediately. "Now is fine. I'm not sure I can handle anything past now," she whispered through her sobs. She repeated how she'd been away at a conference. She gave the name of the conference and where it was held and added, "You can check with my office to verify it."

The tears still ran down Alana's face, breaking Kate's heart.

"I was gone for six days," Alana explained, then frowned. "I think it was six. My flight tickets and the hotel bookings are documented as well, so my office should confirm that too."

Kate just nodded and took down the company name and all the other given information, and then she turned to the father. "And you, sir."

He immediately provided the information that she asked for, cooperative and willing, but not necessarily 100 percent truthful. She sensed him holding something back.

When they were done, Kate looked at the wife and asked, "Now, what is it that you're not telling me?"

Alana looked at her in surprise, then burst into tears.

Kate waited. "I'll just stay here until you tell me." Then she looked over at the husband. "You too, Mr. Smith, because you're both hiding something."

His shoulders sagged. "I did time for domestic violence,"

he shared, defeat in his tone. "All I can tell you is that it was a long time ago. I've been doing anger management for what seems like forever since then, and I swear I did not kill my little boy." He started to cry great big heaving sobs of sorrow. "I didn't do this."

Rodney looked over at the wife and frowned.

Kate understood. Rodney had seen the physical damage done to the little boy, including the different color bruises.

Rodney spoke to the father. "But you do admit to having hit him recently."

Adam gasped and nodded. "Yes, but not hard. Honestly, it wasn't." He winced and then shook his head. "It wasn't hard enough to kill him."

"That's a different story," Kate noted, staring him down. "Because what you think might kill a child and what might actually kill a child are two different things," she pointed out, "and that will be up to the autopsy to determine."

"I wasn't home all night," he admitted suddenly. When his wife stared at him, he shrugged. "I went out with the guys."

"And you can prove that?" Kate asked.

"Yes, I can prove that. We went to a local bar because one of the guys from work was leaving. So I joined them and had ... a few beers."

"And who was looking after the child?" Kate asked.

He hesitated and frowned. "My brother." At that, his wife turned to eye him in horror. "I know. I know, but Sammy said he would look after him just for the night," Adam cried out. "I didn't see the harm."

"Now apparently you do," Kate declared, turning to look at the wife.

Alana stared at Kate, then back at her husband. "Sammy's not very stable," she began. "He does a lot of drugs, and I won't have him around my kids." She turned and glared at her husband. "And you knew that."

"Honey, he's been clean for months," Adam protested. "You never would believe me, but he's been clean."

"Clean maybe," she muttered, "but how clean? Look at what happened when you left our boy in his charge."

"And when did you get home?" Kate asked them both. "We have a time line to work out here."

"I flew in around eleven. My husband was home." She turned to face him, and he replied, "I'd just gotten home. I'd only been here for maybe ten minutes."

"You didn't tell me that though, did you?" Alana asked Adam.

"No, I didn't. You went in, and we both found Andrew," he shared. "After that, I wanted to tell you how much I regret leaving my brother in charge."

"Where is your brother now?" Kate asked.

"I sent Sammy home." Then Adam frowned. "And honestly, he wasn't in very good shape."

"When you say he wasn't in very good shape, what do you mean?"

Adam shook his head. "Sammy was slurring his words a little bit. I asked if he'd been drinking. and he told me no, how he hadn't had anything to drink, and I believed him."

"You believed him?" Alana shrieked, staring at Adam with anger and mockery. "You fucking believed him?"

"Yes," he roared. "I believed him. I believe in second chances."

"It will be interesting to see what the autopsy turns up then, won't it?" Rodney asked, his tone suddenly hard. "Because now we have three suspects."

"Suspects?" the father asked, turning to look at him. "What do you mean, suspects?"

"I hate to be bearer of the news, but your child did not die by natural causes," Rodney pointed out, trying to tone down his own anger. "So, someway, somehow, we need to find out who's responsible for Andrew's death, and that is the person who will be charged with murder."

Adam, the color fading completely from his face, sat down hard on the step beside his wife. "We didn't do anything," he muttered, hanging his head. "We've been working so hard at getting me back to normal and getting everybody back to normal. We wouldn't."

"Maybe not," Kate conceded, trying to find some sympathy. "Still, somebody, somehow, did kill Andrew, and we need to find out who that was."

THE REST OF his day wasn't too bad. Simon was busy with various issues, problems, and challenges. Yet he hated to even say it out loud, lest he jinx himself, but, in general, he felt as if he had gotten through most of the day relatively unscathed. That just made him a little more worried about what could come tomorrow. Good days tended to be followed by crappy days, and he really wasn't in the mood for any crappy days right now. There were just way too many of them sometimes.

He walked through the alley and headed over to the women's center. He knew that the owner, Lisa Sands, needed money, even if people didn't think she deserved it. That blame should be put on her business partner, not on Lisa. So Simon didn't want to punish all the women who went through the center for one bad egg. He knew a huge investigation was going on concerning Lisa's former business partner, but he hoped Lisa came out of it in the clear. In the meantime, he took a couple quick corners and ended up right where he needed to be.

He walked up to the side door and knocked. When it opened hesitantly, Lisa was there, the relief evident on her face. He immediately handed her a roll of bills, and she took it gratefully. "How has it been?" he asked.

"Honestly, it's been pretty tough," Lisa admitted.

"Of course," he noted, "and not everybody will understand what I'm doing."

"No, of course not," she said bitterly, "but I'm just trying to help these women."

"I know that," he replied, "but trying to help can damage your reputation when things go wrong."

"It wasn't so much for me."

He nodded. "I know," he murmured.

"You're a good person," she muttered, staring at him. "I wish more men were like you."

He just smiled and didn't say anything.

She was in the business of helping women who were recovering from various abusive scenarios. As such, her response was fairly typical.

"I'll be back when I can," he added, and, with that, he backed away.

She stepped back inside, watching him until he disappeared.

He felt her gaze on his back, and he knew that she had to wonder why he even continued to come, but the reasons for coming were the same as they had always been. These women and the children needed help, and Simon was more than happy to participate. Yet he always preferred to do it quietly and in his own way.

He headed back, taking another shortcut through the alley. He was hoping to get home in time to sit down and to do something constructive—such as trying to contact the person who kept socking him in the gut, which had happened several more times. Thankfully the blows had been of lesser strength, at least today.

He also wanted to try contacting Kate's brother again. To even think that was a possibility still sent him out to left field as he considered doing such a thing. To do it successfully was one thing; to try and fail was another, and yet failure was often the mother of invention. So he couldn't ignore the possibility that he could get through. It was also confusing as hell to him to even figure out how this could possibly work.

He wanted something to work. He wanted to help lessen Kate's torment, and he'd held off doing anything about Timmy all this time, mostly because he didn't know what to do. Now here he was in the position to maybe do something, yet he wasn't sure that anything would work. All he could do was try. He headed home, taking the small sea-pass across, and then headed to his apartment building. As he walked in, his doorman Harry frowned at him, checking his watch.

Simon smiled, then nodded and acknowledged, "I know. I'm home early for once."

"Hey, you should do it more often," he suggested, with a bright smile. "You work too hard."

Simon laughed. "I'm not against doing less work. It's just hard to make that happen."

"If you don't make it happen, nobody else will," Harry noted, with a knowing look. "You learn that one pretty-damn fast."

"And that is true, isn't it?" Simon asked, as he contemplated this man who had become his friend over the years, a man who had far more insight into what was going on in Simon's world than a lot of people.

"Unfortunately, it's way too common," Harry noted. "You know it as well as I do. Look after yourself. Otherwise, nobody else will."

Simon thought about the sad life lessons people learned as they moved through the world that existed around them. Harry was correct about that. It was up to them to focus and to make everything work the way they needed it to, but it wasn't always that easy. As a matter of fact, most of the time, it wasn't easy at all.

Simon headed up to his place and quickly tossed off his jacket and put on a pot of coffee. When it was ready, he poured himself a cup and then sat on the couch. He didn't know how to contact these spirits and wanted to attempt something new without anybody peering in to see how he was doing.

He knew Kate would respect his boundaries if he had any way to tell her to butt out and exactly what those boundaries were. But the problem was, he didn't really know himself, and, therefore, he felt this constant sense that he needed to do something, but what that something was, he didn't know.

With his coffee done and a notebook close by, he laid down on the couch, closed his eyes, and mentally reached out. He called out specifically for Timmy to respond. Simon remembered his grandmother's words in the back of his head, telling him that, once he opened that door, it would not close anytime soon. Yet he pushed aside that warning because that door had already been opened. Plus, he couldn't just walk away from everything that had happened up until now, even if he wanted to. That option was long gone.

He would like to do so many things with his life, and it wasn't past him yet. However, that deadline loomed. Simon knew there was definitely a time and a place, and he had missed the markers and had already gone well past all of those.

Resting here, leaving himself wide open for any communication, felt strange, and maybe a little disconnected from the real world raging around him. But he opened up, now calling out for anybody who needed to talk to him. Preferably the one in particular who kept slugging him in the gut. Simon stayed here for a good thirty minutes, but nothing came. He felt the frustration starting to build. As soon as he felt frustrated, he knew that would make it worse. That wasn't helping, but then again he had to do something, and this was the only thing he knew to do. If this didn't work, what else would?

It's not as if Simon knew of a psychic school on how to handle this or some specialist he could call. However, Simon knew other psychics were in the world. He didn't know how successful they were. Maybe if he knew any personally, he might contact them to get some pointers. Then again, he didn't know anybody who was particularly interested in helping him. That was one of those hard lessons. If somebody was there, did they care enough to assist?

As an afterthought Simon put a protective guard around himself, then immediately felt more centered, more secure in some weird way. Feeling more confident after that, he sent out the call yet again for Timmy or the gut-slugger or just anybody who could help Simon. There was no answer, yet he felt something. What was this feeling?

He wasn't sure, but he felt some weird sense of movement somewhere. He waited, then called out again and again. Then came laughter and something that he couldn't fully understand. He wasn't sure what that was.

Frowning, he stepped off to the side mentally and gave it some room, gave it time to dwell and to expand and to do whatever it thought it needed to do. More laughter came, as if somebody were playing a game with him. He didn't really appreciate that, but considering everything else that had gone on, he would take it.

*Of course you will,* someone said, as a snicker swept through Simon's mind. *You're the one calling out this time.*

He frowned, not sure who had spoken.

*I said it* came the harsh voice.

"Okay, and who are you?" Simon asked.

After a moment of silence, the voice answered, *Nobody you care about.*

"Then what should I call you?"

*Doesn't matter.*

Simon sighed. "I'll call you Jessie then. So why are you talking to me?" Simon asked.

There came that laugh again. *Because I can help.*

"Maybe you can," Simon conceded, "but maybe you're just here to cause trouble."

*Maybe I am at that,* he admitted, almost in a mocking tone, *but that's up to you to decide. Who do you want to talk to?*

"I'm looking for Timmy," Simon replied, and then groaned a bit. "I don't even know, ... for sure, if he's over there. Do you know anything?"

The voice in his head seemed surprised. *If you don't know, how am I supposed to?*

Simon frowned, admitting, "I thought maybe you would know something, anything. Who are you?"

*Somebody you don't want to know*, the voice replied, turning sad.

"And why is that?"

*I'm here because of things that I did while I was over there*, he shared.

"And yet you could leave if you wanted to."

The voice, disembodied, turned angry. *Maybe I could, but, but maybe I don't deserve to.*

Simon winced at that. "Maybe, so what then? … You'll just stay there in limbo your entire existence, hating yourself?"

*Maybe*, the voice snapped. *Maybe that's exactly what I'm doing. Maybe that's exactly what I should do.*

"Sorry, I can't help you with that," Simon muttered. "I'm looking for somebody specific."

*If it's not me, I'll leave you in peace.*

"Wait," Simon called out. "Are you the one hitting me in the gut?"

But Jessie was gone.

Simon frowned, thinking about that. If this guy he had dubbed Jessie had nobody else to talk to, was it Simon's responsibility to try and talk to him? He didn't know how any of this worked or what his roles and responsibilities were. He needed something from somebody out there who could give him that information. Yet what he really needed was to connect with the child Timmy himself.

Simon shook his head, having a hard time dealing with it himself. And just when he was ready to give up on this for the day and go grab another cup of coffee, a small shaky voice called out, *Hello?*

# CHAPTER 7

THE RAIN HAD started at about two o'clock in the afternoon. So, by the time Kate made it back to the office, she was soaking wet, irritable, cranky, and fed up. She had just come back from a session at the morgue. Everyone in the department looked at her as she walked in, shaking her head like a wet dog, but nobody dared to mention anything. She knew she was running on empty, but some days that's just what was required.

As she sat down at her desk, Rodney frowned at her. "I thought maybe you would take off the afternoon and work from home or something."

"One completely contradicts the other," she snapped, staring at him. "I could take off the afternoon and work from home, but that would not be taking off."

He blinked and then nodded. "Okay, you're in that kind of a mood."

"No, not really," she muttered. "I was thinking about my mother."

"Oh, ouch," he muttered. "That's definitely not a topic I would want to work on."

"Last I heard, she was in a full care facility." When he frowned at her, she nodded. "So, the question is, how did she get out? When did she get out? And why did she get out? How can she afford any of this?"

Lilliana spoke up. "That's a really good point. I'll check into that."

"Thank you," Kate said, turning to her. "It's not that I'm trying to get her locked up again, but I want to know that the world is safe from her particular brand of poison."

"Is she that difficult with others?" Rodney asked, with a heavy dose of sarcasm. Kate looked over at him, one eyebrow raised, and he nodded. "Okay, point taken, not a good time for humor."

"It would be interesting to know," Kate added, "considering it was a change in her residence, and a change that might affect the case."

"You're right," Lilliana agreed. "It is a change, and anything that's a change in this world right now, we need to keep track of." And, with that, she added, "I will get the details and am pulling the files right now." She got up, and, as she walked past Rodney, she nodded to him. "You can come help."

"Sure," he replied, as he hopped up and followed her.

Kate wasn't sure whether they were deliberately trying to stay out of her way or just generally giving her a bit of a space. She didn't really need either. Yet having both was very helpful. She groaned at the thought because she didn't really want anybody on her team avoiding her while she was here at work. That wouldn't be the answer that she needed.

However, something had occurred to her as she walked back into the office. If her mother had been here all this time, what was she doing, and how was she doing it? Was it wrong to track down her past?

No, not at all.

If it were any other suspect, Kate would have done this already. It just never occurred to her and, therefore, gave her insight into what else didn't occur to her when it came to suspects. Did she really think her mother was behind this? She didn't think so, but her mother was a wild card, and that wild card could often cause trouble.

When Lilliana and Rodney returned not very long later, they stopped at her desk.

"What's up?" Kate asked, lifting her head from the notes in front of her.

"Your mother was released from a facility a good thirteen years ago," Lilliana stated.

She stared at them and nodded. "Wow, that's interesting. That's way longer than I expected you to find, so obviously I didn't get updated information myself." She frowned at that. "Honestly, it sounds as if I didn't get any updated information at all. I guess they weren't required to tell me when she got out, and obviously she didn't contact me herself."

"Which in this case is probably a blessing," Lilliana noted.

"Possibly for me," Kate agreed, with a nod. "Yet nothing good could be happening in that scenario."

"Exactly," Lilliana replied. "Your mother was kept under the supervision of a halfway house for quite a while, two years, and then she was released on her own."

Kate nodded. "Good, sounds as if she has come a long way."

"And yet look at how she was when we saw her, uncooperative and belligerent." Rodney chimed in, at her side. "And combative when she saw you."

"Maybe," Kate pointed out, "she was incarcerated against her will and holds it against anybody in authority, just on principle."

Lilliana nodded. "And that's a good point too, and it's definitely something we need to consider. If she is clear from this mess, then it's not an issue at all. And I guess that's one of the questions. Do you think she could be involved in the puzzle box note?" Lilliana asked, and Rodney watched Kate like a hawk.

Kate winced at that. "I was really hoping that wouldn't even come up," she muttered. "Yet I suspect that it needs to be discussed. Do I think she could have done this? Yes. Do I think she has the craftiness to do this?" She pondered it for a moment, then replied, "I don't know. I only have a child's view of her. Do I think she would want to relive everything that happened with her son? Only if for revenge, if she thinks that I did something to my brother and that I've gotten away scot-free," she suggested.

"Then maybe revenge would be enough of a motive for her," Lilliana noted.

"But you were seven," Rodney reminded them, staring at Kate in disbelief. "That's hardly fair."

She nodded. "I was seven, but, for some people, with the loss of a child, … there's no time frame, no age distinction, there is only *I did something*," she shared, looking at him. "And, for my mother, that could be a mental block she never really got past."

"It is an interesting concept though, isn't it?" Lilliana asked, looking at Kate. "I mean, if Selene was so fixated on your paying a price, she would have lost track of everything else."

"And that could be," Kate acknowledged. "I don't know. You saw her reaction to me when she saw me at the door."

"Yeah," she muttered. "Believe me that it'll be a long time before Rodney ever sees that in a very different light,"

Lilliana said, giving Rodney an eye.

"It's hard," Kate admitted. "I would just as soon not have any of you see anything to do with my world," she muttered. "Yet I also can't stop the fact that my mother is who my mother is, and maybe she does still have some major hate on for me. I have no way of knowing."

Lilliana pointed out, "You are not responsible for your parents."

"I know," Kate replied, with a nod, "but I'm still a private person."

"And you're entitled to your privacy, until you get targeted, and then all bets are off."

"Which is also something I thought might be deliberate."

At that, Lilliana turned to eye her in surprise.

Kate shrugged. "Anybody who knows me is aware that I'm a really private person. Anybody who wants to make me uncomfortable would expose whatever it is to make my personal and private world very public."

Lilliana pondered that and nodded. "That is a pretty ugly thought."

"I've put a lot of consideration into it," Kate said, shaking her head. "And, no, I don't have an answer. I wish I did."

"Of course you do," Lilliana agreed. "We all would. That's just life. So, let's get past that part fairly quickly."

"If you say so," Kate muttered, with a note of humor. "Is there any getting past it?"

"There is," Lilliana declared. "Forensics came back. The note's clear of any forensics, as is the puzzle box itself."

"Of course." Kate groaned. "No reason for the sender to do this if they'll get caught."

Lilliana laughed, "Exactly, but what is interesting was

that it was hand-delivered, and we do have the kid who was paid to deliver it, and both Rodney and I interviewed him. The kid told us how he was given fifty bucks to drop it off at the station."

"And, of course, he can't really identify who asked him to drop it off, right?" Kate asked.

Lilliana gave her a smile. "Let's just say that the information he gave us isn't very helpful, in that the guy wore a baseball cap, he was about medium height, and the kid couldn't tell about the hair. He noted it was a white man, with a smoker's voice, and that was about it."

"Right," Kate muttered, "so not exactly helpful."

"And yet, in its own way *not unhelpful.*"

"Keep me posted, please."

"Will do."

Kate buried herself in her own case on the little boy whose father claimed that he had nothing to do with his son Andrew's death. She was still waiting for forensics from Smidge, and, of course, the more she pushed in that direction, the less she would get. So sitting back and waiting was the best course of action. It was also the hardest.

She got up for more coffee and walked past Rodney's desk, accidentally hitting a corner of it and making a file fall to the floor. She bent to pick it up, only to freeze when she realized it was a file on her brother's case and within it were pictures.

She reached out a finger and slowly traced her brother's face, looking at it with tears in her eyes, realizing what she was up against. Of course they would have pictures of him. It was part of the case file. Rodney immediately dropped down and scooped up the pages. She held on to the picture of her brother for a long moment.

"Those were the days," she murmured. "Days of innocence, days of thinking that the world was your oyster and that nothing bad could ever happen." She shook her head. "They sure didn't last."

"Not in your case, no," he agreed, "but, for a lot of children, they do."

She nodded and straightened up, then handed him the photo. "I want copies of these, if you have any more. I don't think I've ever seen this one before," she said, tapping it.

He looked at her in surprise. "And yet you have a file."

"I do have a file, but this wasn't in it." Frowning, she walked over to the file she had, opened it up, and double-checked, then nodded. "Not in here."

"Sure, you can have a copy," Rodney replied. "It's your brother after all."

Kate frowned. "Now I'm wondering why I don't already have it."

Rodney smiled. "Some of the stuff was archived, and some of it's been brought online. So a few pieces may need to be added to your file, as everything gets digitized and updated."

"That's possible," she noted, yet still frowning at him. "Actually it's quite feasible, isn't it?" She walked over to his file, and, taking a deep breath, she flipped it open and checked everything in there. She frowned at a couple spots, stopping to read the notes before carrying on.

Rodney didn't say anything and just watched as she went through it.

When she got to the last page, she found several more photos. She picked a couple of them, staring at them for a long moment, trying not to shatter with pain at some of them. When she got to the last one, she frowned at it, long and hard.

"Why that one?" he asked.

"Again, it's one I don't remember, one I hadn't seen," she murmured, as she stared at it. "These are different, and that makes me want to know why and how."

"Of course," he agreed, looking at her. "Maybe you forgot."

"No, I haven't forgotten," she stated immediately. "It's different." She tapped the picture. "This is six of us. Six innocent children from way back then."

"Sure," he replied, "and do any of those faces mean anything?"

She tapped one of them. "This one, I don't remember who he was, but we used to play with him a lot."

Rodney looked down at the person she tapped in the photo and noted, "He looks much older."

"He is much older, was much older," she corrected. "He was a neighbor kid. He got along better with the younger kids than the older ones. The older ones used to bug him."

"Was there a reason for that?"

"I'm sure there was," she stated, "but you know what kids are like. As long as they have a reason to dis somebody, they'll go in there and do it in a big way."

"Of course," he murmured. "Do you remember what this kid was like?"

"Nope, I sure don't." She stared at the photo, turning it sideways.

"And yet something about it bothers you."

"I presume that everybody back then was spoken to," she shared, shaking her head. "The kids themselves might have a better recollection now, but then memory plays tricks on all of us over time."

"And yet, if they had something to hide, you would think that maybe time would also loosen their tongues."

"Absolutely," she agreed. "Have you spoken to any of them?"

"No, not yet. I'm going out tomorrow to talk to a couple." She nodded, then hesitated. He immediately spoke up. "I don't think that would be a good idea."

She looked up at him. "Maybe not, but, if they see me, it might loosen their tongues."

"And it might clam them up," he pointed out. "It seems as if not everybody is happy that this case is being looked at."

"Of course not," she muttered ruefully. "The ones who are unhappy will be the ones who have something to hide. Who would have thought that it would take some asshole to bring this case back up into the eyes of the police again?" she muttered.

"Did you ever ask to have it opened?"

"I did," she confirmed, "and I was always told that nothing was new, so there was no reason to open it and to waste the man-hours."

"And that's not wrong," Lilliana interjected, as she stopped by.

"No, it wasn't wrong," Kate murmured. "Yet now apparently it is reopened, and that's the part I don't understand."

"What part is that?"

"Did they know that this would open it all up again, and that partly was why it was done this way?"

"I don't know," Lilliana replied, looking at her, "but it would seem to imply that they wanted it open."

"Exactly," Kate stated. "We're always looking at these cases as if they're wanting to be closed, but what if that isn't it? What if, in this case, somebody wants it opened for answers."

"And that would bring us back to your mother again."

She winced at that and nodded. "I'm not saying my mother couldn't be behind it. I'm just saying that it would be unusual for her to care at this stage. … If she's healing, if she's gone through any kind of therapy, maybe it was her back then. If not, maybe she is still looking for answers. Maybe, … maybe she needs answers in order to move on," Kate suggested.

"Just because she's my mother doesn't mean she's not a human being who also lost a child. The fact that I was the one who ended up losing my childhood is not her fault. It's purely the fault of whoever kidnapped my brother." Just then her phone rang. She looked down, frowning, as she didn't recognize the number but answered it. "Hello," she said, her gaze on the other two as they waited for her to get off the phone and to continue the conversation.

"I need to talk to you." The hoarse voice from years of smoking, alcohol, and drug abuse sounded like stones grating. "And this time without your pokey little friends." And, with that, she hung up.

Kate sucked in her breath and looked over at the other two. "That was my mother. She wants to talk to me."

Lilliana immediately shook her head. "That's not a good idea."

Kate nodded but sighed. "I know that, but I'm not sure how to handle this."

"I'll go with you," Lilliana offered. "This is not something to mess around with, … particularly if it's related to the case. You definitely shouldn't be there alone."

"She did say to come without my *pokey friends*," Kate

shared, with an eye roll.

"Of course she did. She obviously has zero respect for the law."

"I think that zero respect for authority comes after a decade of trying to avoid them," Kate pointed out. "Or a lifetime of trying to avoid them," she corrected. "I'm just not sure what the answer is right now."

At that, Colby walked in, right on time. "What's going on?"

When she told him about the phone call, he frowned. "You're definitely not going alone. Honestly, I would just as soon that we brought her in and spoke to her here."

"And I think, if you did that," Kate suggested, "she would clam up and would stay that way."

"Do you really think she'll be of any help now?" he asked, studying Kate intently.

She hesitated before responding. "I doubt it, but can we take that chance?"

"Then you need to go with somebody we trust."

"That's great, but, if Lilliana comes with me, or Rodney, ... my mother won't open up."

"Maybe not," Colby conceded, looking around the office as if trying to decide.

"She should take Simon," Rodney suggested.

Colby turned to him first, then faced Kate and asked, "How do you feel about that?"

She opened her eyes wider. "Are we really thinking that a civilian is the best person to go with me?" she asked in astonishment.

Her boss frowned. "The thing is, you can't be alone, and he is at least somebody who ... we do trust."

"That's something," Kate muttered in a dry tone. "I'm

sure he would be thrilled to hear that."

Colby flushed. "It would also give you some backup, if she turns out to be completely off her rocker."

Kate frowned as she considered it and then nodded. "Fine, I'll take Simon."

"And you're to report in immediately afterward," Colby ordered, giving her a stare. "No going off and thinking this is all about you."

She laughed. "It's not about me at all," she declared, staring right back. "This is about my brother."

FRUSTRATED, SIMON GOT up and poured himself a second cup of coffee. He made several more attempts to contact either person, the older-sounding voice or the young timid one. But nothing.

It was always nothing, as if everything happened on someone else's time. That was one of the most frustrating things about any of this psychic work. He wanted answers, so why couldn't he get answers? Instead, it seemed, if anybody else wanted answers, they reached out, and they got them. He knew it didn't quite work that way either, but it sure wasn't easy for him. It was damn frustrating.

As he took his coffee and sat back down on the couch, his phone rang. It was Kate. He immediately answered it. "Hey," he greeted her. "Are you coming home anytime soon?" When she hesitated, he replied to his own question, "I'll take that as a no," a note of humor in his tone.

"Actually, I have a request, but it's Colby's suggestion."

"Oh," he replied warily. "What does that mean?"

"That they trust you, at least to a certain extent," she quipped, humor seeping through her tone as well.

"Okay, he trusts me about what?" When she explained, he immediately agreed. She winced. "It won't be nice, and it could get really ugly, pretty fast."

"And you want to keep me out of that. I get it," he said, "but, if your mother has answers, we need to find out."

"Maybe, but she might *not* have answers. This could just be her yanking my chain to get another chance to blame me for all those years that she spent in the psych ward."

"Did you have anything to do with it?" he asked in astonishment.

"No, of course not," she stated, with apprehension, "but I was fairly truthful as to my childhood when it came to my mother. ... So, I'm sure they took a lot of that into account."

"Of course they did," he muttered, "but that's not your fault. She was a useless parent. Even worse, she was abusive."

"I don't think she would consider herself abusive," Kate noted calmly. "Anyway, if you're okay with it, I suppose I owe you dinner afterward."

He wanted to laugh out loud at her sorting through the debits and credits that were in her mind, in terms of favors. "There's no debit or credit for this one," he declared. "We help each other because we need help."

"Maybe," she said crossly, "but you know how I feel about that."

"I know you don't want to feel beholden to anybody," he stated. "Still, I would think that this situation completely eclipses any of that."

"Maybe," she muttered.

"Besides, a couple new restaurants are in that area, so, if you want, we can go try them out afterward."

"Okay, that would be good," she agreed, "and gives us a good reason to not want to scream for hours on end instead."

He chuckled.

"Do you want to meet me there?" she asked.

"No. Why don't I swing by and grab you at work. Then we can both go there, have a meal, and I'll give you a ride back to work in the morning." She hemmed and hawed, and he offered, "Or, you can drive here, and we can leave from here."

"Or you can drive me back to work, and I can bring the car home afterward."

"That too," he replied agreeably. "Whatever makes you comfortable."

"None of it makes me comfortable," she muttered.

"I know, so … whatever makes it easier, let's put it that way."

"You're always so damn accommodating," she snapped, and then she groaned. "I'm sorry."

"Don't be. Maybe you need to go to the dojo and … kick a few butts after this."

"Yeah, that's not a bad idea. … I'm sure they're wondering what happened to me."

"It hasn't been that long, has it?"

"Maybe not, but I used to go all the time, back before you were in my life. Now I spend a lot of my off time with you instead," she pointed out. "So, less going to the dojo and kicking ass."

"I won't say I'm sad about that," he admitted, smiling, "I'll be there in"—he checked his watch—"say, twenty minutes?"

"Good enough. I may or may not be outside, depending on how buried into work I get."

"I'll assume you won't be outside," he replied, with a chuckle. And, with that, he ended the call and headed to pick up his keys.

The thought of meeting her mother was something he was innately curious about. He knew Kate wouldn't appreciate it, but her mother would say an awful lot about Kate. If the situation were reversed, and Kate had a chance to meet his mother, he knew she too would say an awful lot about him as well. Those times had come and gone, but, in Kate's life, some remnants were still there. At least if he saw her mom, he might understand Kate a little bit more.

Then again, knowing her, Kate would probably block him completely out, so he couldn't get any further understanding as to any of what her mother said. He figured he was more or less there as a safety line, just in case her mom got physical. But then again, Kate was quite capable of kicking ass if she wanted to. Not exactly a good thing in this case either. He was still thinking about it when he drove into the police parking lot. As he hopped out, he saw Colby standing there, talking with Kate. She walked closer to Simon, and Colby came with her.

Colby smiled at him. "Hey, it was my idea, but I've been kind of second-guessing it."

Simon shook his head. "Don't bother. I'll go. I need to see who this woman is for myself."

"Maybe, but you've got to realize we can't have anything compromising the case."

"Of course not, but my understanding is that her mother asked Kate to come."

"I know, and that's the part that concerns me."

"It'll be fine," Kate said, "unless you want to call her in for some official visit."

"No, I don't want to do that, not yet," Colby replied. "We don't have any reason to, and, even when we do have a reason, *you* won't be talking to her."

"Good," Kate replied. "I don't want to talk to her now either."

He just patted her on the shoulder and watched as she got into Simon's car.

When they drove away, Simon shared, "Colby seems to be quite concerned."

"Yeah, I think he is," she agreed, shooting him a look. "Then again, if it was one of your staff, you would be too."

He had to agree he would definitely be upset about it. She gave him the directions. "I thought she was in a facility."

"She was, but apparently she got out quite a few years ago—as in thirteen years ago."

Simon frowned. "That means she has to be doing halfway decent."

"Doing something halfway decent or avoiding a certain level of trouble at least," she clarified, with a sigh. "Do people like that ever truly get out of trouble?"

"I don't know," he murmured.

"How is Danny, by the way?" she asked.

Simon smiled at her. "He's doing just fine."

"He's happy to be back at work?"

"He's definitely happy to be back at work. He also knows that my foreman and I are both keeping an eye on him. We don't want him taking that suicide pathway again."

"And yet if that's what he is determined to do," she pointed out, "it's pretty hard for any of us to stop him."

"I know, and that's one of the things that my foreman is all over. Joe really likes Danny. Joe's even had him over to his house a couple times for beer and pizza."

She chuckled. "If you can't get adopted as a child, being adopted as an adult is pretty damn nice."

He glanced at her and burst out laughing. "I hadn't thought about it in that way, but you're right. So far as Joe's family goes, Danny's doing all right."

"Good, seems to be a connection that'll keep Danny alert."

"And that's all he needs. It's a chance to stay grounded and to not go spiraling downward. So he's got that with Joe and his family. Yet it's not that easy to stop once a spiral starts," he pointed out.

"No, so we do everything we can to avoid them getting there."

"I presume Roger has professional help, adapting to real life. And surely his court case won't take long, will it?"

"His should be open-and-shut and will convince the jury that he had been robbed of his life, drugged unconscious by his own brother, serving as his doctor no less. Now the facility itself, Haven Center? That case will take years because they did this to so many other patients as well," she grumbled, as she settled more comfortably into the seat. "It won't be fun either way. All kinds of people are screaming now, after they found out the center was paid quite handsomely to keep their family members locked up and comatose in that facility," she murmured. "It just proves that people are assholes."

He chuckled. "*Some* people *are* assholes," he reminded her. "Then there are all the rest."

"*Right*," she quipped, looking over at him with a big smirk. "They're even bigger assholes."

He snorted and very quickly they were up at the address she'd given him. He looked up at the apartment building and nodded. "Not bad. Obviously not a wealthy area of town, but, if she's in here, she must be holding it together to some degree."

"That's what I'm hoping. I don't wish her any ill will through all this," Kate shared. "I just don't want anything to do with her."

"Sometimes that, in itself, makes things even worse," he pointed out.

She didn't say anything and was already out of the vehicle and walking up to the main entrance to the building. He hurriedly caught up. When they got to the correct apartment number, she knocked on the door. She got no answer. She knocked again harder, and again no answer. She frowned at him.

Simon asked, "Do you think she pulled a runner?"

"I don't know." She tested the doorknob, and it opened under her hand. She poked her head in and called out, "Hello, anybody here? Hello?" There was no answer. She frowned. "I'm on time."

"Sure, but does she have a habit of being on time herself?"

She winced. "No, that she does not."

As she stood here, deciding what to do, he offered, "I can go in, if you want."

"No, no, no, no. I need to. And it needs to be official."

She immediately pushed the door open farther, then called out, "Police, I'm coming in."

As she stepped in and walked through to where the kitchen was, she found her mother collapsed on the floor, her arm outstretched, a needle shoved into it. Kate raced to her mother. She was alive but barely. Kate looked back at Simon. "Call 9-1-1."

Simon, who had followed her in, took one look, swore, and immediately pulled out his phone.

"Call Colby too. And now"—she looked at him—"stay clear of this."

She pulled out her phone as well, and he half listened while he made his own calls. Very quickly, the room was full of paramedics, all racing to save the woman he'd hoped to one day call his mother-in-law.

# CHAPTER 8

KATE SAT IN the hallway of the hospital, waiting for somebody to give her an update on her mother's condition. Colby had just left, and, even now, Rodney paced in front of her.

"I should have gone with you," he snapped.

"But everybody was okay with Simon coming."

"Yes, but you shouldn't have been alone, when finding her like this."

She looked over at him and realized he was worried about her. "I'm fine, Rodney."

He frowned at her and snorted. "I doubt that."

She wanted to laugh. She wanted to cry. She wasn't even sure what the hell she could do here, so she sat, just wondering and waiting. "Has anybody gone back to her apartment?" she asked her partner.

Rodney nodded. "Lilliana and Colby are there, doing a full sweep of the place."

"Good." She dropped her head into her hands, as fatigue swept over her.

"Are you expecting them to find something?"

She lifted her head to frown at him. "Honestly, I'm not sure she did this."

He froze and asked, "What do you mean?"

"She was expecting me. I don't think she would have

done this if she was expecting me to show up any minute. It doesn't make sense."

"But she's a junkie, … so nothing they do makes sense."

She had to ponder that because he was right. If it were anyone else and not her own mother in there, Kate probably would have had the exact same answer. But was she a junkie still? She thought back and noted, "The door was unlocked and unlatched."

"Meaning?" he asked, standing there with his hands on his hips in front of her. "How can you think she didn't do this?"

"I guess I have to consider it," she conceded, staring at him, "because of the renewed investigation into Timmy."

Rodney immediately frowned and turned away to contemplate her words. "That would imply that somebody was afraid of what Selene would say."

"Exactly."

"Given the fact that this is a cold case, we don't know who that could have been."

"Or what she was planning on telling me," Kate pointed out. "If somebody thought she would say the wrong thing, they might have done this to prevent it, to make her word worthless potentially making this either an accidental or deliberate overdose," she explained.

Rodney nodded. "That would make sense."

When he started to pace again, she studied him, then frowned. "You might as well leave. I'll stay here anyway."

He stared at her. "Out of love for your mother, right?" he asked, with a sardonic tone.

She winced and shrugged. "She contacted me, and she's still involved in a case that I'm involved in," she murmured. "So I don't really feel as if I can just leave."

"No, of course not, sorry. That was a really bitchy comment."

She smiled. "Given the circumstances we're in, I'll let you off the hook on that."

He shrugged. "You used to come across as such a bitch, and now you come across as ... way too nice." As she frowned at him in astonishment, he nodded. "In some ways, I almost like the other response better." And, with that, he stormed out of the hospital, leaving her staring after him.

What the hell was that all about? She didn't know, but it made zero sense. Yet that was his issue, not hers. At least she hoped not. God, ... what a mess.

Just then her phone rang. *Simon.* She quickly answered, without even saying hello, "No update."

A sigh came on the other end. "Not shocking, I guess. Do you want me to come by?"

"Not unless you're bringing coffee and food," she muttered.

He laughed. "I can do that too, you know?"

"You don't exist just to feed me," she muttered. "I can always grab something from the hospital cafeteria." She swore she heard his wince.

"I don't think so," he declared in shock. "That would be worse than anything."

She chuckled. "You do know people live on that stuff here."

"Yeah, they also die there too," he snapped back immediately.

She wouldn't argue because he was right. She was in a hospital after all. "I'll give you an update whenever I have something. ... I just sent Rodney home."

"I'm surprised he was still there."

"I think he was looking to support me."

"And I suppose you told him that it was fine and that you didn't need any support."

She sighed. "In a way, … that's kind of how I feel."

"Numb?" he asked.

"Maybe," she conceded. "I don't know whether it's numb so much as just trying to figure out what the hell's going on with this case and why she would have contacted me. I think that's the part that bothers me the most."

"You're thinking somebody did this to her?"

"I have to consider it, don't I?" She sighed again. "I mean, if she decided to bare her soul, and somebody would be affected by that, some potential conspirator or somebody she may have been hiding all this time, then they aren't left in a good position."

"Are you thinking Selene had something to do with your brother's disappearance?"

"No," she replied immediately, "I honestly don't. Yet I'm worried that she knows who did. And, rather than dealing with it all those years ago, she's finally decided that now is the time."

"Interesting," Simon muttered. "That could be tough, breaking through decades of some conspiracy to keep it quiet."

"And potentially exposing someone who thought they were safe and moved on," she pointed out.

"Until now."

"Exactly. Therefore, I plan to stay here, waiting for her to wake up—until the next emergency breaks."

"Understood. I'll be by in a few minutes."

And, with that, he was gone, leaving her staring down at her phone and wondering if she really should have brought him in or not. As much as she wanted to have him around sometimes, he wasn't necessarily the easiest person to include because he made her look at things in her life that she didn't particularly want to deal with. Yet there really wasn't any option when it came to him.

Just then the doctor walked out of her mother's room, saw Kate was still here, and frowned. When she raised an eyebrow, he nodded. "Selene will make it." He hesitated, then asked, "Does she have a history of drugs?"

"She has a previous history of drugs," Kate clarified. "I don't know about the last ten years or so."

"Right." He nodded. "I have a very up and down history for her."

"Yes, and again I don't know how much of this history is still valid. She was, … I thought, getting help and had potentially moved on."

"Do you know what happened to set her off?"

"She was a drug addict when I was growing up," she explained, "so what set her off initially, I don't know. What I can tell you is that, when I was seven, my younger brother disappeared, and we never saw him again. He was five years old. That sent my mother into a spiral from which she never recovered."

"Not many do," the doc confirmed, as he looked back at the woman in the hospital bed, with a complete change in his attitude now.

"Afterward she was eventually remanded for mental health and substance abuse treatment," Kate shared, trying to keep the irony out of her voice. "We ultimately lost touch. I was put into foster care and made a life for myself."

"Without her?"

"Yes, without her," Kate declared, her tone hardening.

"She blamed me for my brother's disappearance." When he looked at her in surprise, she shrugged. "I was seven and didn't take kindly to having the blame put on my shoulders."

"Put on your shoulders because she had to have a target, and you were available," the doctor suggested, with a nod. "We see that a lot too."

"Maybe, but, when it's on your shoulders, it really sucks."

"It does, indeed," he agreed, "but you're a cop now, aren't you?"

"I am, and we currently have a reason to reopen my brother's case," she said. "The police tried to talk to her about it yesterday, and then she contacted me later to come talk to her. When we got there, we found her like this."

"Interesting, since it begs the question, was she really ready to talk to you, or did she change her mind at the last minute and panicked?"

"I don't know," Kate admitted. "However, I very much want to hear what she had to say."

"Of course," he replied. "It'll be a while though. Don't get your hopes up that she'll be terribly willing to talk when she first wakes up."

"Right, I understand. If she changed her mind and did this," she noted, "then obviously she may wake up with that same mind change."

"Exactly," he murmured. "Anyway, she'll be out for hours yet, so you can't talk to her. If you want to go ho—"

"I'll stay," she cut him off, her tone inflexible.

He nodded. "That's what I figured you would say." And, with that, he turned and headed down the hallway.

Only a few minutes later came Simon, walking toward her. When she raised her eyebrows at him, he shrugged.

"I was already on my way over."

She groaned. "Of course you were." However, the smell of food woke up her system in a big way. Her stomach growled as he approached.

He smiled. "It does seem that I need to feed you on a regular basis."

She shook her head but reached eagerly for the bag. "I didn't used to eat this much"—she rolled her eyes—"until after you showed up."

"And that's not good," he declared, eyeing her. "In theory, you should be eating steadily."

"Sure, but it was never a big issue before. Besides, I had to provide my own food." She sent him a cheeky grin.

That made him laugh. He added, "I'm glad you're in decent spirits."

She shook her head. "I'm not really. Even though they've told me that she'll survive, I'm not convinced she will."

"Meaning?"

She shrugged. "I don't understand what's going on, so I really want to know what she has to say and whether that had anything to do with her actions afterward."

"Or did somebody else do this?" he pointed out shrewdly.

She nodded. "Or did somebody else. At the office, everybody else is trying to do an investigation into this," she murmured. "That's got its own set of hazards."

"Nobody else was at her place?"

"No, but still somebody could have been accustomed to spending a night or two."

"Ah, that's also very true. Do you want me to go over there and take another look?"

She immediately shook her head. "No, I want to. They've already sent forensics over there, but I want to make sure I'm in on that final sweep."

"And can you be?" he asked.

"I hope so," she muttered, as she unwrapped a sandwich. "That's the plan anyway. *My* plan. And I know they all have ideas of what I should and should not be doing in this one, but it's pretty hard to just sit here and to do nothing but wait."

"And that's what they want you to do?"

"They want as much as they can to keep me out of the investigation," she shared, with a wry look at him.

"And, of course, you'll thwart that, won't you?"

"No, I won't, at least not deliberately." He just rolled his eyes at that, and she shrugged. "I mean, I'm not even the best person to talk to about her, but, if she has somebody who's staying over there, or coming and going on a regular basis, that is someone we need to talk to—not to mention her coworkers and other potential contacts."

"And you will do a bunch of that yourself, but not as a cop, right?"

"I was thinking about that," she admitted, with a nod. "By rights I could go do something constructive tonight." She frowned as she looked down at her watch, and almost immediately Colby contacted her. She skipped the usual greeting and went with the update. "She's doing okay, and they say she'll come around, but she'll be out for several hours, so I can't talk to her yet," Kate began. "I want to go to her place and take a closer look and see if she's had anybody else living there or visiting regularly, plus talk to the neighbors and see if anybody saw anything." When Colby hesitated, she sighed. "I know, but we're also shorthanded, and, in this case, it makes sense that it would be me."

"Until there's a problem, and then it doesn't make sense at all."

"Of course," she murmured, "but, if we were to keep to that standard, we would never get anywhere. I've got Simon here with me, and we can just take a quick look through her place and ensure forensics didn't miss anything."

"That's what forensics does," he reminded her. "They don't miss stuff."

"They don't *intend* to miss things," she clarified, "but you also know that they often do."

He hesitated.

"I'll let you know if I find anything. Obviously I didn't get a chance to look around at all because of how we found her. So I want to at least go back and take a look at what, in my mind, *should* have been there."

"Are you looking for something specific?"

"No, not specific, but it does feel as if we're missing something."

"Fine," he relented, "but you let me know when you get there, and you let me know when you leave."

"Will do." She hopped to her feet as she put away her phone. She looked at Simon and added, "You don't have to come."

He raised his eyebrows. "I'm your ride, remember? Plus, you already told your boss that I was going with you."

"I know," she admitted, with a smile. "He seems to think you're a calming influence on me or something."

Simon snorted. "That just says he doesn't know you all that well, doesn't it?"

"I'm sure he wants to think he knows me very well," she noted, "but this is unfamiliar territory for all of us."

"Meaning?"

"Meaning that it's my mother," she acknowledged. "It's *my* mother. It's *my* brother, and it's a whole mess of emotions. I understand his point. I get it. Yet I still just need Colby to give me a little room to maneuver."

Simon asked, "Do you want to go in and say hi to Selene?"

"No, she'll be out of it for hours yet. Plus, they're still working on her. Let's just go. I'll come back afterward." When he frowned at that, she shrugged. "What else am I supposed to do? I need to check out her apartment now, with a fresh perspective."

"Right," he replied, staring her down.

She frowned. "I'm not saying that as a daughter. I'm saying that as a detective."

He rolled his eyes. "Whatever you want to believe," he muttered, as he nudged her down the hallway.

"Good sandwich too," she shared, as she took the last bite and dropped the wrapper into the closest bin. "Did you want one?"

"I'll eat later." When she frowned at him, he added, "It's fine. Let's go."

"How was your day?" she asked him.

"My day was fine," he said, "but this is all about you."

"I don't want it to be all about me." She moaned. She knew she was being difficult, but it was hard to manage all the emotions brought up when dealing with her mother and her brother. Everybody seemed to be walking on tenterhooks around her, and she didn't like that either. Then again, there wasn't a whole lot to like about any of this.

She walked out of the hospital, then stopped and took several deep breaths. "I really hate those places."

He smiled and nudged her to his car up ahead. She hopped into the passenger seat, and he drove the relatively short distance to her mother's apartment.

As they got to Selene's door, several neighbors came out of nearby apartments. Kate asked them if they knew the woman, keeping it tucked away that it was her mother.

One of them shrugged, and he replied, "I've seen her around. Why?"

"She's in hospital at the moment," Kate shared. "We just wondered if she had any regular visitors or any friends."

"None that I know of," he said, "but I wouldn't know because I don't keep track of her." He looked around at his neighbors. "Honestly, I don't have a lot to do with anybody in this place."

"Right," she noted, as the neighbors all headed toward the elevator, laughing and talking among themselves.

Nobody looked back, and nobody seemed to care as she turned to her mother's apartment.

Kate sighed, as she watched them leave. She turned to Simon. "You don't realize how isolated the world is, until you run into somebody who's got an issue. Then you find out that nobody even knows they existed."

"What's that now, pity?" Simon asked.

"No," she declared, glaring at him. "But it's not just about my mother, it's everyone. How many times do we come across people who don't have family, friends, or anybody who gives a crap?"

He just nodded.

She came to the door, then groaned and pushed it open. Almost immediately the memories assaulted her. She took a deep breath and stepped through. She was glad that Simon didn't say anything but just watched her. She looked around, frowned, and muttered, "Forensics has obviously been here."

"Of course they have. Isn't that what you expected?"

"I did, but I guess I also half expected to see some evidence of some crime."

"Yet you also might have to ultimately accept that there was no crime and that it was self-induced."

"I know," she muttered. "I know that but not yet…"

"However, just because you know your mother was a junkie, doesn't mean that you're ready and prepared to see the evidence of a slide back into that same state again. And, in this case, we don't know that's what happened."

"No, we don't," she agreed. "I'm just trying to be objective." She walked into the kitchen, her gaze turning sharp as she carefully studied one thing after another.

She stopped inside, then frowned. "She hasn't been living alone. That's for sure." There in the bathroom were multiple toothbrushes and several other male trappings—shavers, razors, and a grooming kit.

"At least not all the time," Simon pointed out. "Doesn't mean anybody's been here recently though."

"That's true too," she murmured, as she kept going.

Getting to the bedroom, she quickly checked under the bed. Inside the nightstand she found boxes of condoms and not a whole lot else. Frowning, she stepped out.

Simon asked, "What's the matter?"

She shrugged. "I get that she lived here." She looked all around. "But there's also not a whole lot of personality here. Seems she's either just moved here or doesn't spend a lot of time here."

NOW THAT KATE had mentioned it, Simon saw the same

thing. "It's possible she just moved in," he pointed out. "Particularly if she has not been out of a treatment center for very long."

Kate nodded and stared around the room. "It's something we'll take a look at."

"Of course."

She went from one room to the other and then headed right back to the bedroom. For whatever reason, that was where she centered her focus.

For him it was fascinating to watch her slide right back into detective mode. It was a little easier to understand her when she was like this. It was easier to see where she was coming from and who she was looking after in her mind. When she turned and headed to the bedroom, he was on her heels.

He stood in the doorway and watched, not sure what she was looking for, but knowing that, until she found it, she would dig away. She opened the closet and started pulling out box after box, three in total, all seemingly packed up and ready to move. She whistled as she opened the top one.

"What is all this?" he asked, as he stepped forward.

She frowned, looking down at the boxes. "Case files," she said softly. "Files on my brother."

He frowned back at her, and she nodded, pointing at them. "Interesting," he muttered, as Kate began sifting through one box.

"Articles, newspapers, all about it," she noted. "Nothing seems to have been disturbed in a while. Maybe she held on to everything, hoping, but then gave up after a time."

"In a way that helps to clear her, doesn't it?"

"Maybe. ... I mean, mentally, if you were this fixated on the case itself, maybe it shows that you aren't related to any of the happenings about it. Yet a lot of people can twist that around to say she was following everything in the news afterward in order to stay abreast of any developments. Then she could get herself out of trouble quickly."

Simon looked startled. "I hadn't considered that."

"Lots of people who commit murder have that same reaction," she shared. "They hound the files. They hound the newspapers. They hound everything so they can stay one step ahead. Honestly, that is what a lot of people would say this is about." She shook her head.

"What does it mean to you?"

She stared at him, and her tone was bleak. "Honestly? A life lost."

"Yours, your brother's, whose?" he asked, not sure why he was pushing her.

"Hers. More than anything, … hers." And, with that, Kate opened up the other boxes, realizing that the contents of all three were related to her brother's case. "How come she has so much?"

"What do you mean?"

"I don't have this much in the official file," she muttered. With that, she took the top box to the bed and started pulling out folders and files. It wasn't long before she turned and looked at him. "She hired a private detective."

"She did?" he asked. "I didn't think she had any money."

"I didn't think so either," Kate confirmed, frowning as she looked back down at the files.

"Do you think she hired the PI?"

"I don't know," she admitted, "but that's what these files are."

"And you're saying that doesn't jive with the woman you

know?"

"Nothing jives with the woman I know," she stated, with a mock smile, "but remember that my information is very old. And I haven't had an update on her in a long time."

He acknowledged that any update would have meant Kate had some contact with her mother, and that was something both of them had avoided all these years. He asked, "Does the PI have a name?"

She went through the folders and nodded. "Yeah." She brought out a report from him, took a photo of it, and read off the name on the report. "John McCauley. Do you know him?"

Simon shook his head. "No, but I don't know very many private investigators anyway." He gave her a wry smile. "No need to use them."

"*Right*," she murmured. She pulled out her phone and dialed the number for the guy. She immediately frowned once more.

"What's the matter?"

"It says the number is no longer in service." She stared down at the files. It didn't take much for the two of them to find an address. She looked over at him. "Are you up for a road trip?"

"Always," he replied. "Do you want to take photos of any of this stuff?"

# CHAPTER 9

S HE NODDED BUT quickly phoned Colby and told him what they found as he listened in.

"Forensics did mention that," he shared, "and we're waiting for a warrant to seize it and to bring it in."

"Right," she muttered. "I hate to leave it all here. However, we do have the name of a private detective, so I wanted to contact him."

"Why do you want to jump on it?"

"His phone isn't in service anymore."

"What's the name?" Colby asked, his voice sharpening.

"John McCauley," she replied. He snorted, so she asked, "Why?"

"Ah, hell," he muttered.

"You want to talk to me about that?"

"He was convicted of fraud, cheating, making up information for his clients," Colby explained. "McCauley would take on cases and then manufacture information, making his clients think he was doing something, but, in reality, he wasn't."

"Ah, so my mother was potentially swindled in that deal too."

"I would think the potential was high," Colby noted. "Yet, as that case is also ongoing, it might be a situation where we need access to those files to prove there were other victims."

"They're right here," she said. "You give me the word, and I'll bring them in."

She heard him talking in the background, then he came back and told her, "Bring them in. If nothing else they'll be ammunition for his future court case."

"Didn't you say he was convicted?"

"Yes, but they're reopening it, wondering if more was involved."

"As in?"

"As in, murder."

"Oh, crap," she muttered. "In that case, we definitely need these."

With a look over at Simon, they lifted the boxes and carried them out. In the hallway, a box in her arms, she stopped, looked around, and realized it was a dead little corner, and really nobody was here. No life, nobody moving back and forth. She put her box down in the hallway, walked to the apartment across the hall, and knocked on the door.

When a woman opened it just enough so she could see through the chain, Kate held up her badge. The woman groaned. "I did talk to somebody earlier today," she shared. "I don't know anything about the woman. I haven't had anything to do with her."

"Right, so you haven't seen anybody coming back and forth?"

She hesitated and then replied, "There has been, but I don't have a good idea who they are."

"Male?"

"Yes, definitely male. That much I can tell."

"Could you give us a description of him?"

She shook her head. "Honestly, the only way you survive

these days is by staying to yourself, so I don't really know anything."

"Do you know how long she's been here?"

"Months, if not years. However, for a while, she wasn't really here," she added, with a wave of her hand. "I don't know whether she's been away or had another place to live, but at least she would come and go. Then she wouldn't come, and we didn't see her for quite a while. But now, after what happened with the drugs, maybe she was in a rehab center or something."

For some reason that seemed to tick Kate off. Still, she shrugged and responded, "It's possible, yes." She was biting back her tongue.

The other woman winced. "It's better than thinking somebody did this to her," she pointed out nervously, as she looked around the hallway.

"Is there much in the way of drug dealing going on here?"

The woman stared at her. "I honestly don't know. I don't have anything to do with drugs," she whispered, as she tried to close the door a little more. "Look. I've got to go. I've got kids here. I don't even want them to hear this conversation." And, with a faint smile, she closed the door.

"That didn't help much, did it?" Simon asked.

"It didn't necessarily help, but it didn't really hurt either. The one thing that was obvious is that she's afraid."

He studied Kate, then looked back at the neighbor's door. "I wouldn't necessarily have thought that."

"No, but that's because you couldn't see her trying to close the door in my face or her white-knuckled grip on the door. Somebody else was in there," she stated, shaking her head. "What I don't know is who it is and if that person has any connection to what happened to my mother."

Simon frowned. "Could it just have been that she was scared because it's the police?" he pointed out.

"It could be," she conceded, yet not willing to let it go. "The thing is, because she's afraid, now she's somebody of interest to me."

He groaned. "That's not fair to anyone. As soon as somebody comes to the door, and there's a problem, everybody goes into defensive mode."

"I understand," she agreed, "but this woman's response was much more." She frowned and knocked on the door again. When no answer came, she pounded on it harder and harder. She looked over at him. "Is that normal to you?"

"It depends. She may have left, or she may be dealing with kids," he suggested, "and she may just not want to talk to you."

"She definitely doesn't want to talk to me," Kate confirmed, "but the biggest question is why. What is the problem with talking to me, except for the fact that she's scared?" She pounded on the door one more time.

This time it opened with a fury, and a huge burly male with a beer gut stepped out, his expression thunderous, as he shoved his face in Kate's. "What the fuck does it take for you to leave us alone? She told you that she doesn't want to talk to you."

"Yeah, that may be," Kate noted, shoving her face right back into his. "Yet maybe it's *you* I really want to talk to."

He stared at her. "I don't know shit," he snapped. "The neighbor woman is nothing but a psycho bitch."

"Really? And you know that how?"

"Because I talk to her. She's always trying to scrounge drugs off me," he sneered. "I don't have time for that crap.

Anybody who does drugs is just one sick motherfucker."

"Really?" she asked, with a mock smile. "I suppose alcohol is your vice then?"

"It's not a vice," he declared, glaring at her. "Alcohol is decent at least. It doesn't turn you into a crazy man."

"If you say so," she said, staring at him intently. "So, what did you see?"

"I didn't see fuck-all," he snapped. "Why the hell would you even think I did?"

"It's hard *not* to think you did. It's pretty clear, especially when you won't even let the poor woman inside talk to me."

"She already talked to everybody she needs to, and now you're just hassling her."

"I'm really glad to know you're here looking out for her," she quipped, with a knowing smile, "because, at this point, we're not exactly sure whether this was an overdose or something else."

"It was an overdose. ... That's obvious," he declared, staring at her. "Anybody could have seen that. She had the fucking needle hanging off her arm."

"Oh? You saw that, did you?" she asked, eyeing him intently. "Kind of interesting that you saw that."

"Not really," he snapped. "They took her out of here on a gurney so hard to miss."

"And you were at your door, watching?"

"I saw some of it, yeah. Why not? We got pretty piss-poor entertainment around this place. So, if somebody offs it next door, you kind of want to see who and what you're dealing with."

"Who and what you're dealing with, or just a gory sense of curiosity?"

"Whatever," he mumbled. "No crime in that."

"Maybe not," she replied, still staring him down. "It depends on whether you can tell us about anybody who might have been there earlier or not."

"I don't know. I didn't get home too early."

"Which is why I was trying to talk to your partner in there."

"You did talk to her," he snapped, "and you won't talk to her anymore."

"Unless I need her down at the station," Kate countered, calmly staring at him. "And then you better make sure she shows up."

He frowned. "Hey, hey, hey, no need for that. She can't afford to get babysitters, … not cool."

"And yet here you are interfering in an official investigation."

"What investigation? She's nothing but a junkie," he argued in frustration. "So, she killed herself. Who gives a fuck?"

"And yet," Kate added, looking at him, "maybe she didn't kill herself. Maybe that was you over there, popping her. It's not as if anybody else would know. For all I know, you weren't even at work today."

"Hey, hey, hey," he roared, but it was obvious he was getting agitated.

"I'll need an alibi from you," Kate stated, with a hard smile.

He stared at her. "Are you serious, man?"

"Yeah, I am serious," she snapped right back at him. "A woman is in hospital, fighting for her life. Whether she did it to herself or somebody else did it to her, we need to know what happened."

"Fucking cops," he muttered, slouching against the door.

"I didn't see anybody before, and neither did she. We talked about it earlier, and she thinks it was an overdose. How anybody can think it was anything but that, I don't know," he said. "You guys are just trying to make a case where there isn't one. Why don't you go off and deal with the bloody drug dealers?"

"That's next," she shared, with half a smile. "I don't suppose you know where she got her fix, do you?"

"No, I don't," he snapped. With that, he turned to go back in to his apartment, and added, "And I was at work." Then he gave her the name of the company. "You can check with them."

"I will," she confirmed, with a smile. "Have a good evening."

And, with that, she turned, picked up her box, and walked down the hallway, leaving Simon helpless to do much of anything as he held the other two boxes. He did nod at the man, as Kate set off. Simon quickly followed her down the hallway.

Kate had reached the car and just deposited her box with Simon's two in the trunk, when her phone rang. It was Colby.

"I got two men on the PI, already heading out to check on the address. So you stay out of it, Kate. Got that?"

Kate grumbled, didn't say a word, and listened to the *click* on the other end of the call.

# CHAPTER 10

KATE WOKE THE next morning with a deep sense of unease. She reached for her phone and called the hospital. Reassured that her mother was still alive but frustration that her mother was still unconscious, Kate laid back down on the bed, wondering what had caused her to wake up with that sense of wrongness. She frowned as she glanced around. Seeing no sign of Simon, she bolted out of bed and walked out to the living room.

He was sitting on the couch, but his gaze was off in the distance.

She stepped up quietly and stared at him, but, when he didn't respond, she whispered, "Simon, are you there?"

No answer came.

Frowning, she walked around so she could get a full visual on his face. His eyes were super wide open, and she wasn't sure what to make of that. She crouched in front of him. "Simon, I'm here," she murmured. "It's okay." He gave half a snort and muttered something intelligible, and she frowned, stepping back ever-so-slightly. Then she realized it wasn't even necessarily his voice. "Who is this?" she snapped.

Simon jolted, surprised into movement, and then he gave his head a hard shake and woke up. He stared at her, frowning.

"Hey," she greeted him. "Are you okay?"

"I'm not sure," he conceded. "By the look on your face, you don't seem to think I am."

She winced. "I'm not sure either. I came out here, and you were staring off into the distance. I spoke to you, and you gave a snort and mumbled something." She then added, "Honestly, I got the impression it wasn't you."

His eyebrows shot up, and he just stared at her.

"I know. I know," she agreed, backing away, holding up her hands. "I don't even believe I said that either."

"It's interesting that you did," he noted, "because I've certainly had a feeling the last few days of something else going on."

"*Uh-oh,*" she muttered. "Going on how?"

He winced. "That I can't really answer. Just … not normal."

"Nothing about you is normal," she pointed out.

He gave her a small smile. "No, but you seem to be okay with the fact that I'm *not normal.*"

"Sometimes I'm okay with it," she conceded, "and other times? Well, … it's a little bit harder."

"And yet you're doing so well," he stated solemnly.

She groaned and sat down on the couch beside him. He looked over at her and the oversized shirt that she'd pulled on the previous night when she got cold. She kept several very unsexy outfits here, and, up until now, he'd been okay with it. She wasn't one to worry about how she looked.

Simon sighed. "We really need to get you some better nightclothes."

"Do we?" she asked, with a wave of her hand. "I'm more concerned about you."

"Of course you are," he said, with a sigh. "I'm not even sure when I came out here."

She frowned at him. "I figured you just couldn't sleep."

"I'm not sure what I figured," he admitted, shaking his head. "Honestly, I don't remember coming out here."

She nodded as he scrubbed at his face. She asked, "What do you remember?"

"I remember somebody laughing."

"Yeah, and that would go along with the snort and the mumbling that I heard."

He sighed. "The trouble is, I'm really not getting much in the way of answers, no matter what I do."

"Are you looking for answers?"

"Yes," he confirmed. "I was hoping to find some … on your brother."

She stiffened, then sighed. "That would be nice, if there were answers to get," she noted. "I certainly won't hold that against you."

"Of course not," he agreed, with a wave of his hand. "That would be very *un-Kate-like.*"

She glared at him. "I'm getting a lot of comments lately about how I'm not the normal Kate anymore," she shared, "and I really don't appreciate it."

He cocked his head at her and then laughed. "So, are you worse or better?"

"According to Rodney, … both."

Simon's eyebrows shot up, and he asked, "How does that work?"

"I don't know, something about … he preferred the old Kate, but this new Kate is nicer," she explained, "and *that* I really can't have." Simon snickered and she nodded. "I don't want people thinking I'm getting soft and am some nice person now," she muttered. She glared at him, got up, and moved to the kitchen. "So, as long as you're okay, I'm putting on coffee."

"Coffee would be good," he murmured, as he got up and stretched. She watched him warily. "I won't explode, Kate."

"That's good," she muttered. "I never really quite know what you'll do."

He smiled at her. "I know. I'm a bit of a trial."

"We're all a bit of a trial," she agreed, with a weary smile. "I'm not exactly my normal self at present either."

"With your brother's case up front and center again, that's true and understandable. … How is your mom?"

"You tell me."

"She's fine, no change," he replied automatically and then frowned, staring at her as if she had horns. "I don't know how I know that."

"You're right. She is fine, with no change," she confirmed. "So, I'm not sure where your information came from, but it's all good." She spoke with a straight face, but she kept a wary eye on him.

He glared at her. "Kate, I really don't know where that information came from."

"Some of the research I find myself doing says that, because I apparently now have a psychic in my world, all this information is out there in the energy field, and you can access it whenever you want."

"In the energy field?" he asked.

"Yeah, don't ask me what that is," she said, rolling her eyes. "I was kind of hoping you would know."

"God only knows," he muttered, glaring at her. "It's not as if I have any experience in this shit."

"Nope, you sure don't, and, at the rate you're going, you may not get any more," she declared cheerfully.

He shook his head. "You're awfully cheerful."

"No, I'm not really," she admitted. "I'm just trying to start with a good mood, so maybe I can get through today."

"I'm sorry. It's a rough time for you right now."

She just nodded and didn't say anything. When the coffee was done, she poured two cups and brought one over to him and sat down on the couch.

"Plans for today?" he asked her.

"Get a lift from you to go to work as my car is still there," she replied, quirking an eyebrow at him more in question if he remembered, but he nodded. "Try and find who's behind this bloody note and see what the hell is going on with my mother," she muttered. "So, no end of crappy things to think about today. And then, of course, I have a current case with a young boy whose parents have absolutely no interest in confessing to abusing him."

"Aah." Simon groaned. "Those are always the worst. And he's dead?"

"Yes, he's dead."

"It will be the end of the poor mother."

"Of course, and the father apparently let his brother look after the child, while dear old dad went out for a bit, while the mom was away at a conference."

"And the child died on the brother's watch?"

She nodded. "Yes, apparently."

"Great, that'll cause all kinds of family drama, won't it?"

"I think it's too late for that," she stated. "According to the interviews, the brother says he had nothing to do with it. But the fact remains, the child is dead, and I'm waiting on Smidge for the autopsy report. I know he wasn't looking forward to it. As far as he was concerned, he already saw clear signs of long-term abuse."

"Suspect?"

"The father has been in counseling and treatment for anger management and has done time for child abuse and domestic violence."

"Jesus," Simon muttered, staring at her.

"Yeah, and now we have a dead child, and we're not exactly sure who to blame."

"And, of course, the law wants to blame somebody."

"We do have a dead child," she repeated, looking over at him. "Somebody did that, so somebody has to pay the price."

"It still won't bring back the child."

"No, it sure won't," she admitted. "For the mother's sake, we will do everything we can."

"And yet she's still with the abuser."

Kate nodded. "As far as I can tell from the reports, it was his child as well."

"Christ," Simon muttered, rubbing his forehead. "How about you just lock up the whole family?"

"I would love to," she declared, shrugging her body as if to shake off an unpleasant feeling. "If it were clear-cut, it would be my absolute pleasure to toss all three of them in jail and to throw away the key," she added, "but I don't get that choice."

"Aren't you officially off all cases right now?"

"No, I'm on limited duty due to personal concerns."

"Of course," he replied, "your mother."

"They'll come up with any number of things to keep me away from active duty," she noted, with a look in his direction. "My mother is one of them, and the fact is, somebody is sending me notes that make no sense but are telling me to rethink everything about my brother's disappearance. As if I haven't already spent a lifetime doing that."

"That's the worst part, isn't it?" Simon asked. "No answers just lead you to question what did everybody miss all those years ago?"

She gave him a wry look. "I've spent lifetimes reconsidering everything I know about my brother's disappearance. ... Once I hit adulthood, almost every year on the anniversary of Timmy's disappearance, I talked to every person I could remember from that time. It always came back as useless. Nobody knows anything. Now here we are, going on twenty-one years later," she muttered. "And now somebody seems to think he knows something."

"But the real trick," Simon pointed out, his hand covering hers, "is the fact that somebody *does* know something, or they wouldn't have tried to silence your mother. Now you must figure out who that is." She waited in silence, as he drank his coffee. He shrugged. "I don't know what's going on, but I did try to contact your brother."

"But no luck?"

"Nope."

"Do you ..." She closed her eyes and sighed.

Simon knew right away what she wanted to ask. "Do I know if he's dead or alive? No," he stated. "I don't. Apparently, some people from the other side can talk to people on this side, but not everyone can. Even if they can, not everyone wants to." Her shoulders sagged, and he nodded. "I'm sorry because I would love nothing more than to give you what you need."

"Of course you would," she agreed, "but that apparently won't happen."

"It will one day," he stated, "but it may not be anytime soon. At least not from my corner of the world."

She smiled. "Anything that happens in that psychic

world is good, and, as long as you're learning to control it, that's also good."

"My grandmother spent a lifetime without a community, without support, and I don't think she resented it. However, during several low points in her life, she could have used a friend. And I don't think she had any."

"Was it that nobody really believed her or …"

He shrugged. "I think everybody just wanted something from her."

She winced at that. "I can see that too," she murmured. "And I'm definitely guilty of that myself." When he looked at her in surprise, she shrugged. "How many times does my office want me to get information that you might have?"

He snorted. "If I had more, I would give more, and I sure don't blame you guys. I just look at the cases you're dealing with all the time and realize how traumatizing it is to do this work and to struggle to find answers. I have enough connections to that shady world myself that I can see it. And I've been involved in enough cases with you that I understand it better."

"Maybe," she conceded, "but sometimes I still feel bad asking."

He smiled and gave her a hug. "And that is what makes you *you.*"

"Bullshit," she said succinctly. He burst out laughing and was still grinning when her phone rang. She sighed, picked it up, and asked, "Hey, Rodney. What's up?"

"Another case."

"Damn." She listened for a few minutes, got the address from him, and replied, "I'll get the details when I see you."

"Yeah, well, you won't like them," Rodney replied.

Kate noted something unsettling in his tone. "In that

case," she declared, "I'm definitely the one who needs to come."

"I would just as soon you didn't," he stated, "as I have this really horrible feeling that it's connected to yesterday's mess."

"The dead child?" she asked.

"Yes," he confirmed, his tone pitched higher. "We have another dead child, older this time, and injured multiple times by the family."

"What the hell?"

"Yeah, in this case we don't have very much in the way of information, but he's dead, potentially from a drug overdose."

"Good God." Kate swore. "So did you mean connected to my mother or connected to the younger child?"

"Honestly, I'm not sure. For all I know, it's connected to both, or possibly neither." And, with that, he ended the call.

She stared down at the phone. "Dead teen," she murmured to Simon. "I'm not too sure of the details, but Rodney seems to think it might be connected to another current case." She got up, tossed back the rest of her coffee. "One thing I do know is that it's time for me to go to work."

On the way there, she called the hospital to check on her mother's status. Selene remained unconscious but the staff were still optimistic that she would make it.

Kate arrived at this newest crime scene in just under thirty minutes. Rodney stood there, a morose expression on his face. "Hey," she muttered, "dead kids are always an issue."

"Dead kids, ... yeah, this one is sixteen," he said.

She walked over to the body and froze because he was lying in the same position her mother had been, with a needle sticking out of his arm. She shook her head at that.

"Well, hell."

Smidge looked up at her and glared.

She nodded. "This is too much reminiscing for me."

"Ya think?" he snapped, nearly biting off her head. And then he did a double-take. "Wait, what did you say?"

"This is how my mother was found."

"Your mother? I don't have your mother on my docket."

She looked over at him and nodded. "We got there just in time. She's in ICU at the hospital."

He frowned and nodded. "That's something at least." He eyed her sideways.

She knew that look. "We've been estranged since I was a child," she murmured.

"Of course," he replied. "I can't imagine you having much to do with a junkie for a family member."

"Yeah, you're right," she agreed, her tone hardening. "I have a pretty-low tolerance when it comes to that. Not to mention I was raised with her constantly shooting up."

He winced. "That's not anybody's ideal circumstance."

"No, it sure isn't," she declared bitterly. "What does bother me though is that this scene looks very much the same. Needle still hanging out and everything."

"Honest to God," Smidge noted, "we see that all the time."

"Right," she murmured, "so maybe this isn't all that un-usual and not necessarily connected to my mother's close call."

He frowned as he looked at the needle in the teen's arm and then shook his head. "I wouldn't have thought so, but, now that you've brought it up, I'll wonder."

"Good," she said, as she studied the teen. "Keep wonder-ing. I've got another child who just passed away."

"I know," Smidge confirmed. "He's on my docket."

"Which is again good because I also wonder if there aren't similarities between these two."

He frowned at her, glanced back at the dead teen, and asked, "What could possibly be the similarities?"

"I'll let you know when I talk to the family," she replied, "but keep an open mind when you get there."

"Always," he muttered. "You do bring me the most interesting puzzles." And, with that, he ordered the body to be moved.

She straightened and looked around, finding the mother sitting off to the side, chain-smoking.

Rodney nodded toward the woman. "Her name's Edna."

Kate walked over and sat down beside her. "Was that your son?"

Hearing Kate's question sent a jolt to Edna's system, then came a jerking nod. "Yes," she whispered, pinching the cigarette butt between her fingers. "God, I can't believe it."

"Did you know that he did drugs?"

"Yes, I did know he did drugs. I was hoping he was being smart about it."

Kate didn't even know what to say to that. Was there any way to be smart about taking drugs, particularly when you were a teenager? "I'm sorry," Kate replied. "This is never easy."

"No, it isn't." The mother groaned. "I told him so many times not to do any of the hard ones. It was one thing to smoke a little weed, but something like this? Hell no," Edna muttered. Her cigarette burned down, and she immediately lit another one off the end of the first.

Kate watched her and realized this was also a long-term habit, not just stress. "Where were you last night?" she asked, "and when did you last see him?"

Edna glanced at her sideways, then back at her son again. "I work night shift at the pub," she began, "and I got in around three this morning. We were open late last night, and I had a crap load of cleaning to do."

"And when did you find your son?"

"This morning," she said. "The door was a little bit open when I got up, so I pushed it wide and told him to rise and shine, that I had to go out again."

"And he didn't answer?"

"No, he didn't answer," she confirmed. "I went down and made coffee, came back up to get changed, called out to him again, realized I still hadn't heard from him, which is really no different than any other time," she muttered. "He was never easy to get out of bed. I went in there, dragged the covers off of him, and saw him like that."

Kate looked around and frowned. "But his body is out here."

Edna faced her and nodded. "Yeah, I called my girl-friend, screaming, and she told me to get him some air, and he would probably be fine. She suggested it was just an overdose and to call for help. And ... I didn't even think about it, I just opened up his French doors and dragged him outside." She started to sob, great big ugly sobs just then. "Please tell me that I didn't kill him."

"No, I don't think you killed him," Kate stated, as she looked around at the layout. Edna just continued to cry. Kate hated this part and winced.

"That's not what"—she cried, making horrible sounds— "The fresh air ... I should have just left him in the bed. Dear God, ... I raced inside, grabbed my phone, and, when I came back out, I thought he'd moved," she added, "so I started screaming at him and shaking him."

"What do you mean, you thought he'd moved?"

"He was slightly in a different position than I had him," Edna explained, "or at least I think so. The trouble is, I can't be sure of anything anymore."

"Right," Kate murmured, looking around. "Is anybody else here?"

"No, … yet the neighbors and whatnot, I'm sure they all heard me screaming. Maybe a couple of them ran over to help. I don't know." She stared down at her feet.

"You didn't see anybody?" Kate asked.

"I saw everybody," Edna stated, "but I didn't ask if they moved the body. At that point in time, I didn't think it mattered, didn't think any of it mattered. He was gone. It was so obvious he was gone, and I just couldn't imagine my life any longer," she muttered.

Edna stared down at the cigarette in her hand and swore to herself. "You go through all those years raising them. You think everything is good. You think it's all fine. You just don't realize that it's these last few years, the teen years, that are really the worst."

"The worst?"

"Yeah," she added, turning to look at her. "The most dangerous. They're off on their own. They're thinking for themselves and making real shit decisions." And, with that, she dropped her head into her hands and sobbed.

⚬⚬⚬

SIMON LISTENED TO Kate on the phone, explaining her latest case with a dead teenager. He winced, as he muttered, "God, that's got to be hard."

"Sounds absolutely horrible," she murmured.

"Sounds?"

"Yeah, sounds. … Why? Did I say something wrong?"

"No, but it was interesting phrasing."

"I don't know about phrasing," she muttered. "I'm not trying to be cynical or anything, but, Jesus, … the job does get to you after a while."

"No," he countered. "It gets to you every day, and that's what makes you human. That's what makes you so very special for this job."

"*Right*," she muttered. "You're just trying to keep me positive, while I track all these down."

"I would say death is an anathema, and this is what you do, but do you really think anything sinister is here?"

"You mean, since this is my department, is it murder? I don't know," she admitted. "The one thing that has me a little concerned is that the body was moved."

"I think a lot of family members would move a body in the act of trying to save their child," he noted.

"You're right. The mother admitted to dragging him outside, trying to get some fresh air in him."

"She did what?" When Kate repeated that, Simon shook his head. "Okay, so that's not the reaction I would have expected."

"No, but somebody told her to get him some fresh air. I guess the kid's room was kind of smelly too."

"Drugs?"

"That's what it appears to be. He's got a needle in his arm."

"Aah, so an overdose is likely."

"Likely, but the problem with *likely*," she pointed out, "is that it's not always self-induced."

"And, of course, you want things all tied up with a bow."

"Which never happens," she muttered.

He sensed the strain in her tone. "Will you be home anytime soon?"

"No, probably not." Then somebody spoke to her in the background. "I've got to go," she snapped. "I'll talk to you in a bit."

He stared down at his phone. Whatever had just happened at the end there had definitely upset her. It was just a matter of what and why. She played her cards close to the vest a lot, but she'd also become a little bit better at loosening up and letting some of the issues go before she exploded from the pressure of trying to keep it all inside. The fact that something was bothering her about the case just meant that she would worry away at it for a long time. Yet it was a second recent case with a child. Then he wondered if this child had also been abused.

She hadn't mentioned anything about it, so, with any luck, they were not connected in that way. But Simon didn't work in law enforcement, so, two dead kids showing up back-to-back, his mind automatically thinks they are bound to be connected. However, Kate did work in law enforcement, and unfortunately two dead kids might just be a normal night for them. Yet, had it been sixteen dead kids, some of them might be connected.

Simon shook his head at the thought. God, just to go through life as a parent and then to get this far, only to realize the child would not survive and would never be anything more was crippling. After so many years and all the effort of raising him, that had to be devastating.

He didn't know what kind of therapy was available for people in that situation, but he highly suspected it wouldn't be anywhere near enough. Losing a child was just too heartbreaking, just too much damage. And that made it easy to understand why so many grieving parents committed suicide, choosing to be with their child who died, rather than be with those left behind.

Simon hoped that wasn't the case here, but it could just as easily have been Kate's mother committing suicide, when Timmy first went missing. Apparently she'd gone to pieces when her little boy had disappeared, but she hadn't turned to Kate for comfort, which was interesting. Instead of turning *to* Kate, Selene had used it as a way to push Kate even farther away, leaving a single hollow spot left for the missing boy.

It was kind of sad because, when Kate really needed her mother, Kate appeared to be the last person her mother wanted anything to do with, ultimately causing more damage to Kate herself. It just brought back how messed-up all this was, and yet there was nothing more on Timmy. Which meant maybe it was nothing?

And yet Simon couldn't really see it. How could losing a child end up being nothing? Why would someone even send Kate a note like that, or pay somebody to take it to the police station anyway? It made no sense to him, but then, as much as he might have known a lot of criminals, and he might understand the criminal mind, what he didn't really understand was the sick mind. Yet he'd gained way-too-much personal knowledge on that recently.

He couldn't deal with his office paperwork at the moment. He really needed to just get up and get out for a little bit. And, with that on his mind, he grabbed his keys and headed to his nearest rehab job. His foreman saw him as he walked in, and a surprised expression came on his face.

Simon shrugged. "I decided to come out anyway and get some fresh air."

"Hey, anytime you want fresh air, feel free," Steven replied, with a smile.

"Ha, you would say that anyway."

"Nope," he countered. "If I didn't want to see your sorry ass around here, I would tell you."

Simon burst out laughing at that because the two of them had worked together long enough that Simon believed him. And, if Simon would be in somebody's way or could cause an interruption onsite, this guy definitely wouldn't hold back. "How are things going here?"

"They kind of suck, but when did that ever stop us?"

"I like the sound of that last part," Simon quipped.

"Of course you do." Steven gave him a smile. "You're all about saving these guys."

"I didn't think so at first," he muttered. "I wouldn't have thought saving anybody was part of my thought process on these rehabs."

"That's just because you're not really consciously thinking along those lines. It's just an inherent part of who you are—saving these buildings and saving these guys."

"I'm not even sure what you're talking about now. Maybe you need some fresh air," Simon teased, eyeing him.

His foreman snorted. "You just don't want to acknowledge being one of the good guys."

"Hell no, I don't," he declared, with a laugh. "You know what they say, how good guys end up last."

"With some of these jobs you've taken on, I wonder if that may not be true as well."

"Right, and, every once in a while, we get one that's a fight every step of the way."

"Seems we always have one," the foreman agreed. "We've just gotta have *the* one that completely blows up in order to make the others work," he muttered, with a sigh. "And today, this is the one."

"What's up?"

"Two guys didn't show up. We've got a leak in the plumbing, and the city came in, saying some of our permits aren't correct."

"Now that's just bull," Simon argued, yet with a smile. "We know our permits are accurate. It's not as if we don't do this every damn day of the year."

"I know," Steven muttered, "but it's not as if I have the permit documentation here in my hands, so that took a bit to get sorted out."

"It's just bullshit, that's what it is."

"I agree with you there, but that doesn't make any of the city people any happier. They just don't like the fact that we're here, fixing up old buildings," he muttered.

"No, they sure don't like it," Simon confirmed, with a laugh. "Anytime you want to straighten them away on that whole issue and get it cleared up, that'll be good."

"Not happening," he shared. "It's a situation where we're damned if we do and damned if we don't."

"Honestly, it seems as if life is just damned in general at the moment," Simon shared, "so I would take anything good today."

"What? Now you sound like some of these guys on the crew who always have girlfriend problems. Trouble in paradise?"

"Nah, but her job's pretty rough. And I want to help, and yet there's just nothing I can do."

"Probably better for me to stay single then," Steven noted. "I'm more on the side of needing help, than giving it," he joked.

"Is that because you're always stepping a little too close to the wrong side of things yourself?" Simon asked, with a laugh.

At that, his foreman rolled his eyes. "Yeah, maybe when I was sixteen and stupid," he muttered, "but not since then. Now it's way-too-much headache to even want to get involved in that crap—especially where the law is concerned."

"Right, I don't even know why anybody would volunteer for that," Simon added. "Knowing people like her would be hounding me, I think it's a lost cause."

His foreman laughed. "And yet here you are, running straight to her, with your arms wide open."

Simon grinned. "Never thought I would see the day either, but don't you worry. The good outweighs the struggle, 100 percent."

"Good to hear," Steven replied. "Now I've got to check on one of the guys up top. I told him that I would be back in about twenty minutes. What will you do?"

"I'll just keep walking around and checking on shit," Simon said. "You know me. You never know when I'll pop up."

"Just as long as you're keeping track of where you're going and who you're going with," Steven pointed out. "Otherwise having you around tends to make the guys nervous."

"Good," Simon stated, his tone serious. "Maybe they'll stop fooling around and take the job seriously."

"Most of our guys do," his foreman replied, "but I would just as soon they weren't nervous because you're here."

"What? You want me to take off then?"

"No, I don't want you to take off. I just don't want you standing here, hounding them."

Simon laughed. "Not to worry. I'll head into the trailer and get some of that paperwork done."

"Oh, fly at it then," his foreman stated. "Please get that shit taken care of so I don't have to."

Still laughing, Simon turned and headed for the small trailer they kept onsite. As soon as he got inside, he sat down at the desk and started working. It didn't take long to get through the worst of it. As was typical of most paperwork, he hated it. So he tended to put it off, until he just couldn't anymore. Yet, once he buckled down, it wasn't all that bad. At least that was the theory, one he always kept hoping for. However, his world was complex enough that it didn't necessarily work out that way.

As he got up to leave, he felt a weird sensation in his stomach. "Oh no, you don't," he muttered. "That shit ain't happening." Just as he went to take a step, there was that punch in the gut again, and he sat back down, hard. "Okay, fine," he muttered. "You've got my attention. I'm listening, but, if you don't have anything to tell me or anything to say, you need to knock it off."

Expecting nothing, he was surprised when instead he heard a tiny voice in his head.

*Help me. Please help me.*

Simon closed his eyes, and sensing it was a child just because of the fear and the tone of the voice, Simon whispered, "Where are you, and what's wrong?"

*Help me,*" the child repeated. *Please, God, help me.*"

And, with that, he was gone.

But just as he faded away there was the faintest of echoes. *Think.*

# CHAPTER 11

KATE WALKED INTO her office and sat down on her chair with a hard *thump*. As soon as she tossed down her phone, it rang. She glared at it, and Rodney smirked beside her.

"Let me know if that works for you."

"What?" she asked, as she snatched it up.

"If you glare at your cell, does it stop ringing?"

"Not likely," she muttered, "at least not in our world right now."

"Never in our world," he pointed out.

She nodded. "Isn't that the truth?" Since it was Simon, she answered it, not even attempting to hold back the weariness in her tone.

"Hey," he began, "are you alone?"

"No," she murmured, "I'm at the office. Why?" When he hesitated, she urged him, "What's up?"

"Maybe I'll just tell you when you get home."

"How about you just tell me now?" she declared, too tired to even beat around the bush. "If it's something helpful, I'm more than happy to hear it. If it's not helpful, well, you know I'll tell you." He laughed, and she had to smile. "Sorry, as you can tell, it's been *that* kind of a day."

"Yeah, it's been that kinda day here too," he admitted. "So, … I spent a bit of time at my rehabs, decided to work in the office trailer on one of those jobs, and just when I was getting up to leave …"

"Come on, out with it," she snapped.

He took a deep breath and continued. "I got a hard smack to the stomach, like before, but I sat back down again and basically told off whoever it was. Then I heard a small child crying," he added.

"Did he say anything?"

"Yeah, *help me*. When I realized it was a child, I asked him where he was, what he was doing, and how I can help, and he started crying again," Simon shared, his voice thickening. "I could get no more out of him, but he eventually repeated *Help me* and then I *think* he added, *Think*. And he disappeared."

She swore.

Lilliana, who'd been walking past her, stopped and turned her way. Rodney, who'd been sitting at his desk position ahead of Kate's, turned and stared at her too.

"Nothing else though?" Kate asked Simon.

"No, nothing else, which is why I always hate to tell you."

"I know," she murmured. "Yet, in this instance—"

"I know. I get it. That's also why I'm telling you. And now that I have"—his tone turned cheerful—"I'll get back to my work."

"*Great*," she muttered, as she ended the call.

"Who was that?" Rodney asked.

"Simon," she snapped, glaring down at her phone.

"Trouble in lovers lane?" Lilliana asked, with a smile.

"Trouble of one kind, but I don't know what the trouble is yet."

"Meaning?"

"He's had a couple of"—she frowned, trying to figure out what to say—"I don't want to call them attacks, yet kind of, on a psychic level. And, yes, I know how that sounds." She glared at them.

Nobody spoke, just continued to study her, waiting.

Kate frowned. "I think Simon would call it some sort of, I don't know, *spirit*, I guess. Anyway, whatever it is, it reached out to him."

"Okay," Lilliana noted, "and what did this spirit say?"

"Well, it knocked Simon in the stomach again. So Simon told them to knock it off or to just tell him whatever he needed to know. Then he heard the voice of a child," she shared. "The child kept saying he needed help. Simon kept trying to get something out of him and did finally, before the connection dropped away." She froze at that point, not wanting to say it.

"What was it?" Lilliana asked, echoed by Colby, who'd walked into the bullpen a moment earlier.

"What did the child say?" Colby asked.

She looked at them both, then over to Rodney. "*Think.*" Silence descended on the office.

"Good God, Simon really knows how to drop those bombs, doesn't he?" Lilliana replied.

"Way too much," Kate muttered, staring at them. "So, this kid could be dead or alive. Do we have something? *Maybe.* Do we know what that something is? *Hell no.* And can I do anything with the information? *Absolutely not.*"

"And that's what always bothers you about what he says, isn't it?" Colby asked.

Kate shook her head. "Jesus, look at what Simon gave us. He's in contact with a child, who's asking for help. What am I supposed to do with that? We would all be more than willing to help if we could," she noted. "But how are we supposed to render any kind of aid when we don't know anything more than that?"

"He couldn't give a location, an age, anything?" Lilliana asked.

"No, at least not yet."

"Not yet," she repeated.

Kate let out a deep breath. "Sometimes, and I'm saying *sometimes*, when he can contact an entity or comes back in contact with the entity, he gets a bit more information. Other times there is no follow-up at all. That's just what it is. Take it or leave it, as far as information sharing goes."

She glared down at her phone and then groaned. "Which is also why he doesn't really like to contact me when he gets those messages because the last thing he wants is for us to think its connected to our current cases—although he had been trying to reach Timmy ..."

"And yet, given that single word, how can we not connect this little boy to Timmy?" Rodney immediately asked. "Wow," he muttered.

Colby looked over at her and nodded. "You need to consider it too."

"No, I don't need to consider anything," she argued, pinching the bridge of her nose.

"You need to consider," Colby repeated, "as to whether—"

"I know," she interrupted, a hard note in her tone, "whether that could have been my brother. I get that."

He nodded. "I see you already have considered it."

"What am I supposed to do though? You know how hard it will be to sleep right now if I allow myself to even consider that could be my brother reaching out, crying out for help?"

"Does Simon know if—" Then Rodney stopped.

She looked over at him, guessing what he would say, then replied, "No, he doesn't know. As we've seen in the past, this person could be alive or dead. Both options are on the table for now."

"Good God," Lilliana murmured. "That really is a twister, isn't it?"

"It's a constant pain in my ass," Kate shared, staring over at her. "We want answers. We need answers. Yet this is what we get."

"We also need to know what else Simon comes up with," Colby added, "whether we confirm the source of the information or not. Maybe I should rephrase that. When we get something from Simon that's concrete and usable, it is just that, *usable*."

"Sure, but I can't use what he just gave us because I have no way to act on it."

"Of course not, but you can file it away," Colby suggested, "and you can keep your mind open. With any luck Simon will get more information with another connection."

"Maybe, but those connections also drain him, and, in some instances, strong physical attacks come with them too," she explained. "That's something else I must keep in mind. The first time he connected with this entity ..."

"The first time? He's connected ... *already?*" Colby asked.

"I'm assuming it's the same one who has been slugging Simon in the gut, but I don't know that," she clarified, holding up her hand. "Simon was basically knocked flat on his ass, not something he needs to happen while he's out walking around, in public, or God forbid, on a dangerous jobsite."

"Good God," Colby muttered. "No warning?"

"No warning, just a gut punch, out of nowhere. It completely blindsides him, dropping him to the ground, gasping for air because he'd just been slugged so hard. Plus, he's been gut-punched about four times now—that I know of."

"That doesn't sound like fun," Colby murmured.

"No, and, for him, who has no answers, it just makes it harder because he wants answers, and yet to get them is damn-near impossible sometimes."

They all considered that.

"And this time?" Rodney asked.

"This time Simon told me that something about it felt as if maybe he would get hit and did. Then he snapped back at the ... spirit," she added, with a wave of her hand.

"Could a child knock him around like that?"

"I don't know if, one, it is a child," Kate replied, "or, two, if somebody is with the child, or if this is potentially something completely different. I do know that their strength is not always proportionate to the age of the spirit. So, if this child was desperate, scared, and really looking for help, thought Simon could be that answer, then he could sock him pretty hard."

"Good Christ," Colby said, staring at her.

"Yes, I know." She nodded, giving him a look. "That's a hell of a way to go through life for Simon, ready to be beaten up by spirits without any warning."

"And he's a big guy," Rodney noted.

"A big guy, a private guy, and one in business, so random blows to the gut out of nowhere really don't go down well. Like, what if he's in a meeting on a jobsite or at a bank or something?"

Rodney winced. "Hopefully that would be seen as an attack of what? ... Gas or something?" he asked, with a frown.

"Yeah, that's not much better," she quipped, rolling her eyes.

"Right," Rodney muttered. "What an interesting life he leads."

"I think he would be more than happy to leave this part of it alone," she noted, staring Colby down.

"Okay then, so a child needs help," Colby repeated, returning them to that topic.

"Yes," Kate confirmed, with a nod. "Yet I don't know which child. I don't know the pertinent time frame, whether a child of past years or a child of right now," she pointed out. "That is why we don't really have anything to work with. Nobody wants to think of a child who needs us," she noted, "and we want to help, but we can't identify anything about the child ..."

Just then Simon called back. "Simon," she answered, while everybody else gathered around, and Kate put her cell on Speaker. "Did you forget something?"

"Yes, ... no," he began. "I just got through to the little boy again."

"Interesting. Normally you can't do that."

"No, normally I can't, but nothing is normal about this."

"Okay," she replied cautiously, "and what did you get?"

"He says he's been kidnapped."

She winced. "Do you have a name? Do you have anything to help us identify him?"

"I asked him, and he couldn't remember."

"Ah, hell."

Colby looked at her. "And what does that mean?"

"In Simon's world, that generally means the boy has been dead a while," she replied dispassionately. "So, he could have been kidnapped, and his body," she winced and added, "most likely his body has been dumped."

Lilliana grimaced. "Not as if we haven't seen our share of those."

"Still, we can pull files," Rodney suggested.

"Of how many kids?" she asked, turning to him. "Absolutely I would be all over this if I had any idea of a name or even a time frame." She spoke to Simon now, asking, "And why the hell did he say, *Think?*"

"I don't know," Simon murmured. "He didn't mention that this time, but he did say something about I'm supposed to help."

"You're supposed to help," she repeated. "Hang on a minute, is he being coached?"

"Yeah," Simon said. "I was kind of hoping you would ask that question. Still, I don't have an answer, but that's what came to my mind too."

"What do you mean, *coached?*" Colby stepped forward. "Hey, Simon. Colby here."

"Yeah, hi, Colby," Simon replied. "Sorry I can't be more help."

"This is pretty damn interesting, whatever it is," Colby stated, "and I get it. We all want answers as to where we can find this child. I don't quite understand what you mean by *coached.*"

"I think somebody told this spirit, this entity, ... that I could help him," Simon replied cautiously, "and before you ask, I don't know who that would be or why."

Rodney brought up another question. "Is there any

chance there's a ..." He shook his head, "Do you have a 1-800 number to dial for help on the other side?"

Simon snorted. "If there is one, I hope to God they never get my number."

"Your grandmother used to do this, right?" Rodney asked.

"Yes," he confirmed, "and she would say that, once you start working in this field, they can come to you as soon as they recognize the work you're doing. But that means they have ..." And he stopped.

"You mean. thoughts, feelings, the ability to understand?" Colby asked.

"Yes, some of them are still quite cognizant, and some of them are less so."

"Holy crap," Rodney muttered, sitting down. "Could somebody you helped before then tell another person—spirit, whatever—who needs help that you're there?"

Silence filled the room at that question. Kate looked over at Rodney in surprise.

He shrugged. "I'm just trying to figure out if there's a system."

"I don't know," Simon said. "It's quite the thing to consider though, isn't it? I've got to go." And, with that, he disconnected.

She turned to Colby. "See? That's the problem. We end up with bits and pieces of information but nothing solid."

"It's solid enough," Colby noted, "for Simon at least. However, it's not solid in terms of our still being unable to move forward with it."

"We don't even have a specific year to go on," Kate complained.

"Ask him," Lilliana suggested. "Ask him if he can somehow get you something to go on. You know how sometimes you send him text messages, and sometimes he has answers right away."

She groaned, picked up her phone, and sent a text. **Time frame for this little boy? Anything to narrow it down. Ten years, twenty years, this year?**

The response came back immediately. **Two years ago.**

She swore. "Now that's a little more tangible."

"What?" Colby asked.

She held up her phone. "According to Simon, this kid went missing two years ago."

"Good Christ."

They all raced to their computers to find anything on a little boy who might have gone missing two years ago, while she opted to turn her attention to something a little more tangible. And that was whatever was bothering her about that teenage boy from today. The officers at the scene had taken statements from several of the people standing around, and she'd picked up those and sat here with a cup of coffee and read through them.

According to the neighbors, they'd heard the mother screaming, had stepped outside, and she was opening the door and dragging her son into the fresh air. Several people raced over to help, only to realize that it was already too late. No comment was made about the body being moved. But just something about it bothered Kate because the final positioning had been so much like that of her own mother.

When asked, several of the neighbors knew that the teen had a drug issue, even if Edna wasn't willing to admit it. But then one of them had mentioned something about *Given his childhood, it was no wonder.* Kate immediately picked up her cell, while everybody else was busy, and called the name on that report. "Hi, I'm looking for a Jack Danielson," she murmured.

"Speaking," the man replied.

She identified herself and began, "On the statement that you gave regarding your neighbor's death, you made a reference to the childhood he'd had. Do you know anything about that childhood?"

"He was abused," Jack declared. "His father was quite the abuser, and, for a long time, so was his mother. Mostly because of the father, I think, if that's an excuse. The teen was a ward of the state for quite a while, and then she straightened up, got rid of that sorry excuse for a husband and father, and the State gave the kid back to her. The kid seemed to be more settled, but I guess I'm just not surprised."

"Right. Have you ever seen him do any drugs?" Then came silence. "Look. I don't care if you do drugs or not," she shared. "I'm part of the homicide unit, and I just want to ensure that this wasn't something I need to pick up as one of my cases."

"You mean. you think somebody might have killed him?" Jack asked.

"No, I don't know that at all," she murmured. "I just don't want it to be written off as a drug overdose without looking at other alternatives."

"Interesting," he murmured. "All I can tell you is that he does have some shady friends, and you'll probably want to talk to them."

"And do you know who any of them are?"

He gave her two names. "Don't tell them where you got the names, please."

"I certainly won't," she declared, with a snort. "What

about the mother? Have you ever seen her do any drugs?"

"No, I haven't seen her do any drugs, but I think I saw the sorry-ass father recently. It really surprised me because I thought he was in jail for domestic assault and abuse, but I guess he could be out by now."

Kate didn't say anything, just letting the man talk, but this sounded all too much like Adam's situation.

Jack continued. "For that matter, if that really was who I saw, and he's out, you might consider him, if you're looking for a suspect. The boy gave evidence against his dad, and that's what put him away. His mom may or may not have as well, but the kid talked to me about it one time. He was really worried and upset, but then he was taken away to foster care. That was quite a few years ago now."

"Right," she said. "I get it. And some people have very long memories."

"They do," he agreed, his tone turning rough. "Damn, that kid had his whole life ahead of him, and, if some asshole did that to him, that's just not right. If I were you, I would start there."

With that, she ended the call, stared at her notes, then decided to tackle this from a completely different perspective. She also needed the autopsy because, if this teen had a history of drug abuse, it would be much harder to prove that anybody else had a hand in his death. As far as her caseload went, Kate didn't have time or energy for somebody who wasn't murdered, a fact that would be brought home to her very quickly by Colby if she didn't get some proof and fast.

She quickly phoned Dr. Smidge.

"What do you want?" he snapped.

She smiled. "I would love to not send you any more bodies, and I would love for a miracle where you tell me that you've completed the two autopsies on the boys I've already sent you."

A hard snort came from the other end.

She chuckled. "So, considering that neither one of us will get what we want," she replied, with a smirk, "I suggest that, when you do the autopsy on the teenager who died this morning, you consider the potential for similarities to the other child who just died."

"So you said earlier, but I still don't see any similarities. One is a very young child and did not have a drug problem, so I don't know why you are thinking his was a drug overdose," he noted.

She frowned. "Quite correct, but I'm very concerned about that one, the five-year-old."

"I'm obviously doing everything I can for that little boy," he explained, "but I don't have anything for you at this point."

"Okay," she murmured. "When it comes back, please consider this other boy, the teenager." When he hesitated, she added, "Please."

"Is Simon behind this?" he asked.

She groaned. "If I said yes, would it lend more credence to it?"

"Nope," he barked, "but it would give me a way to understand why you're getting a little bit weird in your old age." And, with that, he ended the call.

She snorted now. *Weird in my old age.* That's not exactly what she expected him to say. As she looked around, frowning, Rodney turned to her.

"Was that Smidge?"

"Yeah."

"Why are you asking him to compare those two? I don't

get it."

She took in a deep breath and shook her head. "Smidge didn't really get it either, and I understand, but … just something is not quite right."

He frowned at her. "Has it got something to do with Simon?"

She glared at him. "No, it has nothing to do with Simon. Believe it or not, I do have a brain of my own, and I can sort out shit without Simon."

Rodney gave her a beaming smile. "You're doing a bang-up job," he declared. "So I'll just sit here and shut my mouth."

"You do that," she muttered, glowering at him, "and maybe next time you want to open your mouth, you'll think first."

Hearing the others laughing beside her, she turned and glared at them, immediately silencing them all. She nodded with satisfaction. The least she could do was get them to shut up about it.

The fact was, she hadn't even mentioned this to Simon but was pretty damn sure that he would be all over it. So she just ignored it for now. Still, she needed something solid, and that would come from the coroner. Even then, she wasn't sure it would be enough to do anything. Because, short of its being exactly the same drug—or something else equally bizarre—it wouldn't have any effect on any of her current cases.

The bottom line was, she didn't even know why she was asking, but she couldn't *not* ask. There had to be an answer on this one, and, if she got lucky, she would find it. Otherwise it would just persist in bugging her, and that was never a good thing.

About two hours later Smidge phoned her. "What the hell?" he snapped.

She felt that inner knowing. "What did you find?" she asked, trying to keep her excitement down.

"The two of you are one hell of a pair."

"Sometimes, yes, and the rest of the time, oh hell no."

He paused at that and started to laugh. "Maybe, but my money is on you guys at this point."

"What did you find?" she repeated.

"I suspect that the little boy may have been drugged," he shared. "So now I've submitted tox screens for both boys. I'll keep you posted."

"And the teenager?" she asked.

"No other sign of drug use. I didn't find any other tracks. I didn't find anything at all. So, either this was his first time or potentially … I just don't know," he muttered.

"Fascinating," she murmured.

"Yeah, I don't think it's very fascinating at all. They're on my table, and now I'm shipping those cases off to you."

"But you're not done with the autopsies."

"No, I'm not, but I will be by end of today because, damn it, now you've got me going on this one too. Anybody who does this shit to a child has got to be stopped. You sure as hell better get a hold of them before they kill someone else."

"Oh, I will. Don't worry."

"I'm counting on that," he declared. "Make these assholes pay." And, with that, he disconnected.

She sat back and smiled.

"How the hell does he actually like you and talk to you, but the rest of us get short shafted all the time?" Lilliana asked her.

"Who?" Kate asked.

Lilliana rolled her eyes. "Are you telling me that wasn't Smidge?"

"Oh yeah, of course it was Smidge," she confirmed. "Not too many other people talk to me like that."

"Yeah, he talks to you though, so I don't think anybody will have any sympathy for you."

She laughed. "He does talk to me, but now we have another issue." She called for the rest of the team and began, "We've got two unattended death cases recently, involving children. One was the young teen this morning, sixteen years old. While it appeared to be an overdose, complete with a needle in his arm, that does appear to be his only drug by a needle, per Smidge.

"The other boy was younger, five years old, I think." She searched through her files for an age and gave up. "While he has obvious signs of abuse, bruises and the like, this child may have a needle mark, which was unexpected. So Smidge submitted tox screens, trying to figure out what the hell happened to this kid."

Everybody stared at her.

"What does that mean?" Rodney asked, looking at her, clearly puzzled. "They were different ages and in different locations in the city."

"Yes," she agreed, "but they did have one connection that I find obscene and am trying to figure it out."

"What's that?"

"Both were in domestic violence homes, where both fathers served time for abuse on these particular kids, and both fathers were no longer in prison but were home with the families."

"Edna never mentioned anything about that," Rodney

protested.

"I know, but I spoke with one of the neighbors earlier today, and he's pretty sure he saw the hubby around the house in the last few days."

"Well, shit."

"Also, in the one case, the teen's testimony put away his father."

<hr>

STILL SHAKY AND a little upset himself, Simon decided that maybe an hour on the boat with some dinner for him and Kate would bring both of them a certain amount of peace today, even if they couldn't get out for very long. He sent Kate a text message. **Dinner on the *Running Mate* tonight, if you can make it.**

She sent a thumbs-up but no indication as to whether she would make it or not. Then again that was Kate. You took her as you got her, and he was resigned to the fact that he would spend his lifetime waiting on her, rather than her waiting on him. It was certainly a big change in his usual dating history, but it wasn't necessarily a bad one.

He ordered a picnic basket from his favorite local Jewish deli, including some hot and some cold foods, just in case the weather turned. It was fall technically, not yet the winter solstice, and it was cold. However, a certain amount of beauty could be had in being out there on the water right now. If he had blankets and a chance to get cozy, he was all for it. As soon as he had everything together, he loaded up and headed downstairs.

Harry, the ever-aware doorman, eyed him toting blankets and nodded. "It's mighty chilly out there, if you are headed out onto the water."

"I know," he replied. "I just needed to get out."

"Ah, are the walls closing in on you?"

"Something like that," he conceded, with a nod.

Harry helped him with the door, as Simon set out for the boat, as it was within walking distance down to the marina where the *Running Mate* was moored. He carried on walking, feeling the bite of the cold weather. Maybe they would eat inside. He didn't know yet, but it was something at least just to have the fresh air, and knowing it was an option to eat indoors or outdoors made life a whole lot easier on him.

As he got there, Simon found Baxter staring at the boat. After all, it had been his once. When Simon called out a greeting, Baxter turned and laughed.

Baxter shook his head. "Okay, you've got to have it bad if you're out here in this weather. You're not going out, are you?"

"No, I'm not," Simon shared. "I wish I could, but work and all that."

"I know. That's part of the problem. So book in regular holidays in order to take good advantage of having her." He waited until Simon climbed onboard and invited him too. As he stepped on deck, he noted, "Doesn't look as if you've made any changes."

"No, not yet," he murmured. "I was kind of hoping to get her out a few more times before I even contemplated changing anything."

"She's in pretty good shape, so I'm not sure you need to do anything anyway." Baxter stuffed his hands into the pockets of the big burly coat he wore. "I used to come down here in the evenings a lot, just to hang out and unwind."

"That's what I'm more or less doing, as it was kind of a

rough day," he shared, looking at his friend.

"And what about your partner?"

"I texted her and told her where I was and that dinner was here with me."

"Oh, that should bring her pretty fast."

Simon nodded. "It's kind of a joke between us, but sometimes she thinks all I do is feed her."

"It doesn't look as if it's taken though. She's pretty lean."

"It's the job."

"She's really a cop, *huh?*"

"Yeah, a detective," Simon clarified, "not that the difference is something I'm particularly worried about, but I know for everybody else, having made detective is an improvement over being a beat cop."

"Unless being a beat cop is what you like," Baxter pointed out. "My uncle was one for a very long time, and he always said there was no other life for him."

"Good, he enjoyed it then."

Baxter stayed there silently a little bit longer, then he announced, "I'm heading home. Enjoy your evening."

Just as the words left Baxter's mouth, the moon cleared above, and Simon witnessed an odd kind of a serene light settle in above. He studied it, wondering if it was just him who could see it.

Then Baxter called back, "There's a spooky light for you. I'm not sure I've ever seen anything quite like it."

So Simon wasn't the only one to see it. Simon nodded and waved his friend off, as Baxter headed down the dock. The light really was something weird. Then this phenomenon happening these days could be climate change, or it could be something else entirely. He was pretty sure his grandmother would have something to say about it. He often wondered why, amid all this he was going through, why he wasn't getting any messages from her.

It was kind of a joke in his head that part of the reason was because she'd worked so damn hard when she was alive, thus the last thing she would do was work when she was dead. He smiled at the thought because that's exactly the kind of person she was. She'd had more than enough of her own headaches when she was alive to ever want anything to do with all this while she was on the other side.

She'd been hell on wheels in her day. She gave no quarter, but she'd always done her damnedest for other people. That was part of what had gotten him so confused over the years. If she'd done so much for other people, why the hell had she ended up so poor and unappreciated and friendless? That would remain a mystery until he spoke with some of the odd people who had known her in that life.

Maybe she'd helped a lot of dead people that Simon didn't know about. It's not as if she'd ever opened up to him about her gift. More to the point, she'd told him that, when the time came, he wouldn't really have a whole lot of choice once he opened that door. Now that he had done exactly that, he realized fully what she meant. But he hadn't known it beforehand. As a matter of fact, it seemed to be damn cowardly on all points. If she'd truly known what was ahead of him, she could have warned him at least.

She clearly had things to say about him and his gift, but maybe she thought it would scare him off. No doubt all of it had scared him off, but life changed when you ended up being able to help somebody through it. And he knew that was what kept Kate going too. She was all heart if somebody needed help, and, if you didn't need help and took advantage of someone, she was hell on wheels against you.

He sat in the weird light, studying the area around him, thinking that because Baxter had also seen it, then nothing could be spiritual or woo-woo about it. Yet, as he sat here, a strange feeling grew and grew. He looked around, a weird sense of being watched. He frowned and wanted to call out, but instead settled in deeper, keeping a bit more distance between him and whatever, whoever, was out there.

A man called out, "Ahoy."

Simon leaned over and found a stranger. "Hello."

The man just stood there for a bit, then added, "I understand you're a friend of Kate's."

"I am a friend of Kate's," he stated calmly, studying him, but the lighting was off, and he couldn't really see who it was. "What can I do for you?"

"I have a message for her," he replied, and he pulled down his baseball cap and looked around a little nervously.

"What's the message?" When the stranger hesitated, Simon asked, "Is it your message or have you been asked to deliver it?"

At that, the man eyed him in surprise. "Now why would you say that?"

Simon snorted. "Because somebody else delivered a message not all that long ago, but it wasn't his message. He was paid to deliver it."

"I hope he got more than what I got paid tonight," the man muttered.

"Maybe you should tell me what the message is and who paid you to deliver it."

"I'm not allowed to tell you who paid me." The man seemed younger than at first, probably because of the fear centered in his tone. At that, the man started to back up.

Simon stepped closer, so he could see him better. "You

still need to tell me what the message is. Otherwise, you won't get paid."

"I've already been paid," he stated.

"That's fine, but you still need to tell me the message."

The man frowned at him. "You're not what I expected."

"It doesn't matter what you expected," Simon pointed out, with a sigh, "but let me guess. I think I already know what the message is."

At that, the other guy frowned at him. "I don't think so, but then maybe you do," he snorted. "Okay, go ahead and guess."

"I think the message is a single word," he declared. "*Think.*"

The other man's jaw dropped. "How the hell did you know that?" he asked, sputtering.

"As I told you, somebody already delivered a similar message."

"*Huh.* I don't know why he needs to do it twice, but, yeah, that's the message." And, just as he went to turn, he ran directly into somebody, who reached out and snagged him, held on to him hard. The young man started to resist. "Let me go. Let me go," he cried out. "I didn't do nothing wrong. I didn't do nothing wrong."

Simon half smiled at her. "Kate, he's the messenger."

Kate glared at him. "That's nice," she snapped in a flinty tone. "He's one I want to talk to."

"I don't know anything," he cried out, and, with a hard jerk, he bolted free and raced into the darkness.

# CHAPTER 12

ONLY AS EXHAUSTION hit did Kate choose to at least get outside and rejuvenate for a few minutes. Even if that meant sitting on the boat and having a bite to eat, that worked. As she walked closer to the *Running Mate*, she couldn't believe what she'd overheard. She looked over at Simon. "Did he give you a message?"

"No, I guessed what it was," he clarified, with half a smile. "And it was exactly as you would guess too."

"*Think?*" she asked.

He nodded. "Yes."

"Well, damn," she muttered.

"And, no, he doesn't know who sent the message, just that somebody paid him to deliver it. He thinks he didn't get paid enough because it was kind of scary down here."

"That weird light is out tonight," she noted. "There's a strange energy." When he smiled at her terminology, she glared at him. "No, I didn't mean it that way."

"I know how you meant it," he said, still chuckling. "Come on board and have some food."

"I was kind of hoping it might be hot food."

"We have both," he stated.

"Good," she muttered, as she hopped on board. "What the hell is he doing sending another messenger?"

"Obviously somebody wants you either out of something

or into something. Your guess would be as good as mine."

"That leaves an awful lot of leeway," she pointed out, "and I'm already sure to get it wrong. So why would they do that? Why can't they just be direct and succinct?"

"Maybe they're already concerned, and that's why they sent the second message," he pointed out.

"Maybe," she muttered, "it still sucks though."

He laughed. "I won't argue that, but at least we now know that an ongoing issue still exists and that you're still at the center of it."

"I am, but I don't know why," she murmured. "It makes no sense to me."

"Nothing makes sense until it does. Remember that."

She glared at him, but he just smiled and then asked, "How about some food?"

He pointed beside her. She smiled once she opened the basket, peering inside to then exclaim in joy. Instead of wine, she found a couple thermos bottles, and a big carafe of hopefully hot coffee.

"We have both coffee and tea," he added.

"Lovely," she murmured and reached for the first package. "Is this curry?" she asked.

"It's something like a curry, but I'm not sure exactly what. I just asked them to pack us up both hot and cold food—enough for four."

She laughed out loud at that. "And you didn't think I would make it."

"No," he countered, with a smile. "I asked for enough for four because I was pretty sure that you would make it here," he stated, chuckling. "The one thing I do know is that, particularly in the evening, when you need food, … you *really* need food."

"I am hungry," she admitted.

"Exactly," he declared. "So now let's park all the rest of this crap and put aside everything else from this day. We can deal with it all, starting tomorrow."

"Is it that easy?" she asked, as she picked up a fork and looked over at him. "I have another connection between my current cases that is equally disturbing, equally upsetting, and I don't think it has anything to do with the Timmy mess going on right now."

"Good," Simon said, "that will at least be something completely separate."

"Maybe," she murmured, "and yet it feels as if Timmy's case shouldn't be one of two strange cases that I currently have."

"Right. The circumstances being what they are, we would probably assume that's not the case."

"Which means we would be looking at them as potentially connected."

"But you don't think they are?"

"No, I don't think they are," she replied, then stopped, "but considering my brother was a missing child, I can't say they aren't for sure."

"Meaning these are other kids?"

"Yes, other kids, both dead, both with abusive fathers."

He frowned at her. "Look. I know it's not a topic you want to discuss, since you've never mentioned it. What the hell happened to your father? Was he ever in your life?"

She stared at him and slowly nodded. "I don't know who my biological father was. He was never around that I knew of. My stepfather was there, ... but he went to jail for domestic violence." With those words, she dropped her fork and looked at the food, wanting to throw up.

How had she missed that?

# CHAPTER 13

T HE NEXT MORNING Kate walked into the currently empty office. She called the hospital for an update and got the usual response. *Selene's still unconscious, but we are hopeful she will wake up soon.*

As soon as everybody else had arrived, she announced, "One thing has occurred to me, and I'm tossing this out as something that someone else will need to pick up and investigate." At their confused expressions, she took a deep breath. "Simon brought up the fact that I hadn't considered my stepfather in all this. Last I knew, he was in jail for domestic violence," she shared. Then informed them about the messages she'd received.

Lilliana stared at her, both eyebrows raising. "That's just lovely."

"Yeah, I don't know if he's out by now or not. Honestly, I put him out of my mind and never thought about him again."

"Do you know if he went after your brother?"

"I don't know that for sure," she replied, and then she took an even deeper breath and winced. "And ... this is damn hard for me to say, but I can confirm that he went after me."

A couple whistles rang throughout the office, as everybody realized the implication of that.

"That's just the shits," Rodney declared. "I was willing to give your mom a pass, but now? … No way."

"She was a victim too," Kate noted, with difficulty. "And that's hard for me to release her from the guilt of that as well."

"Of course," Lilliana muttered. "I'm sorry."

"Yeah, me too," Kate murmured. "Somebody, one of you," she suggested, "if you come up with some questions, I'm trying to write up some memories I have about him," she murmured. "I am very sorry for not having considered it."

"Honestly," Lilliana noted, frowning at her, "we didn't consider it either. But why the hell is that a thing?"

Rodney looked over at her and shrugged. "Probably because it's Kate, and we thought that, if anything was there, she would have mentioned it."

"As we already know," Lilliana stated, "when there is trauma, we do everything we can to block it out."

"Yes," Kate agreed, "and apparently I've been really good at doing that."

"And you're not to blame either," Rodney said briskly. "Give me a few minutes to reorient myself on this one, and we'll go from there."

She nodded. "I'll get to work on the two kids."

"And do you …" Rodney stopped. "This just adds to the kids, doesn't it?"

She nodded. "Yes, and yet I don't know how."

"Or why," Lilliana added. "There still needs to be a why."

"There's always a why," Kate declared. "We're never really sure what that is until the end."

With that, Kate went to her desk, sat down, and buried her face in her hands for a moment. Then, after a hard mental tug to get her ass back together, she lifted her head and got to work. There had to be something that connected all these cases, and, until she got into this ... She froze, as the thought kept hitting her.

She spoke to her team again. "Due to the fact that I am as scattered as I am, damn it, these other two cases are really not coming together because I can't get a grasp on it."

Rodney slowly turned and asked her, "You're thinking that's what it is?"

"I don't know," she admitted, "but I have to consider it. Which means I'll really dig deep into this one."

"Better you than me," Rodney muttered. "I can't imagine why anybody would kill these kids."

"And yet I'm not sure if that was the intent, or something else," she muttered.

He frowned at her and asked, "They're dead. What else is there?"

"I don't know," she replied, with a hard smile. "Yet definitely something is going on."

He shook his head. "I'll work on your stepfather. You work on dead kids."

"Yeah." She nodded. "We might end up finding they're all connected."

On that note she got back down to going through the witness statements. She picked up the written statements from the beat cops, who'd gone to all the neighbors, asking if they'd heard anything and if they had any relationship with the victims' families. Unfortunately, there was this litany of reports of it being a good family. The neighbors hadn't heard anything wrong, didn't understand what was going on, and the drugs were a surprise, and they'd never seen any evidence of them.

She always wondered about that because she heard it so frequently. As if there was never any evidence of drugs in this world? Or was it just a question the cops asked blindly, hoping that somebody would say, *Hey, yeah, I saw him shooting up last week*, because who the hell ever told the cops that?

She stared down at her witness statements but pushed them aside. She then got to searching for other similar cases. Yet there wasn't really anything she could drill down on to narrow her search. She had typed in *dead kids and teens in the last six months* and came up with sixty-two hits. She winced because that number was way too high. And it didn't matter that she had gone for the entire Lower Mainland. It was just a number that would never sit well for her.

Biting back her own responses, she kept digging, looking to see if anything else popped. A couple things did, and she wrote down notes to check them out. Just when she was about ready to pick up the phone to call some of the neighbors—who had apparently seen *nothing*—Dr. Smidge contacted her.

"Hey," she greeted him. "Find anything?"

"Too much," he lambasted her through the phone. "You need to stop bringing these cases to me. They're upsetting."

She winced. "Yeah, they're upsetting for us too."

That calmed him somewhat, and he added, "The same drug was used in both cases."

She stared down at the phone. "So, the little boy was definitely drugged?"

"Yes, he was drugged, no doubt a new designer version."

"What the hell?" she murmured.

"Yeah, both of them. This is over to you in a big way now. Good luck with that." Then he slammed down his phone.

Kate called out to her team in the bullpen, "For those keeping track on the two dead kids' cases I'm working on, Dr. Smidge just confirmed that both the little boy, who was left in the care of the deadbeat uncle, and the teenager, home alone with the needle in his arm, died from overdoses of the same drug."

"The same drug? Really?" Lilliana asked, startled.

"Yeah, worse yet, it's one of these new designer drugs," Kate murmured.

"You're kidding." Lilliana could only stare.

"I know, and that fact is pissing Smidge right off."

"Better you than me talking to him then," Lilliana said, with a smile.

"Yeah, he's pretty pissed, but then again so am I." She stared around the room. "I'm not exactly sure what's going on here, but you can bet it's a whole different story." She got up, grabbing her wallet and keys. "I'll head over and talk to the teenager's mother again, now that we have that confirmation."

"And then to the five-year-old's parents?"

Kate nodded.

"What about the uncle?" Rodney asked.

"He should be available to talk to by now, and, if he's not, we'll get him picked up," she stated. "This isn't something we can ignore. That little boy didn't do this to himself."

"He might have," Colby suggested, from the far corner where his office was. "I know it's a long shot, but just remember that kids imitate what they've seen."

Kate stopped to consider that. "Seriously?"

He nodded. "It wouldn't be the first time where a little

kid injected himself because he saw his parents do it."

"*Great*," she muttered, "and here I was thinking we were safe from that avenue on this one."

"I'm not saying that's what happened, just that you cannot ignore the possibility."

"Are you sure?" she asked, as she stormed past him. "Because that's really not one I want to consider." But Colby was right, and, if anything needed to be considered on that angle, she would deal with it somehow.

She strode to her vehicle and got inside, when her phone rang. It was Rodney.

"Do you want me to come with you?" he asked.

"No," she responded. "I can do this. I would rather you stay on the research into my stepfather."

"Actually that's one of the reasons I wanted to come with you."

She hesitated, then groaned. "Fine, get your ass out here fast."

He snorted. "I'm standing right beside you."

She looked up, surprised, and there he was. She ended the call, unlocked the car door, and let him in. "You could have mentioned something as I walked out."

"You didn't really give anybody a chance," he pointed out. "You took off really fast."

"Yeah, … I like nothing about this one."

"I don't think we ever like anything about these cases," he muttered. "However, as long as we keep searching for information, we'll get to the truth at some point."

As soon as they arrived at the teenager's family home, Kate knocked on the door, but she got no answer.

"Did you call ahead?" Rodney asked.

She shook her head. "No, I didn't." She knocked again

and nothing. Frowning, she looked over at him. "Now I'm wondering if something is wrong."

He nodded and pounded hard on the door.

One of the neighbors stepped out and shared, "I haven't seen her all day." Then he shrugged and shook his head. "Honestly, I haven't seen her for longer than that."

Kate immediately turned back to the door and tested the knob. It was unlocked. She pushed it open and called out, "Police. Edna? Are you in here?" Still no answer. "Keep the neighbor back," she told Rodney. The neighbor was already on his way over, and Kate had an increasingly bad feeling.

She stepped inside and called out several more times. With that sense of wrongness building, she raced through the lower part of the house, and then up to the bedrooms. As she reached the master, she felt that sense of urgency as she dove into the main bedroom, finding Edna curled up on her bed, not moving. Kate immediately raced to her side to check. She found a pulse. She tried to wake her up. When she got no response, she immediately called for an ambulance. Rodney joined her few minutes later.

She looked over at him. "I'm not sure," she began, "but it looks as if life got to be a little too much."

He nodded. "He was her only child."

"I know," she replied, "but I was really hoping she had a support system."

"Lots of people don't," he murmured, "and when they don't ..."

Kate didn't need to be told because she already knew what happened. While Rodney went back downstairs to wait for the ambulance, she checked over Edna, looking for needle marks and, indeed, found a few. Frowning at that, she looked for anything close by that would indicate what she had done, whether there was any connection to her son's death.

Kate noted a little paraphernalia around, but more than that were other drugs that she didn't recognize just from the packaging. With a heavy heart, she waited for the paramedics, not sure whether Edna would make it or not. Kate knew she surely wouldn't get thanked for saving Edna. However, this was definitely *not* a suicide. Yet, given the circumstances she was living with right now, it certainly made sense.

The paramedics raced upstairs and immediately took over Kate's position. As she stepped back, Rodney stood in the doorway. He looked over at her and said, "I'll go talk to the neighbors."

He quickly disappeared, but she stayed and watched the paramedics work on the poor woman. Edna was stabilized and taken away very quickly, but, as one of the paramedics faced her, he gave her a headshake.

She winced at that. "Please save her," she said, "if there's anything at all you can do. Her son just died of an overdose."

He winced and nodded.

They'd all seen it, the reactionary grief where someone just didn't want to live anymore, not seeing the point. Kate knew the feeling herself and had been there at one point in time. It was always so sad to see this happen, and it would also be incredibly difficult to get answers from a corpse. But that was her cop brain speaking, and she knew nobody would appreciate her bringing that up.

She slowly walked through the house and noted barely any food was in the fridge, and the kitchen itself looked as if nobody had been there to cook, just to toss stuff—largely an accumulation of coffee cups and cigarette butts everywhere. She remembered Edna smoking at the crime scene. Seemed she'd gone into overdrive. It was hard to blame her. She'd been through one of the worst scenarios that anybody could endure, and right now Edna obviously had no will to live.

Yet considering the larger circumstances, it was also presumptuous of Kate to assume that, so she focused on her due diligence, looking to see if anything beyond the ordinary stood out here, very aware that she hadn't been on her game. She needed to be alert and to maintain a little more wariness in this case.

Just because it seemed to be a suicide didn't mean it was one, and, if somebody had taken out the son, maybe the same person came back to take out the mother. Frowning, Kate searched through the bedroom, looking for anything to indicate something was off. The fact that drugs were in the night table spoke volumes, but she hadn't seen long-term signs on the woman's body. So, maybe it was just a case of drugs to get through the worst of the aftermath of her son's death. As Kate checked out the bathroom, it seemed that only a single woman lived here. Kate found no signs of other visitors staying overnight. It looked as if a lonely woman had decided on a lonely pathway.

Trying to keep her brain open and functioning in terms of possibilities, Kate walked through everything, and, when Rodney finally returned, he looked at her, and she shrugged. "It looks as if she did this herself," she shared, "but I'll leave it open for the moment."

"Of course," he agreed, "I just feel for her. Her only son dies of an overdose." He looked around and noted, "If this was an overdose, I wonder if she thought that would work for her too."

"Or if she thought she needed to experience it because he had gone that way," Kate offered. "I don't know."

"Do we ever know?"

"Or maybe it was just the easiest way for her to get some relief, any avenue to buy some time and to not deal with this pain."

"Quite possibly," Rodney agreed. "Nothing is sadder than a life gone to waste, but even more so when one tragedy leads to another."

She looked around and asked, "Did you talk to the neighbors?"

"I talked to three of them. They're all out there now, upset and worried. Of course, nobody had talked to her very much during the last few days. One woman did mention how she'd come over to talk to her and told her, if she needed anything, to let her know."

"But, of course, she didn't let her know."

"No, she didn't," Rodney confirmed, "and I presume the stats will probably show that's fairly typical. For anybody who doesn't have a support system, this might not be an unusual outcome."

"It might not be an unusual outcome," Kate conceded, "but it sure is something we don't want to see." With a heavy heart, she locked up and headed back to her car, where she sat for a long moment.

When Rodney joined her, he asked her, "Are you okay?"

"Yeah," she murmured. "I'm just trying to think of what to do next."

He frowned. "Maybe you should go home."

"I'm fine," she muttered, looking at him. "I could go to the hospital and wait to see if my mother regains consciousness, if they can save her, that is. Or I can carry on to the next family."

"I suggest we do that. We'll follow up with the five-year-old boy's family next," Rodney stated. "At least then you'll feel as if you were doing something to help."

And, with that, she headed over to see Andrew's family. When Kate got there, the mother, Alana, opened the door and stared at her.

"Did you find anything?" she asked.

Kate heard almost a note of fear in her tone. "We're still investigating," she replied, "but I do need to talk to your husband."

The woman winced. "Sorry, but you won't find him here. I kicked his ass out." When Kate silently stared at her, she went on. "He left my boy in the charge of that man," she snapped. "I'm not doing this again."

"Again?" Kate asked, puzzled.

"Yes, I had another child who died when he was two."

Kate winced. "I'm so sorry for your loss. What happened?"

"He was left in my husband's care, and, unfortunately, he had drugs on the counter. My little boy saw them, got into them, and ended up dying."

"Good God." It hit her like a ton of bricks.

Alama started to tear up. "And I know you're wondering what I was even doing with my husband after that, but you don't know what it's like. He was the only one who could understand that loss, and, like it or not, you are bound together in a way that you wouldn't expect."

Kate remained silent, watching tears slowly run down Alana's face as she continued.

"And even though you think that you would never do something like that again, over time, this man slowly becomes a lifeline because you just can't deal on your own. When I got pregnant the second time, we both felt as if it was a new day, a whole new beginning, something that we could move on with," she explained, tears streaming down her face now.

"And I was so careful. I was so good. My husband did time, and he came home. He was good, and it seemed as if he was good. He got into a bit of trouble, but again he seemed to pull back out of it, went to classes, and I kept giving him chances," she shared. "And I know that this time it wasn't his fault, yet it was," she snapped, regaining some of her earlier ferocity.

"And his brother?"

"Sammy's a loser," she declared. "I didn't want him around the house at all, and they knew that. It's one of my rules."

"Why is that?"

"Drugs," she stated. "That takes him down a really bad pathway, and I didn't want that influence around our home, around my child. My husband knew that, but he obviously thought that the one time would be okay."

Kate couldn't imagine. Taking a breath to steady her own voice, she asked, "Where can I go to speak with either or both of them now?"

"I don't know," she said, raising her hands. "When I say that I kicked him out, … I really kicked him out, and I haven't spoken to him since." She wiped away her tears. "And honest to God, if I saw him right now, I might kill him." She wrapped her arms around herself and stared at Kate. "So, if and when you do find them, it might be best if you don't tell me where they are."

Kate nodded. "Do you have any idea where your husband would go?"

"Probably to his mother," she snapped, "and that woman's just brilliant too."

"And where is the mother?"

Alana provided a phone number and an address that wasn't too far away.

Kate nodded. "We'll go check it out."

"Good." The tears still ran down Alana's cheeks. "In the meantime, I'm arranging a funeral."

Kate hesitated and then nodded. "You do realize that until the body is released …"

She nodded. "I know, but honestly, it gives me something to do. One last thing to do for my son, you know? It's really all I can do. This should never have happened, and I should not be in this position," she murmured. Kate hesitated for a moment, and Alana eyed her. "What?"

"The abuse on your son's body, the bruising."

Alana winced and nodded. "That was my husband," she stated. "We had another huge row, and I did call the police about it. I ended up not pressing charges because he was going back through anger management." She shook her head. "God, I've been such a fool. Once an asshole, always an asshole. They don't change, do they?" She shot Rodney a hard look. "Or maybe it's just all men," she snapped. "Maybe they're just no good, through and through."

Kate ignored the comment, unwilling to engage in the woman's attempt to tag Rodney with the same brush as Alana's husband. "Some of those bruises were more recent," Kate clarified, unwilling to be deterred.

Alana frowned and asked, "How recent?"

"I don't have a full autopsy report yet that will tell us that," Kate explained. "However, the other thing I do know is that drugs were in Andrew's body."

Alana stared at her, a cry escaping as she collapsed to the

ground. Rodney caught her before she hit the floor and eased her down gently.

Kate shuffled in the hallway beside her. "I gather you didn't know."

"No, of course I didn't know," she exclaimed, staring at her in so much pain. "When you say drugs ..."

"Yes, hard drugs. It was a modern designer drug. I'm wondering who would have had access to that and who would have given the little boy drugs?"

"Are you saying that someone ..." She hesitated. "I'm thinking of my first toddler."

"I can't speak to that, but, as to Andrew, again I'm waiting on the autopsy report." It was a good question because now there was that doubt about this woman's previous child too.

The crying woman just stared at her. "I can't do this right now," Alana murmured. "Please leave."

Kate and Rodney stepped outside, turning to look at Alana when she closed the door on the two of them.

Kate looked over at Rodney. "We need to go find those two men."

"Yeah, you're not kidding," Rodney agreed. "Imagine losing a toddler, then going back to the same man."

"And that is something she'll have to live with."

"Also, how was the child given the drugs?" Rodney asked. "We need to know whether he was injected or—"

"I know," she murmured. Kate picked up her phone and dialed Dr. Smidge. When he answered, she asked, "Delivery of drug to the first child?"

"Oral," he replied, "and needle for the second one."

"Right, but the same drug?"

"Yes, a variation of a new designer heroine for both of

them."

"Do we have other cases of overdoses with this same drug?"

"Way too many of them," he noted. "It's hitting the streets hard and not quite providing the experience that people wanted."

"What's the point of selling these drugs when you kill off your customer base?" she asked.

"Exactly," Dr. Smidge agreed. "So, we've got a dealer out there who's giving these drugs to the users but not caring about the business side of it."

"Maybe they're trying to clean up the streets."

"I don't know what they're doing," the coroner admitted, "but the fact is, it's now had fatal consequences for children twice. I don't understand how and why these children are getting involved."

"No, I don't know either," she added, "but I intend to find out."

⁓

SIMON WENT TO work, his mind preoccupied to the extent that even his foreman asked if he needed to take a break and to do something else for a while. He gave his head a shake and said, "Sorry, I've got other things on my mind."

"Oh, I get it, and, for what it's worth, no problems are here. So you might as well take off and do something else." Simon stared at his foreman, who repeated, "Yeah, I mean it."

"You can't mean it. All kinds of shit is happening."

He laughed. "Sure, but when isn't there? At the moment, everything is on schedule, and we're okay. So, if you've got other places to go and things to do, have at it."

He suggested it in such a good-natured tone that Simon considered it. "It might be a good thing to do," he admitted.

"Seems like it. Go on. I'm not sure what is bugging you, but, if you've got something to deal with, you know you're better off getting it resolved."

"It's not quite so easy as that though."

"Those are the ones you really need to deal with then," he added, "before they turn around and bite you in the ass, and you end up with bigger problems."

Simon laughed. "The good news is, it's got nothing to do with business."

"That is good news," he confirmed. "I never quite know what's going on in your world," he shared, "whether you're strung up buying something new or you're dealing with finances or whatever."

"Finances are solid," Simon stated immediately. "I mean, the rehab delays aren't good, and none of the rest of the usual mess that we deal with helps, but I'm not going broke, if that's what you're worried about."

"Good, because I do still want to get paid."

"You'll get paid," Simon declared. It was kind of an old joke between them, but it had validity.

Simon took the hint and headed away from the job. He still had another site to check in on, and it would be remiss of him to avoid it. He headed over there next, and, almost as soon as he reached it, his phone rang. He looked down to see a call coming in from his stalker realtor who had made it her mission to continually pester him, with mixed results.

She tended to get in his way more than anything. When he answered, she said, "They dropped it another hundred and fifty."

He frowned, considering it. "That's interesting. How

did you manage that?"

"Nothing that concerns you. You should be excited. You said you wanted them at the table with a serious price, and here they are."

"That might be what I said, but the fact that they've dropped it again so soon makes me a little worried as to what's wrong."

"Oh, for crying out loud," she snapped.

He laughed. "You do know this is business, right? This isn't personal. This is all about business. Yes, I'm interested in the property, and, yes, at some point in time the price may be low enough to make me smile and sign on the dotted line, but am I there yet? No. Frankly I've got bigger fish to fry right now."

"So, what do you want me to tell them then?" she asked, her tone snippy.

"I don't care if you tell them anything," Simon replied. "When I'm ready, I'm ready. Until I'm ready, I'm not." And, with that, he ended the call, pinching the bridge of his nose.

He would do some number crunching. A reduction of one hundred fifty was minor when the cost of the repairs would go up exponentially. With the cost of materials, cost of labor, trouble finding labor, not to mention the seemingly inevitable supply delays, he wasn't sure how much he wanted to invest right now.

His stalker realtor wouldn't like that answer, but it was a whole different story dealing with people who got it, versus dealing with people who didn't. She seemed to be constantly going from one extreme to the other on that point, something that drove him a bit crazy because she should get it by now. This wasn't exactly rocket science.

Vowing to put her out of his mind again, he walked

deeper into this rehab and spoke to his foreman. This one ended up requiring more attention than his previous rehab project, so he was here for a good couple hours. By the time he was done, he'd eaten into the window of time he had allotted to deal with some of Kate's stuff.

Still, he walked over to one of his favorite coffee shops, grabbed a coffee, and sat down at one of the outdoor tables. It was a newer business for him to frequent, looking more like a little bistro, but it was a bustling space, with people coming and going on a regular basis. It was good news for them, and an enterprise he'd never really considered getting into. The thought of running a coffee shop and dealing with the staffing issues and everything that went along with that business had never appealed. Yet he drank enough coffee that maybe he should.

A couple people had mentioned that idea to him, and he'd just smiled and shaken his head. The last thing he wanted to get involved with was a customer-centric coffee house. And really, to be honest, nothing had changed. He still didn't want to get involved.

As he settled in his seat and drank his coffee, he considered the small series of benches and tables. They could be pulled inside if the weather got ugly. Considering this was Vancouver, the weather did get ugly, but luckily for him it was dry right now. He inhaled and relaxed, got inundated with a few phone calls right away, including one from Bartlett's estate, which he was pretty well done with, but not quite because of probate. When it came to business accounts, that was a whole different story.

When he was finally done with that, he realized his coffee had gone cold. Swearing, he got up and ordered himself a fresh cup, this time determined to put his phone on Silent, even though it was a damn hard thing to do. He settled down to destress a bit. He wanted to open his mind and figure out what the hell was happening with Kate's cases and whether Simon could do anything there to help her.

Almost as soon as he had taken several long, slow breaths, that same child's voice slammed into his head. Only this time it was petulant and half angry.

*You haven't helped.*

Simon looked around and sighed. "No, not yet."

*Why not?*

"Because you haven't given me enough information to help with."

First came silence, then a response. *Oh.*

"Can you tell me where you are?"

*No,* he replied.

"Okay, can you tell me what happened to you?"

*No.*

Simon winced at that. "Okay."

*I guess you can't help then, can you?* the boy asked.

"I'm not saying that," he said, trying to keep his voice calm. "Can you tell me something about your mom?"

*She loved me,* he responded immediately.

"Past tense?"

*Yes.* There was an odd tone to his voice.

"Okay." Again not sure if the child was alive or dead, Simon asked, "Do you know what happened to you?"

*No.*

"Okay." He kept asking questions, just trying to get somewhere. "What's your name?"

*Peter.*

At that Simon felt his own gut clench down deep. Now he was getting somewhere, even enough for Kate. "Did you have a father?"

*No.*

After that, Simon went through a series of more questions, writing down the answers as they came. Part of him still felt as if he was just making this all up. How could he possibly be talking to somebody this way? He didn't know, but he kept working his way through it. He asked, "Do you know where you lived?"

*In a house.*

"In a house," he repeated, with a laugh.

Finally the voice in his head went silent, and Simon checked his list. He asked one more question, "How old are you?"

*Five.* And then, with fatigue in his tone, the little boy disappeared.

Simon frowned at that, thinking about a five-year-old boy lost out in the ethers. Simon texted what he had to Kate.

Meanwhile, Peter's being lost in the ethers was just terrifying for Simon. As he sat here pondering what the odds were of this even coming up in his world, he realized that, as long as he was open to it, more of this would likely happen. Whether he really wanted to acknowledge it or not, he was giving himself the leeway to do it. A little shaken up at that understanding—and realizing that this is exactly where he had put himself—he finished his coffee, also cold, then got up and headed back to his penthouse apartment.

As he approached his building, his phone rang. When he looked down at the phone to see a work call coming through, everything around him changed and swirled. He sank to his knees, catching himself and blindly following his way to a set of stairs, where he collapsed, not sure what he heard around him, but definitely hearing something. It came through, and he recognized the voice of Harry, his doorman. Somehow Simon got close to home, yet not close enough to get himself inside his own apartment.

Pissed off at being in this compromising position in public, he pulled himself back out into his consciousness and sat up, staying here for a long moment.

His doorman asked him, "Do you need a hand?"

"I don't think so," Simon muttered, "but I'll just sit here for a minute."

"It's a nice day for it," Harry noted in that same offhand tone.

Simon snorted. "Maybe, but I can't say that I'm a big fan of this happening in public."

Harry smiled at him. "Yet whatever is going on in your world seems to be something you don't have a whole lot of control over."

"Yeah, you noticed that, *huh?*"

"I did, and, in case you're worried about it," Harry shared, shaking his head, "my gran had the sight. So you don't need to be afraid of my saying anything."

"That's good," Simon replied, "because I'm not sure just what the hell I've got."

"Oh, I would say it's the same thing," Harry muttered. "Not terribly comfortable to have either, at least that's what she would say."

"Is she still alive?"

"She is. ... Are you looking to talk to her?"

"I don't know," he admitted. "I'm not exactly sure what I am right now. Just a little confused."

"Confused is not the worst thing you could be," he murmured. "Sometimes this comes to us for a reason."

"Maybe, but trying to deal with it? Now that's a different story."

"That is much harder," he acknowledged. "Sorry about that. Let's get you up to your place." And, with that, Harry helped Simon up the front steps, into the main lobby, and even assisted him right up to his apartment. He hesitated before leaving him there alone, asking, "Will you be okay?"

Simon nodded. "I should be okay from here." Harry still hesitated, but Simon waved him off. "If nothing else, I can go collapse in bed."

"Maybe you should."

"Is that what your grandmother would do?"

"No, she spent a lifetime helping people, not that anybody ever appreciated it."

"Right," he muttered, "and I think that's part of the problem. My grandmother also had the sight," he murmured. "And it's not the easiest thing, knowing that everybody out there is scared of you, yet at the same time wanting something from you."

"Agreed." Harry remained, obviously torn about leaving Simon alone at this time. Yet, at Simon's continued urging, Harry went back downstairs.

Simon crashed onto the couch, swearing.

He looked at his phone, reviewing the notes he had taken when he spoke to the little boy. Frowning, he realized something else had been added there. Had he added it? He didn't think so, or at least he didn't remember doing it. He had an address, at least part of an address. Sure enough, it was local. He immediately called Kate.

When she answered, her voice was distracted, "Is everything okay?" she asked.

"Yes, but I have an odd thing to request."

"Of course, as if anything isn't ever odd with you."

He gave her a short version by way of explanation, then added, "The thing is, I now have in front of me what appears to be an address."

"And you wrote it?" she asked, her tone deepening.

"Maybe," he suggested, having trouble trying to explain it to himself.

She went quiet for a minute. "Give me the address." As soon as he gave it to her, her breath sucked in deep and hard.

"What's the matter?" he asked.

"That … is the house where I was raised. That's my old home."

# CHAPTER 14

IT WAS HARD for Kate to focus after that. She searched the database of case files for that address, but nothing came up, except the one involving her brother. She needed to talk to her mother again, and that wouldn't be much fun. She'd called the hospital, and her mom was slowly waking up but refusing to see her. Now Kate needed to make it official.

She got up and looked over at Rodney. "I'll head over to the hospital and see my mother, and I'll check on Edna while I'm there."

"Edna?"

She winced. "The single mother of the teenage boy, who we found with the syringe in his arm."

"Right," Rodney muttered. "The attempted suicide. At least she's made it this far."

"She did, but I suspect she won't be very thankful that we saved her."

"No, I imagine not," Rodney agreed. "What a mess. It's all just so tragic."

"Tragic. Very sad," she noted.

She walked out, stopped for a minute, and took a deep breath. Just something about all this was so painful. These poor people, going through all this pain and trauma, and nobody was there for them. But she understood because that had been her early life too, and nobody had been there for her either. Her mother had gone to pieces, had blamed Kate for Timmy going missing, and that had more or less been it for her. It made no sense. Her mother just could not look at her own actions—or inactions. Better to blame somebody else than look at herself.

Kate drove to the hospital and parked in the big parking lot. As she got inside, she flashed her ID and asked for the condition on the woman she'd brought in earlier—Edna— and got pretty well the same answer as before. *Cautiously hopeful.*

She nodded, then headed up to the floor where her mother had been moved to. As she got there, she realized that she hadn't had her mother's blood sample checked for the particular drug given to her, and that needed to be done, if someone else hadn't already done it. It wasn't an autopsy kind of tox screen, so it would need to go through a different chain of evidence process, authorized through proper channels. That was one of the first things she asked about when she came to the nurses' station near her mother's room.

The nurse checked her mother's records and confirmed that a sample had already been taken and sent to the lab.

Kate smiled and nodded her thanks, then headed to her mother's room to speak with her, except her mother appeared to be in a deep sleep. Kate hesitated, wondering if she should push it and wake her up, forcing her mother to share whatever she had been dealing with.

She walked toward her, and her mother's eyes opened, and she freaked out.

Kate immediately raced to her side, her hands out as she whispered, "It's okay. It's all right. Calm down. You're not alone. You're in the hospital."

Her mother stared at her, frightened and trembling, her eyes wide as she looked around.

Kate repeated, "You're in the hospital. It's all right."

Her mother sagged back onto the hospital bed and stared at her.

"We came to find you because you wanted to talk," Kate began, "but, when we got there, you were, … you were on the kitchen floor, with a needle in your arm."

Her mother stared at her, then shook her head. "No, I wouldn't have done that."

"I don't know whether you did or not," Kate stated. "What I can tell you is that's how we found you." Knowing her mother wouldn't believe her, Kate brought up the photos taken at the site and held them up for her to see.

She stared at it, immediately shaking her head. "I didn't. I wouldn't."

"I'm not saying you did. I'm just saying this is what we found. I came to talk to you but found you like this instead."

Selene stared at Kate, that same shock in her gaze.

"Do you want to talk now?"

She shut down immediately, like watching all the lights go out inside. Selene stared out the window. Finally, after a long moment, she shook her head.

Frustrated, Kate replied, "It would help a lot if you would talk to us."

She immediately shook her head again.

Not sure what to do, Kate asked, "Then why did you call me?"

"It was a mistake," she snapped.

Swearing at that, Kate replied, "It couldn't have been that much of a mistake when you called me to come talk to you."

"It was a mistake. I told you that."

When she was in this mood, Kate knew it would be hard to shake anything loose, so she changed her tactics. "Any chance that somebody else did this to you?"

She just shrugged and didn't say anything.

"I'll take that as a yes."

"I don't know," Selene snapped again, glaring at her daughter. "I obviously don't know anything, because I didn't think I did that."

"And maybe you didn't," Kate conceded. "Is there anybody in your life who might have done this?"

She stared at her, bit her bottom lip for a moment, then shook her head. "No, … no one."

That was clearly a lie. Kate frowned at her mother. "You haven't had any visitors since you've been in here, except me."

"And why are you here? Oh, right," she grumbled, "because somehow now you're a cop."

"Yes, I am a cop."

"But you didn't find your brother though, did you?"

"No, not yet," she stated, "but I haven't given up either." Her mother turned to stare at her. Kate nodded. "His file stays on my desk all the time. There is always hope that something will break in the case and that we'll find him."

"Really?" her mother asked, a distinctively odd note in her tone.

Kate leaned forward and stated, "Yes. I will find him." She wasn't sure if her mother was seeking reassurance or something else, but something was off. Kate couldn't place it.

Even long after she'd left the hospital, that feeling wouldn't leave her. "What the hell was that all about?" she mumbled to herself.

If she could just figure out what her mother *wasn't* saying, it would help. The fact that her mother wouldn't talk now was even worse. If she hadn't put herself in the hospital with this stunt, then who the hell had? Kate was pretty damn sure, once her mom had woken up and had seen Kate, that's when her mom had first realized that something was going on. Kate just didn't know what. She didn't see fear in her mother's expression. Instead she found one of resignation, as if Selene understood that the end was coming regardless.

And that made no sense at all to Kate.

Frowning, she stood outside the hospital for a long moment, wondering what was going on. Then she realized she'd forgotten to ask her about the address Simon had just given her. Had they owned the house?

She didn't remember. She walked back up to her mother's room and walked in just in time to see her mother up, dressed, and trying to pack to leave.

Selene stopped as soon as she saw Kate and glared at her. "What are you doing back?" she snapped.

Kate noted a completely different woman now, compared to the one she had left just a few minutes ago. "I forgot to ask you a couple questions. Where were you thinking of going?"

"Home, of course. I'm not staying here."

"Why?"

"I'm not staying here," she repeated. "It doesn't matter why." With that, she grabbed her bag and walked calmly to the door. "You can tell the doctors I'm checking out."

And yet it did matter. It mattered in a big way. Kate walked beside her in the hallway and took a stab in the dark. "Do you think you'll be any safer at home?"

Her mother froze, then turned to Kate, and she now saw the fear in her mother's gaze. Kate nodded. "You may not be any safer at home, and you need to consider that."

"It's not as if you'll protect me," she snapped, followed by a harsh laugh. "So, it doesn't matter, does it?" And her mother took off toward the elevator.

"The mistakes we make," Kate said, "they travel with us."

"Don't I know it," her mother snapped. "You don't need to lecture me about that." She stepped inside the elevator, with Kate dogging her the whole way.

"Maybe not," Kate conceded, "but that house we used to live in?" Kate gave her the address, trying to jog her memory.

"What about it?"

"Did you own it?"

"Yes, we did." Her mother stiffened as if against impending doom, and Kate saw her hunching her shoulders. "Did you sell it way back then?"

"I did," she confirmed. "I got the house in the divorce and sold it." When the elevator door opened, Selene headed for the big double doors and stepped outside and kept on going.

And that gave Kate the first indication as to why her mother might be scared. "Do you think he'll come back after you for money?"

"I don't have any money," she stated, staring at her. "So, even if he does, it won't make a damn bit of difference."

"That might not save you anyway," Kate noted. "You need to tell me why you're so scared."

"I'm not scared," she snapped, glaring at Kate. "And, for a cop, you're not very smart."

She didn't have any reason to hold her, outside of the

overdose, so she offered, "Let me drive you home at least."

Selene frowned at her. "Why?"

"Because I'm not done questioning you," Kate explained. "So, we can either do it while we're driving, or I can make you come down to the station, and we'll discuss the overdose there. You will be checked up on for that anyway."

"If I leave the hospital, nobody can make me do anything."

Kate laughed. "You think it's that simple? If you are deemed a danger to yourself, then definitely people will be calling you," she pointed out, "whether you like it or not."

Her shoulders slumped. "No, I don't want that. I don't want or need anybody in my world. I just want you all to go away." With that, she shoved her face into Kate's. "All of you, got it?"

"Oh, I got that when you slugged me in the face the other day," Kate replied, staring at her. "And trust me that I don't want anything more to do with you than I have to." She thought a flash of hurt appeared in her mother's gaze, but Kate wasn't too worried about it at this point in time. "I still need questions answered, so you will answer my questions." She pointed in the direction of her car.

"You don't need questions answered," Selene snapped. "You're just trying to make my life difficult."

"And how am I doing that?"

"All the shit about your brother," she said. "It's done and over with."

"Really?" she asked, as she opened up the passenger side of the car. "You would think somebody who lost her son would be the first to want answers."

"There are no answers," she snapped. "Some stranger snatched him, and, if you'd been a better sister, you would know that."

Kate smiled, realizing that, for the first time in a very long time, her mother couldn't hurt her this way. "I'm not seven years old. I'm an adult now. I know better than to believe you, and I reject that shit."

"And I don't have to listen to your shit either," Selene snapped.

"Actually you do, and we can either do that here or down at the station, your choice."

Still glaring, her mother hopped into the car and muttered, "Just get me home, then you can walk out of my life and stay out."

"Happy to," Kate agreed, "at least until we solve our current situation. However, if I need you back in for questioning, believe me that I'll have you back in for questioning."

"That's harassment," her mom snapped.

"Not likely," she countered, with half a smile as she got into the driver's side. "When it comes to needing answers and getting them, turns out I'm pretty good at it," she shared, turning to look at her mother. "And I don't care what kind of excuses you try to pass off this time."

"I didn't have any excuses last time either," she declared, glaring at her daughter. "You're the one who lost him."

"I didn't lose him," she clarified, "and it's nice of you to still try to blame a seven-year-old."

"You were old enough to know better."

"Yeah, and what does that say about you?" she asked, turning to look at her mother. "The adult in all of this, the drug addict, who was forever blaming her partner for that too?"

The color drained from her mom's face. "You don't

know anything," she roared, immediately trying to open the car door, but it was locked.

"Maybe I don't," Kate conceded, "but what I do know is that you're still withholding information, and for that I guess we'll need to take you down to the station. There you can scream and swear and talk all you want, but this time? ... This is well past the point in time for more of your lies. We want answers, and we want them now."

When they pulled up to her mother's apartment building, Kate parked and went to turn off the engine. Her mother immediately bolted out the door, glared at her, and spat, "You're not welcome here. If you need to talk to me again, and I can't get out of it, send one of your cohorts instead. I don't want to see you again."

Surprised that her comment stung as it did, Kate watched as her mother, albeit a little unsteadily, walked straight up to her apartment.

Kate could see the windows from her place right from the parking area, which is one of the reasons she had stopped here, thinking maybe she could keep an eye on her mom as she got up to her apartment. Kate knew her mother. Selene wouldn't let up. While Kate could force the matter and could take Selene to the station, Kate didn't really have any more questions to ask of a mother who apparently no longer had anything that she wanted to say to her.

As she kept watch, she noted the curtain twitched, and her mother's right center finger came up to give Kate the eternal signal to get lost. Shaking her head at that, she slowly drove away, wondering what she was supposed to do with that.

As she got back to the station, Rodney was just walking in. She looked over at him and asked, "Any progress?"

"Some," he replied carefully. "How's your mom?"

"Refusing treatment. She walked out of the hospital, so I drove her home," she shared. "Not sure I should have, but she wasn't staying either way."

"So, she's okay then? Did she tell you what she wanted? What she'd wanted to tell you, I mean."

"No, and not only that, I got the finger and was told to never come back. So, if the police need to speak to her, I'm to send one of you guys, not me," she shared, with studied carelessness.

He just looked at her and shook his head. "Wow."

"Yeah, sometimes families are like that," she noted.

"And sometimes they're not," he added.

"Did you find out anything?" she asked him.

He let loose a long sigh. "I know you might not appreciate this, but I did pull your birth certificate."

"Yeah, that's interesting," she said, looking at him. "I can't say I've ever seen it."

"So, the man in prison isn't listed on your birth certificate."

She paused, contemplating that information. "I'm not terribly surprised at that. I don't even know if she knows who my father actually is."

He winced at that. "A name is on there though."

She frowned at him. "Wait. My father's name is on it, and it's not the guy who's in prison?"

"Right, that's what I'm saying."

"Okay, so who is it?" He gave her a name, and she shrugged. "That's not a name I know. I don't think I've ever even heard it. Wesley Crane," she repeated. "I can't think of ever hearing that name come up in conversation. Too bad I didn't know that earlier. I could have asked her about it,"

Kate said, with a laugh. "That would have pissed her off even more."

"They were married, and I did look for a death certificate."

Kate nodded, waiting. He wasn't telling her something. "Come on, Rodney. Out with it."

"Apparently your real father died a few years ago."

"A few years ago?" she repeated, her eyebrows shooting up.

He nodded. "Yes, about seven."

She frowned. "I didn't even know anything about him."

"And I suspect that was your mother's doing."

She nodded, a little surprised to be shaken by that news. "It would have been nice to know I had a father out there."

"No guarantee that he even knew about the pregnancy. Remember that."

"But you said they were married."

"Yes, but I don't know at what point he disappeared from the picture."

She frowned and acknowledged that possibility too.

"What was your mom even like back then?"

"I only have the perspective of a seven-year-old," she murmured, "and unfortunately it's fairly twisted by the circumstances. So, I would say, *rough*. I think she was a good-time girl, and, when she couldn't find a good time, she made one."

He nodded. "Any chance that your brother might not have the same father?"

She snorted. "There's a damn-good chance. I don't have an answer for you."

"I'll go pull that next," Rodney stated.

"You do that," she muttered.

Lilliana took one look at Kate and said, "Aren't families great?"

"No, not at all," she muttered, as she sat down at her desk. "I just dropped my mother off at home."

"She's okay then?" Lilliana asked.

"Let's just say she's fighting mad and was rather desperate to get home."

"Interesting."

"Yet she seemed afraid, but she won't talk about it, and she won't tell me what she wanted to talk to me about before."

"So, you think somebody is trying to keep her quiet?"

"It's possible. Right now she's incredibly uncooperative and told me flat-out that, if the police want to talk to her again, to send somebody other than me."

Lilliana shook her head. "Well, that clears that up."

"Clears what up?"

"Whether she harbors any motherly love."

"There's none. Apparently there never has been. Today she blamed me again for losing my brother."

Lilliana slowly turned and frowned. "Seriously?"

Kate nodded. "She told me that it was my fault for having lost him. I told her that I was an adult now and didn't take on that BS and that she had been the adult back then, so it was her job to keep him safe. Obviously it wasn't something she did deliberately, and Timmy and I used to walk home together all the time," she noted. "Yet I wasn't about to take that from her again."

"No, of course not," Lilliana agreed, yet with a curious smile. "Do you think she's doing it on purpose?"

"Of course she is. It stops her from facing her own guilt."

"True, but it's still an odd thing to say, considering you were only seven."

"Exactly, and she's never really eased up on that story, so I don't imagine anything's changed."

Rodney walked over, a piece of paper in his hand. "Your brother does not have the same father as you, at least based on the birth certificates."

She nodded. "Not a surprise."

"And he's the one in prison right now," he stated, turning to look at her. She winced, as he went on. "Do we know where he was at the time your brother disappeared?"

She shrugged. "According to the case file, he was already in prison, but, whether that's true or not, I don't know." With that, Kate grabbed the file that she always had on her desk and asked Rodney for the date that Ken was incarcerated. "Yes, according to those dates he was in prison, although that doesn't mean he didn't have a day pass."

"The fact that they even give those out is pretty amazing, especially if they're doing it to commit further crimes."

"He may not have been convicted yet at the time, and they do tend to be more lenient if they are not a flight risk and if he couldn't make bail," she pointed out.

Lilliana nodded. "So, somebody needs to contact your mom."

"You're it then," Kate announced, with a bright smile.

Lilliana rolled her eyes. "Fine, let me see if I can get her on the phone." At that, she walked over, sat down at her desk, and went to work.

Kate turned to Rodney. "So, Ken's listed on Timmy's birth certificate?"

"Yes."

She nodded.

"You didn't know?" he asked her.

"I wouldn't have had any clue, and honestly, I've never questioned who our fathers may have been," she shared. "But really, it's no surprise, knowing my mother."

He just frowned at that, and she knew he was having a hard time with the harsh realities of her childhood. She smiled. "There are so many other things in life to worry about. So, the failings of my mother are not worth wasting my energy on."

"I agree," he muttered. "Your mother is a piece of work."

"I think maybe long ago she had dreams and hopes and wishes, just like everybody else, but what I don't know is what happened in the meantime."

"And it could just as easily have been a divorce—or two," he pointed out, "particularly if she had a certain lifestyle she wanted to maintain."

"I think it's not so much the lifestyle as potentially just some fun in life." Kate frowned. "There were a couple girlfriends in the picture back then. They were very vocal about defending me, telling Selene how I did not have anything to do with my brother's disappearance. They were kind to me. I don't think they approved of Selene throwing me to the wolves," she added in a half-mocking tone.

"Do you remember their names?"

She opened her file again, flipped through, and found their statements. "These two," she murmured. "You might shake something loose now, after all this time."

"Done. Do you want to come with me when I interview them?" he asked.

"No. I'll focus on these two current cases and stay away from that as much as I can."

"And can you?"

"I don't know," she murmured. "However, I do know that somebody could be trying to use it as a distraction, and we do have two dead kids, and that's something we really need to solve."

With that, she sat down at her desk, needing to contact the hospital regarding what drugs had been in her mother's system. A phone call later, she sat here, stunned, wondering how the hell her mother had anything to do with Kate's current cases.

Rodney walked by with a hot cup of coffee in his hand, took one look at her expression, and asked, "What?"

She shook her head. "The drug they found in my mother's system is the same one found in the two boys."

His eyebrows shot up, and he sat down with a hard *thump*. "Wow, that changes things."

"Does it though?" she murmured. "I'm not sure it changes anything."

"It sure does," he declared. "There's your connection."

"Right, meaning they all may have the same drug dealer. However, beyond that, I'm not sure. Why would anybody give a rat's ass about my being involved, when I'm not even on the drug squad?" she asked. "I've been in homicide for long enough that anybody who did two minutes of research would know that."

"So, you think they were trying to hide a homicide?"

"No, I think they fear any connection with me would trigger my interest, regardless of what department I was in," she suggested, giving him a hard glance. "I would be on top of it regardless."

He cracked a knowing smile. "They're right in that sense."

"Maybe," she murmured, "yet I also have to consider

that this is a setup, pure and simple."

His eyebrows slowly rose as he studied her. "A setup for whom?" he asked.

"Me," she snapped. "Just for me."

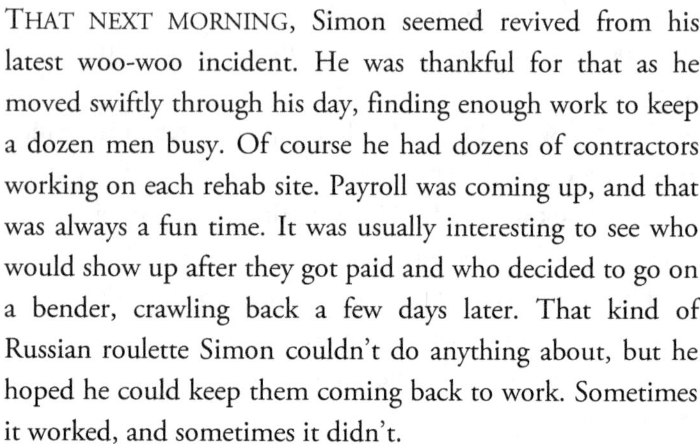

THAT NEXT MORNING, Simon seemed revived from his latest woo-woo incident. He was thankful for that as he moved swiftly through his day, finding enough work to keep a dozen men busy. Of course he had dozens of contractors working on each rehab site. Payroll was coming up, and that was always a fun time. It was usually interesting to see who would show up after they got paid and who decided to go on a bender, crawling back a few days later. That kind of Russian roulette Simon couldn't do anything about, but he hoped he could keep them coming back to work. Sometimes it worked, and sometimes it didn't.

As he walked through the main office of his accountant, the paperwork settled and the pencil-pushers happy—at least as happy as they ever were—Simon headed to the nearest rehab building. With that quickly handled, he headed off to the next one. By the time he was done with his visits through each of his rehab projects, while ignoring the latest calls from his stalker realtor, he headed over to a coffee shop.

As he walked up to get a coffee, the realtor stepped in front of him. "I'll buy it."

He turned around and asked, "Where did you come from?"

"Hey, I know this is one of your regular coffee joints," she shared, with an eye roll. "And since you haven't answered my calls, I figured we could talk here."

"You're still hounding me about that one building,

*huh?*"

"My clients really want to sell," she replied simply.

"That's nice, and I do want to buy, but I won't do that until I have an idea of where I'm at."

"Ooh, does that mean you're broke?" she asked in a half-joking manner, but her gaze was searching.

His eyebrows shot up. "As you should know very well by now, I don't talk money ... ever," he stated coolly. "If I wanted to buy right now, I'm quite capable of buying, but I haven't yet done a cost analysis, and I'm a little busy."

She frowned, realizing that she'd overstepped and tried to laugh it off. "Hey, I was just teasing, and I meant no offense. Don't worry. Everybody knows you're loaded."

"I'm a working man," he declared, staring at her. "*Loaded* isn't part of being a working man. I work my ass off financing these rehabs, and, with any luck, at the end of the day, money is left over to do it again."

She gave him a coy look. "No way you would do this if you weren't making money."

"You might be surprised at what drives me," he countered, with a coldness still in his gaze and in his tone.

"Then tell me," she whined in exasperation. "You're always looking at buildings. You're always looking for something to do, and yet the buildings that you end up choosing are often the ones that nobody else would touch."

"A lot of times that's exactly what they are, but I don't touch them because other people won't," he clarified. "I touch them because they need it."

She frowned, clearly not understanding, something he was up against all the time. It was one of the reasons he didn't discuss it, particularly with people like Ariel. "I'll let you know if I come to a decision on it," he stated. "Other than that, get them down in price. As soon as I reach a point where I can't *not* buy it, I'll come up with a cost analysis for it."

She groaned. "They want to sell, but they still want to get something out of it."

"Yet they've been sitting on it for how long? Twenty years?" he asked, staring at her. "If they wanted to get something out of it, they could have sold it much earlier, at any point in time."

Simon walked from one area to another and sat down at a table again, trying to kick the stupid realtor out of his mind. She was one of those people who seemed to always be there, and it was starting to drive him nuts. When he looked up, she stood in front of him, tapping her foot on the ground. He glared at her. "Seriously, have you got nothing better to do than hound me?"

"Not if you're interested in buying."

"If I buy, I buy," he stated, his patience running thin. "Why are you so pushy?"

"Because I need, I need, … want to make the sale."

"That's nice," he muttered, staring at her. "Lots of other buildings are out there."

"There sure are," she agreed, shrugging, "but this one needs to be done, and you're the right person for it."

His eyebrows rose at that. "And what makes you say that?"

"I don't know," she muttered, frowning and looking around, "but I can't seem to leave it be."

"I see that," he noted, "but it's a little concerning that you're hounding me so much …"

She laughed. "As if you care."

"You don't know anything about me," he stated. "Of

course I care. I don't want anything weird to happen here."

She eyed him in surprise. "What could possibly happen that's any weirder than already is around this place?"

He studied her carefully, trying to assess what she knew, for she was acting odd.

"Besides," she added, "I've heard you have some … abilities."

He just stared at her, the smile falling from his face.

She nodded. "And that you don't like to talk about it."

"I don't talk about much to anybody," he declared, cutting her off. "I've learned the hard way that most people aren't honest when they say what they're after, so now I really don't know what it is you're after."

She smiled. "All good things."

"Now," he replied, standing up, "I'm off to work, and I suggest you leave me alone." And, with that, he turned to walk away.

"If you do have abilities," she added, walking behind him, "I could use some help."

He froze, then turned to her. "Interesting that you would even ask," he muttered.

"The situation requires that I be blunt."

"And why is that?"

"Because," she hesitated, then shrugged, "my nephew is missing."

"Good Christ. What has that got to do with me?"

"Nothing, but I did hear that you helped somebody else get a little boy back."

He stared at her and replied carefully, "Maybe, but that was a fluke."

She gave him a ghost of a smile. "I wonder what that even means in your world."

"It means that I won't be pushed into things."

"Of course," she agreed, with a nod. "You don't want anybody to know, but there's got to be a reason why you buy all these buildings."

He laughed. "I buy them because I want to."

She glared at him. "You could help."

"Maybe, but so could a lot of people."

She shook her head at that. "No, this is bigger than that. I don't know what happened to him."

He didn't even allow himself to contemplate that. "Now, if you'll excuse me."

"Don't you care that a little boy is lost? Peter's never done anything to hurt anybody."

At the name *Peter*, Simon froze, then pivoted to face her.

She nodded. "He's innocent. I don't know what the hell happened to him, but it's bad."

"What did you call him?"

"Peter. Peter Bigwood is his name, and I think it's bad."

"And how do you know it's bad?"

"He's missing, Simon. He's a little boy, and he's missing," she repeated.

For the first time, her demeanor cracked, and Simon saw real emotions. "I don't know that I have anything I could possibly help you with," he replied, studying her intently. He'd become even more jaded after working with Kate. People wanted stuff all the time, and, if they found out what Simon's involvement had been with the police, that would change his life entirely, and he was not up for that.

"I don't know if you can help. I don't even know if you will," she muttered. "I just know that I need help."

"Have you gone to the cops?"

"Of course," she said, with a glare in his direction.

He shrugged. "We see all kinds of things."

"And I do too," she stated, with a nod. "Sometimes I walk into empty buildings, and I'm afraid that another dead homeless guy will be inside. It's not supposed to happen. I'm not supposed to be the one who finds them, but somehow it ends up being that way."

"Seems to be an occupational hazard. Maybe it's time to change jobs."

"Oh, I've thought about that lots of times, trust me," she muttered, glaring at him. "Yet it doesn't change the fact that, rumor has it, you helped the cops find that little boy."

"Even if I did help find a little boy, that has nothing to do with being able to help you."

"No, but I'm hoping," she whispered.

He groaned. "I don't know anything about it."

"Look. All we know is that he didn't come home from school."

"And how long ago was it?" he asked.

She hesitated and then replied, "Two years." When he frowned at her, she nodded. "I know. It's been a while, too long, but we want to bring him home, dead or alive."

"And that really doesn't help in any way if you haven't got anything to help the police find him."

"I know, and that's what they say too," she admitted, with a note of desperation. "After so long, you give up. I even hired a private investigator. My sister, she's going crazy, and she wants answers."

"So often," he noted, "there are no answers."

She immediately nodded. "I know. I know. The police told us that too, but what are we supposed to do? It's not as if we can just turn it off."

"Is that why you've been hounding me?"

"No, but ..." She shrugged. "I figured, what the hell? The only thing you could really do is say no. And everybody else has said no already."

"Of course," he noted.

"I know that you don't want anybody to know and that you probably really wish I hadn't even approached you. Regardless, when you're desperate, you do whatever you need to do, and you don't care. You may think that I'm crazy, but I don't care about any of that."

"What happened to him?"

"He just wasn't there to be picked up at school one day. Nobody saw him. They didn't have any cameras at the right angle in the playground area where he always got picked up. He just wasn't there, and we never saw him again."

"Who was supposed to pick him up?"

"My sister was, but he wasn't there," Ariel explained, "and the police checked. ... They say *everywhere*, but obviously not everywhere because they never found him."

Simon sighed, his brain already working overtime. "I'll call you."

"Please, please, if there's anything ..."

"No promises, all I can do is check all the same sources I did last time."

Relief washed over her face. "Yes, please do, please. Anything is helpful."

"Not necessarily," he countered.

She frowned and whispered, "I know. I'm pretty sure he's dead."

He nodded. "I suspect he is, but that's not what you want to hear."

She winced. "No, I really don't want to hear that, but, if that's what you tell me, it is what it is, and we need to know."

He sighed. "Let me think about it."

She immediately backed off but stared at him anxiously.

He realized how much it had taken for her to take that step forward. He swore.

"I know. I know. I know," she cried out. "But please, if you come up with anything, call me." And, with that, she turned and raced away.

He watched her retreat, knowing that now he must contact Peter, the same little boy he had spoken to before. What the hell was he supposed to do with that?

This was not exactly how he thought his day would go. And the fact that Ariel had mentioned *Peter*, and that was the name of the little boy Simon had been talking to was something he could not ignore, even if he wanted to. Peter wouldn't let him.

# CHAPTER 15

"PETER BIGWOOD," KATE repeated into the phone. "What about it?" When he hesitated, she groaned. "Don't tell me somebody contacted you."

"This little guy has contacted me a couple times," Simon reminded her, "and the best I could tell you was that his name was Peter and he went missing two years ago. You saw my text from last night, I presume?"

"Right."

"But now my stalker realtor contacted me."

"Okay, and what's that got to do with this?"

"She was following me around the city, under the guise of nagging me about buying a building. Finally, I got half mad and asked her what the hell was really going on, and she told me how she'd heard something about my helping to find a little boy."

"Oh, crap," Kate muttered.

"Yeah, you could say that."

"The end result is that little boy I have been talking to is her nephew, and apparently the realtor's sister is not doing very well."

"Of course not," Kate replied compassionately. "But to contact you …"

"I know. Believe me, … I know. I'm not exactly sure what I'm supposed to do with this either. She looked desperate."

"So, what is it you want me to do?"

"Now that you have Peter's last name, could you look into the missing person's case and ensure that it's valid and that this Peter is still missing?"

"What? You're thinking that she's lost her marbles?"

"No, just another lost little boy," he said.

"Crap. I'm inundated with dead little kids."

"Yeah, in this case, I'm pretty sure he's dead."

First came silence. "So often they are," she muttered.

"I know, and I didn't have the heart to tell Ariel that outright, but I did warn her that it could go that way."

"Oh, you probably said a little more than that. You can't help yourself."

He winced. "Maybe," he agreed, "but I didn't tell her anything either way."

"That's good because, if he's dead, it won't be a good answer."

"No, but it is still an answer."

She went silent again. "I'll take a look, but no promises." And, with that, she disconnected, staring at her phone in confusion.

Lilliana stopped by her desk. "That sounded unusual."

"Not when you live with Simon," Kate noted. "Somebody he knows mentioned that their nephew is missing and has somehow figured out that Simon may or may not have a line into helping with such things. So, he's asked me to see if it's a real case and whether anything is there would preclude him from going ahead with it."

"Ouch," Lilliana replied. "I mean, you can't even win with that deal."

Rodney sat nearby and had heard it too. He nodded.

Kate agreed. "I know it, and, if I say no, and a little boy named Peter is missing, then it sucks for everybody. However, if I say yes, then Simon gets involved in another missing child case."

"Which could obviously have repercussions in terms of maybe finding him, but also maybe not."

Rodney turned away from them, cleared his monitor, and brought up the database, then asked, "What's the name?"

"Peter Bigwood," Kate said.

"Oh, I know that case," Lilliana replied. "It was all over the news. Little boy, out on the playground in Surrey and supposed to be with other kids at the time. He just wasn't there at the end of the school day. He was supposed to be on the playground, and school's over, and there's a monitor, and kids are being picked up all over the place. The mom comes to pick him up, and he's gone, never to be seen again."

"And, of course, she knows nothing."

"Right, she knows nothing," Lilliana confirmed. "She had a breakdown afterward, thinking she was responsible, and hasn't been doing well ever since."

"Do you know her?"

She winced and nodded. "Yes, not close, but I knew of her at the time."

"It's not the easiest thing to deal with in any case."

"Exactly," Lilliana agreed.

Rodney asked, "Did Simon say anything about it?"

Kate turned to him and grimaced. "Simon thinks the boy is dead."

They both winced, but no surprise was there because generally, when children are picked up, they are used and abused and then discarded. There was also the sex trade to consider, and, while neither one of them wanted to see anybody go into that, at least it could mean that the little boy might still potentially be alive.

Rodney sent something to the printer and then got up and shared, "I sent you an email copy as well, but this is the file on it."

Just as Lilliana suggested, there was really nothing to go on. "They did check into the parents, but the father was away at a conference, so he was cleared immediately, and the mother was at work. She was off right on time, but the traffic held her up. So, by the time she made it to the location, there was no sign of him."

"Crap," Kate murmured. "That'll be something that weighs on her the whole time too."

"Exactly," Rodney said. "I mean, it's bad enough that you already hate traffic, but to know that being late on one particular day may have contributed to the loss of your son would be awful. Not to mention that I believe the family broke up over it all as well. The father blamed the mother. The mother blamed the father, and it's been a shit show."

"A realtor Simon works with is the one who got in on this. The sister of the mom, I guess."

"Ah, I remember that. She was pretty active in the search I think."

"Too active?" Kate turned and asked directly.

"No, I don't think so. I think she just realized that her sister would go to pieces, and something needed to happen. Otherwise, they were in danger of losing her too."

Rodney nodded. "Which all of us can understand."

"Yeah, especially considering the fact that I'm already dealing with two dead kids right now," Kate stated, "and now we have a third one."

Rodney dropped the printed pages on her desk. "Is there any chance that these are connected?"

"If they are, I have no idea how," Kate admitted. "So far, I don't have anything to speak of, except the same designer drug keeps showing up, and nobody understands how either kid got it—except for the teen, since he could have obtained it and taken it on his own. Yet he has no history of heavy drugs, according to the neighbors and the mother."

Lilliana added, "And we also know that the mother would lie as much as any mother will, in order to save herself, or maybe save her son."

"Did you stop in at the hospital and see her?" Rodney asked.

"Edna? No, I got sidetracked by my mother," Kate replied, "but I can go now, particularly since we have yet another child, missing, presumed dead. And yet—"

"I know," Rodney interrupted, "and yet it shouldn't be related. It's just that when it involves Simon ..."

"Exactly." Kate raised both hands. "When it's Simon, all bets are off."

She grabbed her keys then headed back to the hospital. As she headed down the hallway to Edna's room, the hospital's Code Blue alarm went off, and Kate raced there. She stood outside in the hallway with her heart in her throat as she waited.

When the doctor came out moments later, he shook his head. "I'm sorry," he murmured. "She's gone."

Kate closed her eyes, hating the fact that she had missed the opportunity to talk to her earlier, something that could have made a difference.

Then the doctor added, "She never regained consciousness."

Kate took a deep breath. "Thank you for telling me that. I was supposed to come talk to her earlier, when I was here to see another patient, but I didn't get it done."

"Sometimes we do everything we can, and still it's not enough. Unfortunately, in this instance, we don't have any answers, except for the fact that grief is one of the most debilitating emotions ever. I guess she went to join her son after all." And, with a commiserating look, he walked away.

She immediately sent Rodney a text message, and he called her a few minutes later. "Do you think it's all on the up-and-up?" he asked.

"We'll wait for an autopsy on that one," she murmured. "Yet, if we think about it, considering what Edna had just gone through, I'm really not surprised."

"No, I'm not either. I'm just sad because …"

"I agree. No point in saying she had so much to live for because, as far as she was concerned, life wasn't worth living if she didn't have her son." Kate hesitated. "Still, I need to sort out if anything else was going on with this case, without her assistance. So I'll go to her house and take a look. We went through the teen's room and talked to the neighbors about him, but we didn't do a full search on her."

"Right. How about I meet you there?" Rodney suggested.

"Sure."

He added, "I've got my other cases here more or less wrapped up."

"Good to know," she murmured. "But having said that …"

"I understand. I jinxed it. Now we'll get twelve murders, fourteen drive-by shootings, and sixteen questionable deaths all in the next twenty-four hours."

"When it happens," she quipped, "I'm blaming you."

He laughed. "I'll meet you there in twenty."

She walked out of the hospital, took a deep breath, then looked back and thought about the pain and the waste, the loss of life and how debilitating it was to everyone. When she sat in her vehicle, her phone rang. As she answered it, a man who she barely recognized spoke on the other end of the phone.

"Kate, is that you?"

"Yes. Who is this?"

The man replied, "Your stepfather."

She frowned as she stared down at the phone. "I wasn't expecting your call today," she noted cautiously.

"No, of course not," he conceded. "Your mother told me what's been going on."

"Did she?" she asked, bitterness in her tone. "Are you calling from prison?"

Silence came again. "I just got out," he murmured, "and I was hoping we could talk."

"Oh, we could talk," she noted. "However, I'm not sure what good you think it would do."

"Your mom never really spoke much about what happened to your brother back then."

"No, all she's ever done is blame me," she snapped.

He sighed. "I'm sorry about that. Obviously that's not been fair to you."

She shook her head. "Why do you want to talk?"

"I ... might shed some light on it. On ... what happened."

She sucked in her breath. "I guess that's a guaranteed way to get my attention."

"I didn't really want it to be for that reason," he admitted, "but I really would like to talk to you about it."

"Or you want to talk to Mom."

"No, I've already talked to her."

Kate swore. "Is that the reason she's so terrified right now? Is that because of you?"

"I don't think so," he said, "no reason for her to be."

"What the hell?" she asked, scrubbing her face with her free hand.

"I know. It's confusing, but I think we should talk."

"Fine. When?"

"Tonight. I need food, and you need to eat as well," he stated, with a note of humor in his voice. Then he named a restaurant not too far from her place.

"Fine, but don't be wasting my time."

"Of course not," he said. "Selene told me that you're a cop."

"Yeah, I'm sure that surprised you."

"I haven't kept up over the last few years," he shared, "but I'm happy for you. Really." And, with that, he hung up.

She hadn't mentioned anything about bringing somebody but knew instinctively that, if she told Simon, he would want to be there too. Was it so wrong? He was connected to the case, yet wasn't. She knew she needed to tell Rodney too. And, with that, she turned on the engine and headed to Edna's house to meet him there.

As soon as she got out, Rodney stared at her and asked, "What happened?" Frowning, she told him. "Oh hell no," he declared. "You're not making that meeting on your own."

"That was my take on it too," she agreed, "but I'm not sure exactly what he's planning."

"Which is also why you're not going alone," he repeated immediately.

"Yeah, you coming with me?" she teased, with half a smile.

He frowned at that. "I guess he won't be too happy to see more authority."

"I doubt it, though I could be wrong. He told me that he's just been released from prison."

"Let's check that out. I'll get Lilliana on it right now," he announced.

"Why don't you get Reese to pull everything she can on him, my mother, and anybody else on the case," she suggested. "We should have done that already."

He looked at her and nodded. "We did do that. I just don't think we have a report back yet, or, if it's back, that it was even shared with you." She froze at that, and he nodded. "Remember how it's not just about you anymore. An awful lot more is going on here than that."

"I agree," she muttered. "It's just a weird feeling to think that I've been kept out of the loop on this case, the most important case for me."

"I'm not sure it's deliberate. I think we're all a bit unsure on who's supposed to report to whom on this one," he offered.

He quickly sent off several texts, while she sent one to Simon. As soon as Simon got it, he called her.

"I'll meet you there," he stated.

"Look. It's fine."

"No, it's not fine," he snapped, "and don't go telling me that it's fine. This guy has been in prison for how long? Now he gets out, and the first thing he does is contact you?"

"Yes, that's apparently what he did, after talking to my mother," she pointed out, with a note of humor in her tone. "And I get it. You don't think that's normal."

"Nope, it's not normal," he barked. "And, if he has something to say about your brother, you'll need somebody there with you. Not to mention he assaulted you as a child."

She groaned. "I was kind of hoping to get through this one on my own."

"Not happening," Simon snapped. "So, you might as well give it up right now."

"Fine," she muttered, "then you might as well come for dinner."

"Thank you. I'm glad you asked." And, with that, he hung up.

She was still glaring at the phone while Rodney chuckled beside her.

"Have we solved that problem? Because I don't want you going alone. Me or him, that's your choice on this one."

"I am a cop, you know?"

"And this is your stepfather, who sexually abused you, who physically abused your mother, and no telling what with your missing brother," Rodney reminded her. "So absolutely nothing is normal about it. Every time something happens, it sends you for a loop. It would send any of us for a loop," he stated, glaring at her.

"Fine," she muttered. "Simon is coming. Are you happy with that?"

"Actually I am. If nothing else, … I trust his judgment."

"Oh, and you don't trust mine?"

"Right now, with this case? No," he stated bluntly. "I don't. You're so involved in the case that you're practically a part of it. Still, this is a good answer. Now, shall we go deal with Edna's house?"

She nodded and proceeded to walk into the poor woman's home and tear apart the rest of her life. The little bit that was left after the death of her son was now about to be completely disintegrated by everybody else in law enforcement. It was a sad fact that, the minute you died, your life became a hell of a lot more interesting than when you were alive.

SIMON SHOVED THE paperwork to the back of his desk to stare out his huge office window. He couldn't stop thinking about Kate's stepfather. This was the man who had sexually assaulted her as a child, and she'd had a part in making sure he ended up behind bars. Why the hell would he be contacting her now? He was sure it was nothing good.

Simon wanted to reach out to her mother and see just what was going on, but, if Kate was correct, and Selene was scared shitless, this could explain why. Unfortunately, it made way too much sense.

He sat for a moment and wrote down the little bits and pieces he knew, just trying to empty his mind. Then, hating what he was about to do, but feeling as if he had to try, he opened up his mind and sent out a message to Peter.

His mind went into this sad, quiet, almost desperate moment where there was nothing but just this weird silence in his brain.

And then that little voice said, *Hello?*

"Peter, is that you?"

His voice was even more frail and wispy than before. *Yes, it's me.*

"Somebody is really missing you," Simon told him.

*My mom,* he replied immediately. *Yes, I think so.*

"Is there anything you can tell me about where you are, so I can help you?"

First came silence, and Simon knew that he'd asked Peter this same question before, and it was frustrating that nobody ever seemed to have any answers. "Do you know where you are? Is it dark or light?"

*Light… I think.*

Right, of course not, a clear answer would be way too easy. "Your aunt is asking about you."

Again came silence. *Aunt?*

"Yes, Aunt Ariel, your mother's sister."

*Ah.*

Simon was unsure whether Peter remembered Ariel, though he was young and may not. "I want to bring you home, if I could," Simon said.

*That would be nice.* His voice was fading.

"Please don't leave."

*I don't think I can stay,* the little boy shared.

"Can I get more information other than water? Are you close to the school? Are you close to home? Are you in the woods? Are you inside a building? Are you outside? Do you remember who you were with? Are you alone now?"

*No, … I'm not alone.*

Simon caught the breath in the back of his throat. "I know this is a very complex question, but do you know who you are with?"

*Other … little boys.*

Simon winced. "Can you tell me anything else? Anything about the other boys?"

*No,* he whispered.

"Are they all dead?" Simon asked, hating at needing to clarify question. Of course dead and together didn't mean they'd died together or were buried at the same place. That was a leap he couldn't make. There were too many variables when it came to the other side.

After a long silence, Peter whispered, *I don't know.* And then the little boy broke into weird sobs, that sounded like crying but not. And then he was gone.

"God," Simon muttered to himself. That was really well done. *Not.*

He didn't have any experience in this. All he knew was to ask questions and to hope for answers. Only when he got up did he realize how late it was, how long he'd talked to Peter. Simon had twenty minutes and only twenty minutes to get to the restaurant tonight. When he finally walked in, he saw no sign of Kate. It would make life a little easier if she was already here.

A man sat at a table in the far corner. He was looking around, as if waiting for somebody. Simon studied him for a long moment, not liking anything about it. He knew when Kate arrived outside because the man's gaze sharpened, and almost a feral smile appeared. Simon realized that Kate might be here for all the right reasons, but this asshole was not.

---

# CHAPTER 16

KATE WALKED INTO the restaurant, tired and sad. As soon as she saw Simon, her heart lightened immediately and then froze. He stood outside the restaurant, but he was not happy. She stepped up and asked him, "Problems?"

He nodded. "Yeah, this guy is waiting for you all right, but, Kate, nothing is good about him."

She frowned, then nodded. "He went to jail for child abuse," she said, "and the fact that he's out makes it doubly hard."

"And you might want to double-check his release date too," Simon suggested, "just in case he may have been the reason your mom was so terrified."

"Oh, I highly suspect it. Apparently some paperwork has issues with dates." He rolled his eyes, and she nodded. "Right, not exactly what you want to hear right now."

He glared at her. "You need to be careful. He looks way too interested in seeing you but in a totally creepy way."

She hesitated and then nodded. "Thanks for the heads-up." And, with that, she strode forward to meet the stepfather she hadn't seen in a very long time. He stood up as soon as she approached the table.

"Ah, Kate," he muttered, "I would have known you anywhere."

She studied him and nodded. "You haven't changed

much."

"Oh, trust me, I have," he stated.

His tone held none of the bitterness she expected. Nothing revealed that he held anything against her. And yet she also saw what Simon had already prepared her for. Unrest, anger, and maybe just the fact that he was free, yet—because of the way the restrictions on prisoners worked, even those recently freed—he wasn't free at all. But maybe it was just her imagination. She sat down at the table and introduced Simon carelessly.

"My partner wanted to come," she stated, with a smile. "This is Simon, and, Simon, … this is Ken Reeves."

Simon nodded and refused to shake the man's proffered hand. The insult did not go unnoticed either.

Ken frowned and glared at Simon. "I don't know anything about you," he said, trying to mask his anger.

Kate immediately raised an eyebrow. "We don't know anything about each other," she declared immediately.

"That's not quite true though, is it?" Ken countered, looking at her with a smile. "You're family."

She stared at him. "I'm not sure that I would call you family." She then asked, "Why did you call this meeting?"

"I wanted to see you. It's been a long time."

"It has been a long time," she replied, realizing something else was definitely going on here. "I'm still not sure what the purpose of this meeting is for after all this time."

"You know that you were wrong way back when," he began, "and I wanted to see if I could get you to recant."

"My statement?" she asked in astonishment. "And you waited until I was thirty for that?"

"I didn't realize it was a possibility," he said, with a shrug. "I've only just had a chance to talk to lawyers, and they explained that you could clear my record."

"No, I couldn't," she declared, staring at him. "That was my statement, given a very long time ago."

"Yes, but I'm sure now that you've grown up, you realize that was not the way it all happened."

She stared at him, shaking her head.

The waitress arrived just then, but Kate wasn't sure she would stay long enough to eat something. Simon ordered coffee for both of them, and Ken didn't order anything. He was too busy talking up a storm about what he wanted. It never even occurred to her that he would request this, and it was repugnant to even think that he thought it was doable.

"It's just your word against mine," he added, "and I've already done the time. However, if I could clear my record, then I could, in theory, start to get my life back together again. I don't hold it against you, all those years ago. … Obviously you were very affected by everything else going on."

"Everything else going on?" she repeated and then smiled ferally. "Like what, Ken?"

"Your mother for one."

"Have you seen her since you've gotten out?"

"No," he snapped. "It's on my list."

"Of course it is." Kate snorted. "Yet you've talked to her on the phone, haven't you?"

"Sure, I did. I asked her for a place to stay, and she told me no." He gave an ugly laugh. "She'll change her tone though."

She stared at him. "She just got out of the hospital."

He looked at her and frowned. "Oh, that would explain it then. What was she in for?"

"It would be up to her to tell you that," Kate replied.

"At least you're still speaking."

"I don't know that I would say we are. She basically told me to disappear and to have nothing to do with her again," Kate murmured, "and that was today."

He laughed. "Yeah, she's such a bitch, isn't she?"

Kate caught a note of anger, and she wasn't sure what else, but almost a touch of hostility in Ken's tone. She hadn't really expected this level of emotion from him, and yet why not? He was now free. He'd served his time. Only the parole restrictions in place would make his life difficult in terms of rebuilding his life.

He repeated, "I need you to retract that statement."

"So you could have grounds to go after the State for a mistrial?"

"Exactly," he confirmed, "and that will give me enough money to get myself set back up again. It's not as if I have a career or a job or anything I can do at this point in time. That was all killed when you put me behind bars."

She stared at him, sensing that same anger. "*I* put you behind bars?" she asked, striving for a mild tone and failing. Instead it came across as accusatory.

"Yes, you did. And you didn't mean to. I know that. I blame your mother. Selene has always been ... weak and easily swayed."

And that would explain why her mother was now so scared. Kate shook her head. "I told the truth back then."

"No, you didn't," he countered. "You may have told the truth that you thought you saw as the truth, but it wasn't."

Staring at him, she replied, "That's a little confusing."

"That's because you were a child. You didn't understand what you were seeing."

"Aah. You mean that I didn't understand the male anatomy in the bed beside me."

She felt Simon stiffen at that, but her stepfather immediately replied, "Exactly. You were just a child. It's not as if you could possibly know any of that."

She stared at him. "So, you came out of prison, and your first stop is to come here asking me to change my statement?"

"Yes," he confirmed. She shook her head. "There's no reason for you not to," he added. "I suffered enough."

"*You* suffered enough?" she murmured. "While you're worried about how much you've suffered, I'm still wondering if you had anything to do with my brother's disappearance."

He stared at her in shock. "What? Good God no. ... Why would I? Christ, your brother disappearing, that was just messed up, and there's been absolutely nothing in the papers about it since."

"Meaning, you're keeping track?"

"Meaning that, being stuck in prison, there isn't a whole lot to do but keep track," he explained, with a wave of his hand. "That's hardly a criminal offense."

"Some people ... keep track of things because it's a curiosity."

"Exactly. Now—" Ken leaned forward, his gaze hardening. "Will you change your statement so I get my life back or not?"

She looked directly at him and, in a flat tone of voice, she declared, "I will not."

Nobody in that room could have missed the absolute fury that flashed through Ken's gaze. Though he didn't say it out loud, Kate could all but hear his voice whispering deep inside about how much she would regret that.

Her stepfather got up and walked to the entrance of the restaurant. Then he turned, looked back, gave her half a smile. "What was the one thing I used to always tell you back then?"

She frowned at him.

"It was a single word," he said, giving her the smile. He pointed a finger at her. "I don't think you could forget it. It was the one thing I said whenever you asked me a question or if you did something stupid. I always had that one comment for you."

Then it hit her.

He smiled the nasty evil smile that she remembered.

"Exactly," he said, then he turned and walked away.

She looked back at Simon, her mind racing, her heart sinking.

"What is he talking about?" Simon asked, leaning closer to Kate.

"*Think*. … That's what he always said to me," she whispered. "It never made any sense until now. But no matter what I was trying to do, or had already done, he would tell me how I was being stupid, that I should think for myself. To use my brain. To not rely on anyone else. So that very quickly became a simple refrain, … *think*."

# CHAPTER 17

KATE WALKED INTO the office the next morning, rubbing the sleep out of her eyes.

Lilliana frowned at her and asked, "Bad night?"

"Yeah, you're not kidding," she muttered.

Rodney walked in just behind her, took one look, and muttered, "Ouch."

She shrugged. "I'll need to bring you guys up-to-date. I'm not sure that it's helpful at all, but, considering the word that was used in that puzzle box message, it could be."

They immediately walked closer, and she explained about her stepfather wanting to meet her.

"Right, you told us about that meeting. How did it go?"

"Yes, and Simon did join us. He was pretty-well ignored, but that's very typical of my stepfather. Ken doesn't like anybody who's capable. He doesn't like anybody who's not likely to succumb to his charm and to his twisted belief system. Anyway, Ken asked me to recant my statement, which is what put him away. He wants his record cleared, so he can prove he was unjustly convicted. Then he figures he can get big money out of the State, and that will set him up nicely."

"Good God," Lilliana replied. "That takes a lot of nerve and a pretty big, … I don't know, ego or something, to think he could pull that off."

Kate looked over at her with a wry smile. "Yes, and one thing he said as he walked away was to remind me of something that he always told me to do back then. Of course I've blocked memories of him so much that I hadn't even thought about it until he brought it up last night. He waited for me to figure it out for myself. Then he laughed and walked off because the one thing, no matter what I asked for, be it help with homework, what was for dinner, or basically anything, it would be the same thing. He would give me a smirk and say this one thing. *Think.*"

"So, I assume a point is in here," Rodney asked.

The two of them just stared at her, and Kate nodded. "Now remember the wording in the note that came in the puzzle box."

Lilliana recited the pertinent line. "*You just have to think.*" She immediately whistled. "So, when did he get out of prison?"

"You mentioned it was just a couple days ago, didn't you?" she asked, turning to Rodney.

"I thought it was a couple days," he conceded, "but I'll make a call to the prison to see for sure."

"He could have gotten a message out earlier," Lilliana suggested. "Just because he might not have walked out the prison doors doesn't mean he didn't get somebody to send you that puzzle box and the note earlier."

"Somebody paid to have it delivered," Kate pointed out, "and that person didn't fit Ken's description."

"That's right," Lilliana murmured, "but then again it was a pretty generic description."

"But, if Ken was in prison, he didn't deliver it or pay to get it delivered."

"Those guys have their ways," Lilliana added, "but now

we have a motive."

"Yes, we have a motive, but it doesn't necessarily mean anything, except that I think Ken's involved in some way."

They pondered that. "He's got to have something if he considers that you'll bend over backward to do this for him."

She nodded. "Maybe so in his twisted mind. I don't know what that is. I didn't sleep a wink last night just thinking about it."

When Colby filed in a few minutes later, Lilliana called him over to discuss this latest development.

Colby asked, "And we're sure it has nothing to do with these other kids, right?"

"Sure? No," Kate replied. "I found out that my mother had the same drugs in her system that the murdered kids had. However, she's so scared that she'll just tell us that she took them voluntarily."

"Of course she will," Colby muttered. "What about your stepfather?"

Kate turned to frown at Rodney.

Rodney nodded. "I'm not sure that he knows a whole lot about the drug trade, but I doubt that anybody coming out of prison is really ignorant of any and all things drugs," Rodney offered. "If we find out that he was out earlier than the stated date, that opens up more possibilities."

"And who else does he have in his life?" Colby asked.

"I have no idea," Kate said, with a shrug. "I avoided him as much as I could, and obviously, once life became even more difficult, I *really* stayed out of his way. It's the one thing my mother never blamed me for."

"Meaning?"

Kate hesitated. "I'm not sure what I mean. I guess it's just, when he was put away, she didn't come home and blame me for having taken away her man."

"That's a good thing, isn't it?" Colby asked.

"Sure," she conceded, "but, when you consider that she blames me for my brother, it doesn't make any sense."

Rodney blurted out that the whole lot of them needed to be shot.

She snorted. "If it would bring my brother back, I would be happy to do it."

He nodded sadly at her. "I'm sorry," he hesitated. "Did Simon do anything with that information on Peter?"

"I don't know yet."

"So," Colby began, "I hate to say it, but, considering all these cases may intersect on the drug angle alone, I think you need to go see our resident shrink and see if you can do anything to bring up whatever connotations these subjects mean for you." When she stared at him in dismay, he nodded. "I know, but you also know yourself that, if this were a completely different case, you would be looking for any possible way to get that information out of your subject."

She winced and sagged against her chair. "*Great,*" she muttered. "It's bad enough that this is my life being torn apart in front of all of you, but now you want to get into my head and dredge up my childhood memories? Wasn't living through it bad enough?"

"Yeah, I think it's way worse than bad enough," Colby noted, "and that's why this has been brought up and around again. So either somebody thinks he can get you to do what he wants you to do by invoking all of what went wrong with your brother, stirring up any residual feelings of guilt, reminding you that you're the one who put him away, or else something else is going on. Regardless it's well overdue for you to talk to Dr. Dudley."

She stared at him, trying to come up with any excuse that would get her out of it.

Even Rodney winced, then looked at her and admitted, "He's right, you know? If it was me, you would be telling me to go do exactly that."

Lilliana nodded. "None of us wants to talk to the shrink when it comes to this very personal kind of stuff, but you seem to be linked in *all* this mess—the current cases, the little boy Peter, and definitely with your brother Timmy and your mother's supposed drug OD. What we don't know is how in the hell all this is connected to the others—or if it connects to yet again something else."

"Ken's probably just yanking my chain."

Colby shook his head. "Which is another reason we need you to talk to Dr. Dudley, to ensure something in there can break free with the doc, not out on a case or driving or whatever, and have you go off the wall on us."

She snorted at that. "If I didn't go off the wall when my brother went missing, when I was blamed for it, I won't go off the wall now."

"You know what I mean," Colby stated.

She didn't know what to say. This wasn't what she expected, and she felt a bit blindsided by her own team. Yet she should have seen it coming. It was almost a standard department policy. She didn't like it happening, and she sure as hell didn't like it happening with everybody here watching.

Colby looked over at her, glanced down at his phone, and said, "Best you do it now." He looked around the room, watching everyone. "I'll let the doc know you're on the way." And, with that, Colby headed into his office.

Kate didn't know what to do, and she stared from one to the other, her shoulders sinking as she realized she would have to dredge up all that crap. All of it. That would be something she didn't want to do in any way, shape, or form.

Rodney sat down beside her, closer than he normally would. "Look. I know this isn't what you want. I know that you would do a lot to avoid facing this, but we must consider the fact that something could be rolling around in your brain that you don't remember. A child's brain, a child's memories, but now you're an adult. So maybe something is in there that we can use for your brother."

She stared at him. "I've spent a lifetime going over everything," she murmured.

"Yes, but you were alone in doing that," Lilliana pointed out, coming up beside her. "However, you aren't alone anymore. It took us a while to get here, but we're here now," she declared. "We understand that you've got concerns over these kids, and believe me that we do too. Now there's a problem with a designer drug that's affecting people, and potentially that designer drug also had something to do with what happened to your mother."

"And now my stepfather shows up," Kate noted, shaking her head. "How the hell did I end up in the middle of all this crap?"

"Not because you're trying to," Lilliana pointed out.

Rodney nodded. "And we get that. Honest we do. We don't want to be in your face and in your life any more than we have to. Honest to God, it's sad enough as it is. Go talk to the doc and get it done."

"Just take the afternoon off," Lilliana added. "And don't even try to tell us that it won't affect you." Now she glared at Kate.

Kate glared back at both of them, and Rodney nodded. "I know how awful it'll be for you. It'll be like tearing off your skin, one strip at a time," he described, "but you still need to go through it, so go."

He spoke in such a way that she automatically stood, hating it, but knowing she had to. With a heavy heart and panic blowing up inside, she headed to the shrink's office. The most she could hope for was that he would be out of town, busy, or something, but unfortunately, as she approached, the door opened in front of her.

Dr. Dudley stood there with a smile and greeted her. "Hi, I heard I should expect you." When he noticed her frowning, he sighed and added, "One of these days you'll learn to trust me."

Kate's eyebrows shot up at that.

"It's okay if that's not today, but maybe just try and understand that I'm here to help, and, today of all days, it sounds as if you need it. Now come on in." With that, he ushered her inside and closed the door behind her. He motioned to a chair and said, "I just got off the phone with your boss."

"Colby wanted me to come down," she stated, keeping her tone calm enough that maybe she was in control, though that was a lie she wouldn't tell him.

"He filled me in on a little that's been going on."

"That's because a little is all we know," she replied.

"Agreed, and it seems as if maybe you have more in your head than you possibly even realize."

"I don't know about that." She stared at him.

"Have you ever done hypnosis to try to trigger some memories?"

"Why would anybody want to do that?" she asked.

He studied her and nodded. "I gather those memories are pretty rough."

"Yeah, they're definitely pretty rough," she stated. "Not everybody had two nice parents, with the picket fence home," she said, trying to keep the caustic tone out of her voice and failing.

He nodded. "I know it always seems as if everybody had that, but it's amazing just how many dysfunctional families are out there. Turns out, it's the norm, more than the other way around." She shrugged in response. "So, do you want to tell me what's going on?"

"You already talked to Colby," she replied, "so there's nothing for me to say."

His lips twitched at that. "Maybe you could just tell me in your own words." She just stared at him, not speaking. He took a long breath and exhaled. "Okay, so let's go over the facts. We know your brother is missing, and we know that your stepfather, the man you helped put away, is now out of prison. Can you tell me how you felt when you saw him?"

"Numb, … as if he really didn't belong in my world anymore."

"Oh, that's good. That means you've moved past it."

"Of course I've moved past it," she snapped bitterly. "I'm not that child anymore."

He nodded. "Right, but it's amazing how many of our inner children"—he shook his head—"don't really get to move out of our immediate world. We keep them close."

"We keep them close so we can keep them safe," she pointed out, "and, when they're safe, we can let them go."

"And where do they go?" he asked.

"Presumably deep into your psyche, where you don't need them anymore."

"I like that too because, of course, they're always a part of us."

"All of our history is a part of us," she pointed out. "It's not as if we can walk away from what happened, but that doesn't mean it's part of my present."

"So, what do you do with all that nightmare that happened?"

She stared at him. "In my brother's case, I'm still working on it. I want justice for Timmy. In my case, I pounded it deep into a dark hole that never has to see the light of day again." He winced at that. "It worked," she snapped.

"It works until something triggers it and rips it wide open."

"Then you slap it back down again," she declared, with a shrug. "It's not as if I can let it go. It's not as if you can ever forget. I just don't want to constantly be reminded of it."

"That's quite true, but dealing with it and finding a way to make peace with it—"

"Making peace with it?" she repeated, looking at him in astonishment. "I've made peace with it in terms of being an adult, and that's the world I live in right now. It's not something I ever want to come back up again. How do you make peace with something like that?"

"And yet look at the work you do."

"Of course," she agreed. "How else would I find out about my brother's case?"

He sat back, looked at her for a moment, then down at the papers in front of him. "I guess that makes a lot of sense as to why you joined the force, doesn't it?"

"It's why I was determined to join the force," she shared, "but it's definitely not why I've stayed."

"That's a very fine distinction too," he noted.

"Of course, doing the work I do helps others," she explained, "and I get to put away assholes, like the one who hurt my brother."

"You're assuming he's dead?"

She pondered that. "A part of me says it's foolish to keep hoping, but, until there's a body, there's always hope." He wrote something down on the pad of paper in front of him, and she frowned. "You'll just sit here and write everything down?"

"For the record, that's the first thing I've written down," he noted calmly.

"Sure, but there's bound to be more."

He flashed a smile at her. "Maybe. That's how I process information. You seem remarkably well adjusted."

"So now you're looking to see whether that's a facade?"

He laughed. "What would you like me to do?"

"Pour me a cup of coffee, sit here for ten minutes, and talk to me about nothing important. Then tell Colby that I'm fine."

He blinked at that, looked over to where the coffeepot sat, and nodded. "You're more than welcome to have a cup of coffee." He got up, poured her a cup, and took it to her. "Don't you have coffee in the bullpen?"

"Sure, but I figured yours might be better."

At that, he grinned at her. "You're right. I'm a little bit fussy about my coffee."

She nodded. "I've known people like that."

"I understand that you have an interesting partner as well."

She stiffened and glared at him.

He nodded. "Ah, you want that to be an off-topic conversation as well?"

"It's not relevant."

"You don't think whether you have a balanced home life is relevant to your mental health?"

"Doesn't matter whether it's balanced or not. When the job calls, I'm there," she stated, "and then everything is off balance."

He pondered that for a few moments and then nodded. "That's very true, but it also helps if you know that you have someplace to go when things get—how shall I say it? … *Difficult.*"

"It's the job," she stated.

"It is the job, but it sounds to me that because you have that relationship, it's helping you do your job better." She glared at him, and his eyebrows shot up. "And that upsets you."

"I can do the job without him."

A small smile played at the corner of his lips. "I'm not saying you need him to do your job. I'm saying that having him in your life is making it *easier* for you to do your job."

"I don't know about that," she argued, frowning at him, not sure she liked where he was going with this. "The jury is still out on that."

"Good enough," he conceded, with a laugh. "Meaning, you haven't been in the relationship long enough."

"Something like that," she muttered. "I'm still trying to figure it all out."

"But you are figuring it out," he noted, "and that's a good thing."

She wasn't sure what to say to that either. It just seemed that mine fields of information were opening up in front of her, and she may or may not have the right answer. It was like school all over again.

"What don't you like about being here?"

"I don't like baring my soul. I don't like having you picking apart my answers. And I don't like the feeling of being tested and giving the wrong answers and, therefore, failing."

He stopped, his jaw dropping ever-so-slightly, before he snapped it closed again. "That was very succinct."

"Sure it is, Doc. Everything I say to you, you're analyzing. Whether I'm fit for duty, whether I need assistance in some way, shape, or form," she explained, with a wave of her hand. "Nobody wants to be put through all that."

"I can agree with that," he admitted, "but I'm not here for anybody else's purpose or benefit but yours."

"Yes, you are. You got me in here because Colby asked you to. You'll report to Colby, whether I like it or not," she argued. "So this isn't for me. This is for you and for him."

He winced. "Let me rephrase that. I'm here to help you, if you have any issues that require assistance."

"I don't," she declared.

He groaned. "Whether you think you do or not, there is also a departmental requirement to go through these sessions on an annual basis," he shared, with a smile. "We could just look at this as being your annual visit."

"We could," she muttered, "but you also know that Colby will be on the phone almost immediately, asking you for an evaluation."

"And I will give it to him," he shared, with a smirk. "You're prickly, a bit sharp. You're guarded because of previous hurts. You don't want to let anybody in because, as far as you're concerned, that's a waste of your time."

She shrugged.

"Am I right?" When she didn't respond, he continued.

"It's not so much that you deny you have things to deal with but you don't want to take the time to deal with them. You want to get back out on the streets and deal with those people instead."

"Sure, because I understand those people."

And, with that, a beautiful smile broke across his face. "Exactly, and I'm here to help you understand the ones that you're keeping buried, so they're not buried anymore, and so you can function without all those burdens. So you can finally be free."

"But you can't remove the burdens," she stated, shrugging again. "So you can't free me of anything. What's the point of dragging them all out and looking at them, when you can't do anything about it?"

"And how do you know I can't?"

She stared at him. "Because I don't think anybody can. These *burdens*, as you call them, are a part of my history, and you can't take them away or make me feel better about them just because they are over."

"Maybe not, but we can work on removing the aspect of guilt from them." At that, she narrowed her eyes and glared at him. "And that triggers you in an awful way."

"I spent a lifetime feeling guilty," she stated, "and these days I work damn hard not to."

"And I agree with that," Dr. Dudley replied, raising his hands in his defense, "because you're not guilty. Not in any way. You were a child, and, if your mother chose to blame you, that's on her. It was a situation you had no control over," he pointed out. "So, the question now is, have you dealt with that and moved on, or does something keep coming around to bite you in the ass?"

She snorted at that. "Of course it'll keep biting me in the

ass," she muttered. "Shit like that always does. However, it's how long I let it affect me that becomes the question."

"Could you explain that?"

"It just means that, when life happens, either you let it keep you down or you pick yourself back up and you move on," she explained. "I won't sit here and wallow about a childhood, or a mother who loved her bottle and her drugs more than she loved her kids. I don't know what it's like to experience what she went through, and I have absolutely no intention of experiencing the life she did. Thus, I can't judge her for it. I already judge her enough for what she did to me, so I don't want to judge her for anything she may have done to someone else."

"Did she have other relationships?"

She shrugged. "Some, but not many after my brother disappeared. Or, if she did, I wasn't part of it."

"You went to foster care, did you not?"

"She gave me to social services," she clarified.

He stared at her. "That must have hurt."

"Yes, but I think it was probably easier on both of us. You really can't blame her for that. I think it was probably a saving grace for me," she admitted. "I don't know much about the foster people I went to. I just developed a hard shell and moved through life."

"And your stepfather?"

"I had to go through the courts with him too," she said, with a nod.

"And what about your mother? How did she handle that?"

"I was in social services at that point in time, so I wasn't around her that much. As far as I know, she never really blamed me for sending him to prison, but what do I know?"

she muttered, with a shrug. "There weren't always men around her," Kate noted, looking back to that era. "Sometimes, but not always. As an adult looking back, I always wondered about that. She didn't seem to be the kind to need a man, and yet there seemed to always be enough drama and chaos to destroy my world. And, of course, who knows about my brother. It should be one of the questions the detectives need to talk to her about." With that, she pulled out her phone and texted Rodney and Lilliana.

When she was done, the psychiatrist looked at her and asked, "Could you put away your phone, please?" She nodded and put it away, then he immediately went on. "Is everything work for you?"

She frowned at him. "Shouldn't it be?"

His eyebrows shot up. "No, other things should be going on in your life, thoughts of the future, hobbies, things that you do outside of work."

She stared at him. "Simon bought a boat, and we've gone out on that a few times."

"And when you say, *he bought a boat* ..."

"He bought a damn boat," she repeated, with a shrug. "It has its own name, *Running Mate*. I don't know anything about it. It's just ... a boat, so I don't know what else to say."

His lips twitched. "And do you like going out there?"

"I love it," she said immediately. "I love being on the water. I love the sense of peace and serenity out there. Getting more and more time out there will definitely be something we work on."

"What do you do for hobbies?" She frowned at him again. "I gather you don't really have any."

"I have some," she replied, choosing her words carefully. She knew perfectly well that the department liked you to have hobbies, and they liked you to do things outside of work.

"So, today when you go home, what will you do?"

"I'll stop off and do a bout or two of jujitsu," she said. "Fitness is important to me, and it's a good way to blow off steam."

"And do you do that often?"

"A couple times a week, depending." She shrugged. "Sometimes I just go home and collapse."

"Because of work?"

"Because of work, life, stress, whatever," she said. "It's not as if we have enough staff to handle all the cases we have, and it's not as if we get enough information to close even half of what we have on our dockets. That's frustrating, and, when you get frustrated, it's best to find a way to deal with it."

"Agreed," he murmured. They talked a little bit more, and then he came back around again. "How do you feel about your mother?"

"She's a bitch." She said it without rancor, and he just stared at her. She shrugged. "What do you want me to say? She lost her son, her only son, and blamed her seven-year-old daughter for it."

"Why did she do that?"

"Because it allowed her to avoid blaming herself," Kate declared, staring at him. "I'm sure you can figure that part out."

His lips twitched. "Yes, I just wondered if you did."

"Of course I did," she stated, with a wave of her hand. "Yet it doesn't change anything. She still made life miserable for me in order to make it less miserable for herself."

He smiled at that. "Have you had any contact with her?"

"Minimal, and she was remanded to some mental health or drug and alcohol rehab for quite a while. I'm not exactly sure on that, since, up until now, we've been out of contact. Apparently she got herself together enough to be released to a halfway house program and then to independent living. Then I had to see her as part of work here, a few days ago. Then again at the hospital after she had an overdose, or something completely different as part of our open case," she explained, never breaking eye contact with him. "The first time, she punched me in the face, and the second she told me to not darken her doors again. If it was connected to the law, to send my colleagues instead."

When he looked at her in surprise, she shrugged. "I mean, if you're expecting a nice warm reunion, that opportunity passed a long time ago."

"What if she no longer blames you? Would that have changed how you feel about her?"

"No," she snapped. "That time has come and gone."

"And you don't see that ever changing?"

She glared at him. "No, that will never change."

---

SITTING AT THE coffee shop, going over scads and scads of papers, Simon decided to sit outside. While the weather wasn't likely to be good for long, being outside was great for a few minutes' break from the rain and the blustery December weather. He also realized how quickly Christmas was encroaching his time table and how that would impact his supply deliveries for each of his rehab projects. He frowned as he turned his attention to that. He needed to schedule time off for everybody and then assess how long he wanted to close down the sites. He knew everybody would want

Christmas to New Year's off, but that wasn't something he was particularly fond of.

He hadn't celebrated Christmas in a very long time and imagined that Kate hadn't either. Yet maybe it was time to do that. Maybe it was time to go out and support that time of year. Somehow it felt wrong to do it. However, it felt wrong *not* to. Frowning, he realized it was way too cold to be sitting outside, so he quickly packed up his paperwork, put it back in his briefcase, stood up, and walked away, his coffee in hand.

He headed to the women's shelter, knowing that Christmas would be even tougher for them. There would be kids in there, still hopeful of some kind of a Christmas. As he got there, Lisa stood outside, speaking with somebody.

She spied him and gave him a little nod. When the person she was speaking to left, Lisa walked over to him. "Hey."

"Hey, yourself. Problems?"

"There are always problems," she noted, with a smile. "I'm trying to get the furnace back up and running. I've got some grant funding for it, but the price has really gone up since I applied for the grant, you know?"

He nodded. "What are they looking at?"

"I don't really know. He gave me a quote but it wasn't a great scenario, as it needs to be replaced."

"You need a new one? Most of the time they just need servicing," he noted. "Generally they tend to go forever."

"And you're right. Generally they do. But, in this case, *forever* has called."

"Aah, so it's at least twenty-five-years old."

"Twenty-three, I think."

"Yeah, so you might limp along for another year or two, but you'll need to replace it. A new one will be a whole lot more efficient and cheaper to run though."

"Cheaper to run would be nice," she muttered. "I'm still fighting to get back to the same funding that I had before, and that wasn't even enough."

"Right, I understand that. Let me know how it goes with the furnace. I might be able to help."

She looked over at him and nodded gratefully. "Your help and continued support are very much appreciated."

"It's about the women in there."

"And the kids," she added, tearing up.

"Did you get any extra funding for Christmas?"

She shook her head. "No, and nobody in the grant world thinks there should be a Christmas for displaced kids," she muttered in a half-mocking tone. "Not the kids and mothers who are here anyway."

"What about the food bank?"

"I've registered with a couple to help," she shared, "and some charities. I'm hopeful something will come through."

"You should have heard by now if they would."

She frowned and wrapped her arms around her chest. "I know, … but, once the news got out, we lost a lot of support."

"Even though it wasn't your fault?"

"Yes, but you know how it is when there is even a hint of scandal. It wasn't my fault, and these women who come for us to help certainly don't deserve to be blamed," Lisa explained. "It's been tough on them too."

"Damn," he muttered. He pulled out his wallet and handed over what he had in it. "I know it's never enough. I'll see what I can do about helping for Christmas. Do you have anybody who could do some shopping?"

She looked over at him. "No, not really. There's just me

now."

"Right," he said, feeling frustrated. "Let me think about it." And, with that, he turned and headed off. It was one thing to not celebrate Christmas, but it was another thing to have these kids not celebrate Christmas. That would upset him even more.

As he walked through the alley, it finally hit him that Christmas was right around the corner, even though the annual build-up had been going on for weeks. That meant a whole pile of BS issues that he didn't want to deal with. As a rehab business they didn't deal with Christmas very well. Everything around them shut down. Supplies wouldn't come in on time, and schedules were just a mess.

It hadn't been very Christmassy in his world so far, and, for that, he was quite grateful, but it would hit others pretty hard. He also needed to think about what he wanted to do with Kate, if anything. He was pretty sure she would probably just look at him and say something like, *I'm working.*

He wasn't sure she even knew what Christmas was, and that just made him feel even worse. Neither one of them really had a life or a childhood where Christmas really mattered or where they could even expect to see anything special at Christmastime.

He thought about that, wondering just how much of a Christmas she'd ever even experienced. Maybe when her brother was still alive, but then, as he thought about her stepfather, he wasn't sure that Christmas was even a safe topic to bring up with her.

As he walked through the back alleys, heading to the street on the other side, his phone rang. He pulled it out and saw it was Rodney. "Problems?" he asked, his tone sharp.

Rodney took a breath. "Look. Kate will kill me if she knows I've called you," he began, "but I just wanted to give you a heads-up that she was forced to talk to the psychologist today."

"Ah, crap," he muttered.

"She didn't go willingly. Colby demanded she go, what with her stepfather in town and maybe behind this puzzle-box note. Plus, she could have repressed or otherwise hidden memories inside her own psyche that are relevant to Timmy's case."

"Of course Colby did, and, if Kate was thinking logically, that's precisely what she would want anyone in a similar situation to do," Simon added.

"Exactly, and that was probably the argument that made her sit up, take notice, and follow through," Rodney shared. "The issue now is that she hasn't come back, and I don't know how long the appointment would last," Rodney shared. "There's a good chance that she is heading home, heading to you, or going to ground."

"Right, and is she expected back at the end of the day?"

"No, at least I don't think so."

"And you guys are taking over these cases that are driving her nuts?"

"Yes, we're working on it, although it's all kind of intertwined. You don't know anybody who is doing designer drugs or anything, do you?"

"No, not in my personal world, no," Simon said, "but I've been fairly diligent at keeping completely separated from people who go that route. It's just not my scene. Unfortunately, I have come across the impacts of drug and alcohol use at various times, just because of employees showing up for work, thinking that it's totally safe to do that. Or not showing up at all, for that matter."

"Right," Rodney muttered. "Of course, you get to be the one who reminds them that a paycheck comes with job safety, or then they don't get a paycheck."

Simon laughed. "Something like that, yes."

"If you do hear of anything out there," he added, "we're looking at Kate's mother as using or given the overdose of the exact same designer drug that we have two kids dead from."

Simon contemplated that in silence. "Wow. Okay, that's not cool."

"No, it's not, but we're not exactly sure how any of these cases are related, or if they even are."

"The fact that you've got the same drug, the same variation of a relatively new drug in all three means that they do relate, at least in some way."

"That's Kate's theory."

Simon stared down at his phone. "If that's Kate's theory, that's the one I'm going with."

He rang off from his conversation with Rodney and stood here for a long moment, wondering what would be the best avenue for supporting Kate. Then he realized that just taking her away and giving her a few hours to assimilate and to digest everything that had gone on might be the best course of action. He quickly phoned her, but when there was no answer, he frowned and called again. Still nothing.

He walked back home and called for a hot meal to be delivered. If nothing else, he could potentially get her out on the boat, where they could just spend a few hours floating. Hopefully she could just forget about everything and relax. It's not something she did very often, but, if he could make it happen, it would be huge for her. As soon as he got home, he smiled at his doorman, who looked at him with a questioning gaze. "I'm fine, honest. If you see Kate, send her right up, will you?"

Harry nodded. "Is there a problem?"

"I suspect that she's had a very rough day," he replied.

"Got it," Harry murmured. "Let's hope she gets here soon then."

As soon as Simon got upstairs, he packed up warm blankets and a bunch of stuff they had planned on taking the next time they went out on the boat. He'd had it serviced and had the heater fixed too. That thought reminded him about the furnace over at the women's shelter.

Frowning, he knew something about furnaces, and he'd certainly dealt with them on his rehab projects, but that didn't mean he had all the details on them. He did have somebody he could ask to check out the heater at the women's shelter. He quickly made that call, and while he was learning about furnaces for houses, he packed up more stuff that he thought they might need. Even just getting out there for a while would help him, and he hoped it would help Kate as well.

As he moved the bag to the front door, the elevator opened, and Kate stood there.

She looked at him, bewildered. "I didn't mean to come here," she said, staring at him.

He walked over, enveloped her in his arms, and just held her. He knew she would never cry, at least not unless he could get her to break down and to let some of this go, but maybe just being held would help.

# CHAPTER 18

K ATE BURROWED DEEP into his arms and muttered, "It was a really ugly day."

"I know. Rodney called me."

She stiffened at that, then sagged and nodded. "I'm hungry," she announced, as she pulled away, looking around. "Do you have anything to eat?"

"If I don't, you know perfectly well that I'll get something," he stated, with a smile. "Actually I ordered something, and I was hoping maybe we could go to the boat with it."

She looked at him in surprise and then delight. "Can we?" she asked. "Even just a few hours would be great."

"Exactly what I was thinking." He smiled as he handed her several bags. "We'll take this stuff down and leave it on board."

"Right—wintertime. I forgot about that," she said.

"What about you? Do you want warmer clothes?"

"I don't know about warmer clothes," she murmured, as she stared down at her outfit, "but I definitely want to get changed. Give me a minute." Then she disappeared from view.

In the meantime, dinner arrived. He didn't even unpack it, since he had pretty well everything he needed to eat onboard, but no way they would eat outside, not given the weather right now. He just wanted to ensure they were cozy inside the boat. As he finished packing up, she stepped out in a heavy sweater. "I don't think I've ever seen you in that before."

She looked at him vaguely and shrugged. "Yeah, I'm not even sure where it came from."

He hid a smile because he'd bought it for her but hadn't mentioned it. He'd just added it to one of her drawers, and he was happy she chose to wear it.

She looked great in it too. It accented her long lean build and her short-cropped hair, which was literally a headshake away from being perfect, which was all she ever did with it. That completely amazed him because he'd only ever known women who spent hours on their appearance. Yet Kate just looked out at the world from a completely different lens, and still made it hers in a way he'd never seen before.

As he packed up the last of the items, he asked, "Are you ready?"

She nodded. "Sure, what do you want me to grab?"

"Anything and everything," he replied cheerfully. "It's all got to go." And, with that, he handed her the dinner.

She immediately sniffed and groaned. "Oh my God."

"The boat first," he declared, with a word of warning in her direction.

She nodded. "Absolutely, but we've got to go *now*. I didn't realize that you had *food*, food."

He chuckled. "When do I never have food?"

"Before I came, I don't know that you ever had food either," she declared. "However, now it's as if we can't get enough of the damn stuff."

"That's because you're always running on empty, and I just seem to be perpetually slammed at work now."

"Yeah, in many ways we're a bad pair."

"No," he argued, yet smiled. "Since we've come together, we both eat a lot better, and, even if it is takeout, at least we get *good* takeout," he noted. "Plus, we're both getting more rest, and we have each other."

She looked over at him and then nodded. "I had to see the shrink today. He wanted to talk about you, and I wouldn't let him," she said immediately.

He studied her. "It's probably better if you *do* talk about me."

"Maybe," she admitted. "I just wanted to keep that separate. I don't want people to tear it apart and to analyze whether it was good or bad or indifferent. I just want it to be ... *ours*." She shrugged, then turned and walked out the front door, leaving him smiling in her wake.

She said the darndest things, at the darndest times, he thought to himself, as he quickly made his way down behind her.

Once the elevator opened on the first floor, and Harry took one look, he chuckled and raced over to help. "You know, if I could leave my post, I would walk you down to the boat and carry some of this stuff, but I'm the only one on shift right now."

"You're fine," Kate replied, as she walked past him. "If we have to make two trips, we have to make two trips."

"Are you that close?" he asked.

She looked back at him and nodded. "He changed the mooring, and that gave us another option."

"Wow, that's nice," Harry said. Then he quickly raced to open the front door for them.

Within seconds, they were outside. Simon called back a thanks to Harry, then picked up the pace so he was even with Kate.

As he moved up beside her, she looked at him and asked, "Do I seem a little anxious?"

"You seem ready to get rid of everything in your world except this right now."

"I am," she admitted, "and I don't think I hate anything more than having to open up, particularly to somebody I don't trust or know."

Simon just nodded and let her talk.

"I mean, it's one thing if it's an official thing, and I have to do it," she shared, "which I do have to do. But it's completely different when he doesn't know my situation, although he wants to know. Still, I don't feel like I should have to tell him."

"But you made it through okay?"

"If that's what you want to call it," she muttered. "I don't think I'll be off the hook forever."

"I thought it was an annual thing."

She looked back at him and nodded. "I think part of it is. I've avoided all of it up until now." When he smiled at that, she glared. "You think I'm foolish for avoiding it?"

"I think you can try to avoid it, but I think there's a reason why it's in place, and it's to stop people from doing just that."

Her shoulders slumped slightly at that.

"But once you've been through it the first time, every other time should be easier."

"*Should*," she muttered. "I just don't understand why they have to dig into everything."

"In this case, I do understand."

She looked at him in surprise. "You're on their side?"

Such a gasp of betrayal in her tone surprised him. "Look.

There are no sides to this. It's literally about you making it through a really difficult period in your life, and, if something could help you do that, I'm all for it."

"But what if it doesn't help?" she asked, glaring at him.

He smiled. "It looks to me as if it already has."

She shook her head. "No, I don't think so."

He chuckled. "That's because you don't want to accept that even talking about this is a help."

"Is it really, though?" she muttered. "It just seems as if all we do is move things around and around and get no answers. … I have cases like that, and I hate it. I don't want to be a case."

It took him a bit to work his way through that preamble in his head. "You're linking this to a case?" he asked hesitantly.

She looked at him blankly for a minute. "I want a solution. I want closure, an end date," she explained. "I have cases where that doesn't exist. I don't want whatever this is in my head to be the same."

"Aah." He nodded, finally understanding what she was working toward. "I'm not sure we ever have end dates for the stuff in our heads. I think we have until-the-next-time dates."

She glared at him. "But those don't work, and just brings it all back around again."

"So, you get rid of what you can, while you can, and, the next time, if and when it comes back around again, it will be less."

"Will it, though?" she asked, stopping to face him. "Will it really be less?"

"Yes," he stated. "Deal with what you can deal with, and the next time it will be less."

She frowned, but the *Running Mate* was up ahead, and she lit up like a Christmas tree and almost ran toward it. He smiled, never expecting anyone to share his love of boating the way that she did.

They hadn't even had a chance to get out and sail very much, but just knowing that they had this place to go to, knowing that they had this escape, all seemed to have made a difference like none other. And, for that, he was absolutely delighted with his purchase.

As they walked up, and she hopped in, he immediately handed her the other bags, and she quickly took them and disappeared down below. He joined her a few minutes later and asked, "Do you want to sit down here to eat?"

"It's pretty cold up there," she noted, looking over at him. "Unless you want to try."

He shook his head. "No. I did have heaters installed in here though." And, with that, he went to the little fireplace, and, to his delight, it was already set up. He smiled when he turned it on, and she stepped up beside him, with a look of awe. "Can we have this on a boat?"

"Yes," he confirmed, wrapping an arm around her shoulders and tucking her up close. "Sometimes you just need to take the comforts where you can. And, when you can't, you just need to understand that it'll wait until next time."

She winced. "You're back to that *next time* thing already."

"Yep, I sure am. This isn't over right now, and it's likely to be a rough day or two, or even a week or two."

"A week or two?" she snapped, glaring at him. "God help me if it goes on any longer than today."

He chuckled. "And that may well be," he conceded, "but

the good news is that, at some point in the future, it will end, and you will still be the same person you were before. Yet hopefully better, with fewer bad memories."

THE NEXT DAY Simon was out walking, having just come from one rehab project and heading to the next, perusing his phone. That was something he tried to avoid, but sometimes he had to deal with just so many emails and things that it wasn't an option. He did stop, look around, reorient himself, then quickly crossed the road and headed up on the other side.

Just as he got across the road, a timid voice whispered, *Hello?*

He stopped, looked around, then frowned and called out himself, "Hello?" He heard almost a sigh. He froze, turned around, and called out again, "Hello?" When he heard another sigh, he froze. *Peter.* "Where are you?" Simon asked. When the boy remained silent, Simon added, "Please, you need to tell me where you are."

*I don't know.*

It was little Peter's voice. "Think," Simon told the boy, his tone filled with frustration. "I can't help if you don't help me, Peter. So think. Think about where you were. Think about what you were doing and who you were with."

Almost immediately, his voice shaking, the little boy wailed, *I can't. I can't. I can't,* and, with that, he disappeared.

Simon leaned against the nearby building, cursing himself for having pushed Peter too hard. Simon realized that he was doing something not so different than what Kate's asshole stepfather did to Kate, demanding that she *think.* Simon was asking this little boy to think, and yet Peter may have absolutely no access to usable information.

It was the same for Kate. Ken was telling her to think, but it required delving into thoughts and memories she wanted nothing to do with. Is that what was going on here with Peter? And, if so, how could Simon get this little guy to open up about it?

He stood here for the longest moment, frustrated at his inability to get the information that Kate needed, but it was always this way. How did one handle it? How did he not go crazy with the need to have information that apparently this little guy just couldn't give him?

Almost immediately Peter came back and whispered through his mind, *I'm trying.*

Simon's heart softened, and he murmured, "I'm sorry, Peter. I shouldn't be yelling at you."

Peter's tone seemed surprised, as he replied, *No, you shouldn't.*

That gave Simon a lot of insight into the life this boy had had when he was alive, presuming he was dead now, which was something Simon just didn't know how to handle. And yet there was still a chance that Peter was alive, if only the little boy could share some information. "Peter, please think. Try to remember."

*Maybe I don't want to remember*, Peter muttered, his tone softening.

Simon winced. "Maybe you don't," he agreed. "Maybe it's too painful. Maybe you know what happened, but you don't want to remember."

*Maybe. ... I think I was loved though.*

That brought another wince to Simon's face. "I'm sure you were," he stated.

*Then why am I in this position?*

Such sadness filled Peter's words that it almost brought tears to Simon's eyes. "I don't know. That's one of the reasons I'm trying to help you, so we can figure this out together."

*I'll think some more,* Peter whispered, and suddenly he was gone.

Peter had left a lot for Simon to think about too. Ken, the stepfather from the past who was tormenting Kate even now, was asking for her to think. Had she blocked out something that she literally couldn't bring to mind? Maybe it didn't make sense to her as a child at that time.

Simon wasn't even sure he could work out in his head exactly what he meant. So, walking to his next stop, he considered all that, while he thought about Peter. Then Simon added, "Think if you can, Peter, but maybe don't think so hard. Don't stress about it. Maybe that's a better way to get any memories."

Peter popped back into Simon's head again. The fact that he was popping in and out could reveal something to Simon as well. He just didn't understand what it meant. Did it mean that he was getting more adept at communicating? Did it mean that Peter was dead and was learning to better manage the world he was in? What did it mean?

Then Peter whispered, *I'm trying to think.*

"I know. Just maybe don't try so hard."

There was a short silence on the other end. *No,* Peter replied, *it's important. Something important is here.*

"Is that why you haven't left?"

Then in that same soft voice, he whispered, *Yes.*

"Are you alone over there?"

No, others like me are here.

And that was again likely more confirmation that Peter

was dead. "Can you see anything around you?" Simon asked the little boy.

Darkness sometimes, sunshine sometimes.

"Can you see? … Can you see where your body is?"

*Yes*, he replied ever-so-softly. *It's here with me.*

"And where is *here*?" Simon thought he heard almost a gasp from Peter.

*I'm close.*

Something was off in Peter's tone. "You're close? Close to what?"

*Close to home*, he said. *I want to go home.* And then he started to bawl, great big terrible gasping sobs.

Simon was forced to stop his questions. Instead he whispered to Peter, "Hey, take it easy. Just take it easy."

*I want to go home. I just want to go home.*

The litany didn't stop until Simon somehow forced Peter into silence, both a gift and a curse because now Simon felt as if he had deserted poor Peter too. That wasn't fair to that young boy who'd already been deserted by so many.

Simon sent Kate a text message, saying he'd heard from Peter again, asking if anybody had had a chance to look into it.

She immediately texted back. **Rodney is, and I'll check and see.**

With that, Simon put away those thoughts of Peter and carried on to work. Yet it bothered him throughout the day, especially Simon asking Peter to think, just as Ken had asked Kate to think.

What could Ken possibly want her to think of? Was she to think she had done something wrong as a way for Ken to blackmail her? She had been a child at that point and couldn't be held responsible for anything that had happened to her. It made no sense, and yet Simon knew he was missing something, and that made him frustrated.

When he finally got to his next jobsite, he saw Danny working off to the side. Danny lifted his head, half smiled, waved, and got back to work. Simon smiled at that. So far that situation was turning out okay. He looked over at Joe, the foreman, who was walking toward him. Simon nodded back at Danny.

"He's doing fine," Joe confirmed. "He's a good kid."

"I hear you. I'm just waiting for the *but* ..."

"No buts," he declared cheerfully. "At least not yet."

"Good. Let's hope he's through the worst of it then."

"I hope so. I hate to see anybody in that position. There's an awful lot of life out there worth living."

"Sure, but when you've been touched by some of the more difficult things in life that really suck, it makes it seem otherwise, and you start thinking everyone might be better off without you in the world."

"I don't know," his foreman argued, with a headshake. "Everyone needs somebody to love."

"And when you don't have anybody to love," Simon pointed out, "it feels really bad because you seem all alone in the big world out there—meaning that maybe you're unlovable. So, if that's true, the world is probably better off without your taking up space anymore." His foreman stared at him, aghast. Simon just shrugged. "That's the downhill struggle you can get into from being a victim to this bad stuff," he explained. "It can be really ugly."

"That's beyond ugly," Joe said, "I've never heard the likes of that."

"No, but lots of people have," Simon stated. "So, when we find somebody we can help, we do our best."

"Oh, you're not kidding there." Joe smiled. "My wife is beyond upset to think that Danny came that close. And to think the doctor was charged for all those murders in that crazy center of his?"

"He won't be convicted of anything because he wound up drowning," Simon noted, "but I hear you. It's all pretty unpleasant and ugly to even consider something like that happening."

He nodded. "I just don't understand why the doctor kept his brother in limbo like that. That kind of hate has got to rot away your insides."

"Which some will say is exactly what happened," Simon pointed out. "I don't think anybody was thinking the doc was sane at the end."

"No, of course not," Joe muttered, with a headshake.

"The good news is that we'll save this one." Again Simon nodded in Danny's direction. "Now I have to consider how many other people out there don't have a chance because of something like this."

"We'll help the ones we can," Joe repeated. "We can only do what we can do for now."

"Sure, but this is starting to feel as if it's not enough."

With that, his foreman nodded and headed back to work.

Meanwhile Simon caught up on phone calls. When he headed back home again, he checked in with Peter.

Just before Simon reached his apartment building, Peter whispered, *I'm thinking.*

Simon winced. "Look. I didn't mean to say that as an order or anything. It's just that, if you remember anything else, it could help."

*I'm thinking,* he snapped. And, with that, he disappeared

again.

The trouble was, now that Peter was thinking, all Simon could do was consider how this *think* command would relate to Kate. And maybe it had no relationship at all, but Simon just couldn't seem to let it go. And, just like Peter, it went around and around in his head. *Think, think, think.*

What the hell was wrong with him that he'd snapped at that poor little boy?

Stepping into his apartment building, he waved at Harry and headed upstairs. Simon had a quick shower before coming back out and putting on coffee. He had paperwork to do and a bunch of other crap to deal with before Kate got in, if she got in at all today. Usually, just as soon as he found a lull in his world, something in hers would burn up. Right now, a lot of that could just as easily be the mess she was dealing with in her own personal world. And that just kept his mind going round and round again.

As soon as he sat down with a cup of coffee, Peter popped in.

*I'm thinking,* he cried out, and then he disappeared again.

"Jesus," Simon muttered, as he got up to pace. "Stop thinking then, Peter. Just let it go. Maybe it's more about *not* thinking."

*Not thinking.* Peter came back, his whisper tired and cranky now, as if he'd been given an assignment that he couldn't do.

"Yes, maybe stop thinking and just let information float around. Let's tell your mind that you need to know about what happened and let it go at that. Then see what it does."

*Okay,* he whispered. Then he drifted out of Simon's realm again.

Simon didn't know if that was better or worse, but, dear God, he needed whatever was going on in Peter's world to stop.

Almost immediately Peter came back and whispered, *I think I got it.*

"You think you've got what?" Simon asked.

*I think I got it. I think I got it. I think I got it. I think I got it.*

"Peter, Peter, talk to me. Just talk to me."

*I think I got it,* and then he was gone.

"Good Christ," Simon muttered with a groan, as he collapsed on his couch. This would drive him mental, and yet it was his own fault in a way. That didn't make him feel any better. As he sat here, sipping his coffee, he wondered what he was supposed to do with this now.

Then Kate contacted him. "Hey," she greeted him. "I'm heading over to the station to talk to a couple people involved in the one little boy's death. I know it's not quite my case anymore, but it is my case in a way. We've got the mother, the father, and the brother-in-law in for questioning."

"Didn't you already question them?"

"Yes," she stated, "but we didn't have the autopsy results at the time, and now we do."

"Right, the designer drugs element."

"Yes, the drugs. However, back then, I thought we were talking about a different delivery method—a syringe—but it seems he may have just ingested them, as in drugs loose on a surface."

"Oh Christ," Simon muttered. "To even think that something like that was available to a five-year-old kid ..."

"I know," she murmured. "And yet it happens. It happens all too often."

"The mother will lose it. Isn't this the second time she lost a son to drugs?"

"Yes, and I think she's past losing it now. We just need to talk to her and to ensure she understands what happened. It took a while to find the husband. She had kicked him out, and he'd gone back home to his mother or some such thing. I don't know exactly. Rodney rousted him out. The brother-in-law had been nowhere to be found, but Rodney's got him now too. So, we'll go in and talk to the three of them."

"In other words, no dinner tonight."

"Not for me," she confirmed, "but ensure you eat."

He laughed at that. "I'm supposed to eat, but you aren't?"

She frowned. "One of us might as well enjoy food," she stated crossly. As she went to hang up, she added, "Oh."

"Oh what?" he muttered right back at her, still pissed at her comment about not having time to eat.

"We tracked my stepfather's communication at the prison just before he left. He did send out a letter which was checked over, although he was in minimum security at that point in time. And he did have a couple people who he saw on a regular basis."

"Meaning?"

"Meaning that we're tracking it down as to whether he's the one who sent the puzzle-box note, potentially wanting to blackmail me or something. It would have been easy enough for him to have gotten a friend to hire the kid to deliver the note."

"Yes, that's true," Simon agreed.

"And Ken did have communication with people during that time, which he was entitled to," she added, "since he was being released."

"Right, so it easily could have been him."

"That's what we're hoping for, ... some kind of an answer on that."

"Good, so you can let that part go."

She chuckled. "Good, enjoy your dinner." And, with that, she ended the call.

No sooner had she hung up than his doorman from downstairs contacted him. "Harry, what's up?"

"Somebody is here to see you, ... He mentioned he had dinner with you the other night."

Simon froze and quickly gave a description of Kate's stepfather. "Yeah, that's him," Harry confirmed, "You want me to send him up?"

"Hell no," Simon said immediately. "I'll come down."

"Is this a problem?" Harry asked, ever aware of security issues.

"Maybe, so you stay close."

"Will do," he agreed, with a cheerful tone. "We don't need any issues here."

"No, especially since this one involves Kate."

"Man, that girl does bring on trouble, doesn't she?"

"She sure does," Simon said, with a chuckle, even as he headed to the elevator. He disconnected and immediately put his phone on Record and got down to the main lobby, pocketing his cell. Sure enough, his visitor was Kate's stepfather. Simon walked over to him. "What can I do for you, Mr. Reeves?"

Ken looked around and muttered, "Pretty fancy digs, Simon."

"Yeah, Ken, and?" Simon kept his voice cool, but the stepfather gave one of those smiles that would make the blood of an ordinary man run cold. No way Simon would let this guy get to him. "What can I do for you?" he repeated.

"You can help Kate sign all those documents because that would be really helpful."

"She already told you no. It's not my decision to make. Plus, I haven't talked to her about it. After all, she's busy. She does have a job."

"Yeah, she's a cop," Ken replied, with a creepy smile. "Who would have *thunk* it?" He just waited, and so did Simon. Ken finally added, "So, the thing is, I think it would be a really good idea for her to sign those documents."

"Ah, here it comes. What kind of blackmail will you try?" He watched Harry shift ever-so-slightly, hearing the word *blackmail*.

"That girl's got some making up to do," Ken declared, with that same smarmy smile that Simon had seen from Ken in the restaurant. "I figured that would be an easy one for her, particularly as a cop, since she could just make all kinds of things go away. Yet, I suspect, she's got whatever the hell that thing is called, ... a *conscience*," he said, with a snort. "However, I am not deterred by that. I spent way-too-many years in prison for something I didn't do, and it's her fault."

"Something you didn't do?" Simon asked. "Meaning you didn't assault her?"

"No, of course I didn't," he replied, anger in his tone. "What the hell? Why would I do that?"

Simon just waited, knowing Harry was sitting off to the side, listening in. Maybe not the best in terms of Kate's privacy, but, if things went wrong, Simon would want Harry on his side. And this Ken guy in front of Simon was just a sleaze. "Kate makes her own decisions, and I stand by them," Simon stated. "So I sure as hell won't do anything to encourage her to sign documents recanting a truthful statement she made when she was seven."

"I think she was close to eight at that time, or maybe six, I don't know," Ken said. "The thing is, she was too much of a child, and trust me. She didn't know what she was talking about."

"Really?" Simon asked, with a knowing smile. "You would say that now, of course."

"Yeah, I would, and I said it back then."

"And what did her mother say?"

He glared at him. "Selene thinks Kate won't recant, but I've told Selene that her life would get a little rough if she doesn't make it happen."

"Considering that Selene's not even talking to Kate, I highly doubt that her mother will help you in this situation."

"That's all in the past, so don't be surprised if she calls and wants to talk to her daughter again."

"What is this all about? You tried to get her mother to convince Kate before, didn't you?"

"Selene set up the meeting, and then she backed out." Ken frowned. "What's up with that? I really don't take that kind of shit well."

"Sounds to me as if you haven't really changed at all, Ken."

"What do you mean?" he snapped.

"It's pretty simple. Here you are, trying to threaten people into changing things into the way you want them."

"If you realized that I didn't do any of that shit Kate said I did, then it wouldn't be an issue."

"I don't believe you, Ken. I believe Kate. So are you telling me that's why her mom wanted to talk to her?"

"Yeah, it sure is, but she got cold feet and refused to go

through with it at the last minute."

"So, I suppose you're the one who helped her have a drug overdose then?" Simon asked.

"Hell no." He glared at Simon, not liking the direction the conversation was heading in. "She's been a druggie all her life anyway, and that hasn't changed."

"*Hmm*, I'm not so sure about that. Seems Selene has been staying out of trouble for more than ten years. You didn't do anything to help her along?"

"No, of course not," Ken snapped, but such a fake grin was on his face that Simon knew that's exactly what happened.

"So, all of this is literally about you wanting Kate to recant her statement from so many years ago."

"She was mistaken," he stated, still smiling that fake grin, "and coerced, which is easy to do with a young child."

"Right, like you coerced her as a young child, but it's not so easy to do to an adult. Kate won't recant. She was honest back then, and she remains honest today. She won't say she was wrong because she wasn't."

"Yes, she can." Then he frowned. "I'm sure she can. She can say it was somebody else entirely. Hell, I've got a whole bunch of guys I absolutely hate. I'm sure one of them was around back then. She can blame him."

"Really?" Simon asked casually. "So, you are wasting your time here with me as you wasted your time with Kate at the restaurant. Nothing has changed. She will not lie. And I surely won't ask her to lie either. I have a conscience too. As far as she's concerned, it's done and dusted. Completely over with." At least he sincerely hoped that was the case.

"For her it may be. She got to make her statement that put my life on hold for all these years. So now the least she can do is make good on it now."

"Make good on it?" Simon repeated.

"Yeah, make good on it. I promised her back then that she needed to think very clearly about what step she was about to take. To think hard before sending me to jail. And I made sure she remembered that."

Simon stared at him. "I see," he muttered. "So you sent her a note, telling her to *think*. And you figured she'd done something wrong that she owed you for, so she would just fall in line and do your bidding? Kate's not a seven-year-old child anymore, Ken."

"No, she sure isn't, and, man, she grew up bony, didn't she?" He shook his head. "Even a guy like you would appreciate more curves than she's got."

Simon stared at the asshole, feeling anger spark inside but desperate not to show it and not to give this asshole any leverage. Simon shook his head. "I don't understand what you're doing here."

"I figured you would have more smarts than she did and would understand where her bread was buttered."

"You think so?" Simon asked. "Do you think I give a crap which side her bread is buttered on?" He motioned around him. "Does anything here tell you that I care?"

"You're not desperate at all, which is why I can't figure out what the hell you're even doing with her. There isn't anything to her, and, Christ, she's a cop. Why the hell would you want to bring that to your door?"

It was all Simon could do to hold back the temper sparking deep inside him. "You've wasted enough time here," he announced. "Kate won't recant because she did the right thing."

"But she didn't, that's the thing," Ken roared. "I didn't

fucking touch her."

At that, Simon studied him. "Seriously?"

"Yeah, seriously," he spat, and then roared again. "Like what the hell? I didn't rape her. I didn't do any of that."

"So, what did you do?"

"Nothing much at all," he replied, giving him that smarmy smile again. "I mean, so I looked a bit. I *dingled* a bit," he conceded, with a wave of his hand, "I put up a few cameras. I was looking at her brother as much as at her." He shrugged. "Then she got all upset because of the videos. I was like, I'll stop the damn videos from happening. I could have made a lot of money off them."

Simon's stomach wrenched, and he wanted to punch this guy until he was black and blue. "Are you serious?"

"Yeah, of course I'm serious, and I won't lie about this. She has the ability to turn my life around, and she damn-well fucking owes me."

"I don't understand the *owes you* part."

"Are you that simple? She owes me because she's the one who put me away."

"What's that got to do with her owing you?"

"I just told you. She's the one who put me away. So how hard is that to understand?"

"But you're the one who was *dingling her*, as you put so very eloquently," Simon pointed out, staring at Ken. "The rest of us call it *child abuse*. She doesn't owe you shit."

"But if she hadn't said anything, my life wouldn't have gone to hell."

"But if you hadn't done what you'd done, it wouldn't have gone to hell in the first place."

The stepfather stared at him in frustration. "See? This is where we'll have a problem," he declared finally. "As far as

I'm concerned, she owes me, and she needs to fix it."

"Or else what?" Simon asked patiently.

"Or else I'll make life difficult for her. And … I know she's responsible for her brother going missing."

Simon sighed. "You *know* that, do you?"

"I do know that," he stated. "And you can sure as hell bet I'll let the world know it too."

Not sure what this threat meant exactly, or in what way a seven-year-old child could be responsible for disappearing her five-year-old brother, Simon said, "You got evidence? Bring it to the police."

"Oh, you should listen to me," he suggested, "because you should never touch that woman again. She's just poison."

Simon stared at him. "Are you talking about her mother or her?"

"Her mother is poison too," Ken snapped, "and I've got enough on her to keep her in line for a long time."

Simon winced. "That's your system? You just blackmail people into doing what you want them to do?"

"You've got to have obedience," he spat, staring at Simon. "Jesus Christ, don't tell me that you're one of those namby-pamby men who have the women's hearts to consider because that's complete BS."

"Is it?" he murmured. "I'm not so sure about that."

"God, man," Ken muttered, with a headshake. "Keep them in line, and they don't give you any trouble."

"So, what part of all this do you consider that Kate screwed up on?"

"It wasn't me," he stated. "That's all she needs to know."

"So you told her at the restaurant, and she rejected you already. Now you're telling me that Kate, as a seven-year-old girl, was supposedly responsible for her little brother going missing. I don't believe it. So you need to give me a hell of a lot more than just your word."

He glared at him. "I'm not giving up my ace in the hole."

"I don't believe you," Simon repeated. "It's just that simple."

Ken stared at him for a long moment. "You really got it bad, don't you, Simon? I can fix that for you," he threatened, "and you won't want nothing to do with her."

"So far, all you're doing is talking," Simon noted, with a bored look on his face. "And I don't deal with bullies or with empty threats."

"Yeah, I get it." Ken snorted and waved a hand around. "You're one of those little rich boys, some trust fund baby who never had to work a day in his life."

Simon laughed. "You don't have a clue," he muttered, "but whatever. You can keep thinking what you want. So far, all you're doing is talking bullshit, trying to cause trouble, and defaming a person who doesn't deserve it."

"Oh, yes, she does," Ken snapped. "She's fucking responsible. I tell you that right now."

"And why is that?"

"Because she told Timmy that she wished he would die. She got mad and told her five-year-old brother that she wished he would die and that he was too much effort to look after."

"Are you sure *she* told him that, or did *you* tell Timmy that she said that?"

Instantly Ken's expression turned to fury. "What the fuck?" he yelled, foam appearing at the corners of his mouth. "Why don't you believe me?"

"Because I know Kate," he shared. "I know kids can say all kinds of things when they're frustrated and fed up, but she and Timmy were close. While I find it easy to believe that *you* might have told that little boy that's what she said, I don't for a minute believe Kate actually said it."

Ken stared at him and then laughed. "You do know her then, don't you?" he muttered. "That's just too funny."

"Why is it funny?"

"Just because you believe in her doesn't mean it's the truth."

"Yeah? I know you're full of shit too," Simon added. "And I can see that you might have told Timmy that. What did he do, Ken? Did he take off from school on his own that day?"

Ken winced and nodded. "That's what he did. I went there to get him, but he got mad and told me that I wasn't supposed to even see him and Kate, and he was right. I wasn't supposed to see him or Kate. That pissed me off, so I told him that his sister didn't love him anymore. You should have seen him. His little face just cracked and filled with tears."

Simon felt sick to his stomach as he listened to that. "And that was the last you saw of Timmy, I suppose."

Ken shrugged. "Yeah, except for the vehicle I saw him get into. ... Once I saw that, it was like, oh well, too bad."

Ken had such a cavalier attitude when he said that. Immediately Simon took a step toward him, and Ken backed up real fast. "Whoa, whoa, whoa," he muttered, his hands up. "I didn't know who was in the vehicle, and I'm not to blame for that. For all I know, he was one of the kid's friends."

"One of the kid's friends? A five-year-old driving a vehicle?"

"Yeah, the dad or whatever. It seemed to be one of the dad's vehicles. So what else could I think?"

"But you didn't think, did you?" Simon asked, staring him down this time. "You just stepped away and ignored it."

"So, he got a ride home? What gives? Afterward I did consider it and realized that was probably the last person to see him alive."

"And you were okay to let Kate and her mother worry all these years?"

Ken sneered. "I'm okay to let Kate, … let's see. How shall I put it? I would be okay to let her worry for the rest of her life. And her mother too, for that matter. There's nothing good about that pair of bitches."

Simon snorted. "So, why now?"

"Because I'm out of that fucking prison, and I want her to do something for me. In order to do that, I'll give her something."

"Yet, if you were only interested in Kate being punished, what difference does that *something* make? Besides, any information coming from you is bogus anyway."

Ken shrugged. "But I'm all she's got, so there."

"Maybe we'll go talk to her mother. Besides, I thought they had people saying he'd gotten into a vehicle that day."

"I wasn't too worried about it. So Timmy got into a friend's vehicle? The thing is, it wasn't the friend's vehicle at all," he said, with a laugh. "And I didn't say anything more."

"But you do know who was in that vehicle, don't you?" Simon asked, staring at him.

Ken shrugged. "I don't know any such thing," he snapped. "And I ain't talking anymore." With that, he headed toward the doorway.

Harry cleared his throat to get Simon's attention. Harry had his hand on the button. He could stop Ken from leaving, if need be, but Simon knew the guy would just get more belligerent if he wasn't allowed to leave.

Simon signaled to Harry to let Ken go for now. Then Simon shared with Ken, "We'll speak to Kate's mom again."

"Oh, you go ahead and do that." Ken laughed. "That should be fun to watch."

"So you'll get her to overdose again?" Simon asked.

"That's pretty easy, now that she's hooked again. She'll do anything I say just to get her next fix."

"These drugs that you're getting," Simon added, "you know they're bad, right?"

He frowned. "I did hear something about that." He turned to Simon, eyeing him oddly. "I'm not sure where you heard that though."

"There have already been a couple deaths linked to that particular designer drug," Simon shared.

Ken's breath caught. "There shouldn't have been. I didn't sell to anybody." And Ken raced out of the building.

That last part came out as a whisper. Simon sure hoped it was caught on his recording. He turned off that feature and immediately called Kate. "I'm sending you a recording. I'm not sure Ken said what I thought he said. Call me back as soon as you've heard all of it." He sent her the audio file, then turned to Harry. "Please don't ever mention any of that to anyone."

Harry nodded. "Yeah, no way. Kate's good people, and, if she put away that asshole, even at that young age, she was already destined to be a cop."

Simon smiled at that. "She did, indeed, put away that asshole. However, her brother has been missing for many decades, and nobody's ever been able to crack the case," he shared. "It's the one big wound in her heart that she would do anything to solve."

Harry winced. "Taking children, … that's just not cool, and that jerk seems to think he saw who did it."

"I'm pretty sure he did," Simon replied, "but, so typical of that breed of man, he wouldn't hand over the information unless he gained something from it. Nobody even knew that Ken was there at the school either because he was already looking at jail time. His court case just hadn't come up yet."

"Christ."

"So, he was mad at the police anyway."

"Yeah, but just think about this," Harry noted. "That was his son, and he was totally okay for that kid to never show up again. What does that say about him?"

"I'm not sure I've got words for a guy like that," Simon muttered.

Harry nodded. "For now, *slimy old bastard* will do."

# CHAPTER 19

K ATE WAS FROZEN. She couldn't believe what she heard on the recording Simon had sent her. Earlier she had tried to explain her stepfather and his request to the others on her team, and everybody had just stared at her, like nobody would really do that. But now? After listening to this tape, listening to what Ken had told her brother, it just permanently etched a new source of pain into Kate's brain. Thinking that her brother had believed Ken was so painful that she was locked in place and couldn't move.

Rodney squeezed her knee. "Ken would have said anything to save his sorry ass and to cause you the most pain," he told her. "You can't believe a word of it. He's just choosing what he knows will hurt you the most."

She looked over at him gratefully. "I'm really hoping he didn't tell Timmy that," she whispered, still struggling to deal with this. "However, Ken's an asshole through and through, so I wouldn't put it past him."

"Yeah, you're not kidding, but what is interesting," Rodney pointed out, "is the part about your brother getting into a vehicle."

"I know, and I do recall ... Well, I'm pretty sure that there were reports on that, saying it was supposedly the father of a friend. However, when he was questioned, he had an alibi and looked to be completely in the clear. I don't know. We never—I never contacted the cop on the case. There were two at the time, and I did try to contact one, but he didn't have anything good to say to me. I never did contact the other one, and I lost track of him. So I don't know where the hell he ended up," she shared.

"What do you mean by that?" Rodney asked.

"I don't remember exactly. He moved, changed countries, something," she muttered, with a headshake. "I didn't blame the cops, … but my mother certainly did. Plenty of other things were going on at the time, but only as I've been an adult and had a chance to go through the files can I see what the cops did, what they didn't do," she muttered. "And it's never easy coming into a case after the fact," she noted. "People don't want to talk at the time, and yet now I was hoping that maybe somebody would loosen their tongue. It's been so damn long."

"Now you have your stepfather as a potential witness, but would you have gone to the prison to talk to him about it? I don't know that I would have," Rodney admitted.

"No way, I sure wouldn't have gone anywhere near him. Yet, now that he's brought up his involvement already," she pointed out, with half a smile, "you can bet that's at the top of my list."

"Do you suspect him of it?"

"No," she replied, shaking her head. "I don't think so, but"—then she frowned—"I also don't like that bit about the drugs. Simon was concerned about that because we've got these current deaths, plus the potential death of my mother. Simon seems to think that those instances might have been related to Ken's remark about drugs."

"I wouldn't be at all surprised if it wasn't related to Ken," Rodney stated. "If it is related, then we may have the seller, *Ken.*"

"Ken used to be into drugs," she added, frowning. "How the hell do I get my mother away from this asshole?" Everybody stopped and looked at her. "Obviously he's back to torturing her again."

"I'm sorry to point this out," Lilliana corrected, "but it is quite possible that he's back to *controlling* her."

Kate frowned, while nodding. "Here's something to consider. My mother's very skinny, so, with a hat, dressed in men's clothing, with a little bit of crafty makeup, what are the chances of her fitting the description of the one who sent that kid with the note in the puzzle box into the station?"

Colby joined them, hearing that last part from Kate. He remained silent as the team members shared a look. Lilliana walked over to the case files and reread the description. Immediately she nodded. "Honest to God, Kate, she probably could pull it off, couldn't she?"

"Yeah, she probably could. Christ," Kate muttered. "Why the hell would she do that?"

"You know the answer as well as I do," Lilliana stated. "If Ken's got her hooked again, she would do nearly anything to get the drugs she needs. She didn't want to but couldn't hire somebody else to do it without putting herself at even more risk, and she had to be careful, knowing it all would bring everybody back to her just because it was your brother."

Kate stared at them. "It explains our *glorious reunion* at her front door. ... Jesus, another element to this shit show I wasn't expecting."

"Of course not," Lilliana agreed. "You don't expect your own mother to be involved in this. Do you ... Do you think your mother was involved in the disappearance of your brother?"

Kate looked up at her teammate. "I sure hope not," she muttered, "but I have no way of knowing. I do think that all this mess stirred up by delivering the note was literally because Ken wants me to recant my statement," she shared. "He had hope that I would do it, and it would show him as being innocent, so he could then be cleared and sue for a shit ton of money. However, … I have a question." Kate looked around the room and let it fly. "Why did he wait all this time to do it?"

Silence. Everybody stared at her, then at each other.

Rodney spoke up first. "That's a really good point."

Lilliana added, "What do you want to bet it was something that your mother might have suggested or something that someone in prison with him thought about?"

Rodney tilted his head, grimacing. "I'm surprised he didn't bring up the vehicle that your brother got into as being evidence suppressed by the police. Maybe he wants to tarnish your reputation—or that of the whole department—by saying you've been hiding evidence this whole time."

"He probably thought it wasn't enough," she muttered, "but I wouldn't put it past him to create other evidence."

He nodded. "I can see that too."

"This recorded discussion was not a twist I expected," Kate admitted. "I've got it downloaded on my computer to send off as needed."

"Let forensics deal with this last bit," Rodney suggested, as he walked out, "because that conversation is something we'll need to question him about. However, as far as I'm concerned, if he's got anything to do with distributing those deadly designer drugs, especially when these two kids died from it," he added, "that'll put him away for the rest of his life."

"Good," Kate declared. "As far as I'm concerned, he never should have gotten out in the first place."

"I hate to ask," Colby said, joining in the conversation, "but it sounds like he thinks you lied."

She snorted. "It's more that he doesn't think he did anything wrong. I didn't lie. I'm just the only one of however many kids who stood up. I tried to talk to several of them back then, and nobody would talk to me. I became some pariah in my world because of this. But, for me, there really wasn't any other option. Maybe he was right about one thing though. I was destined to be a cop even then." She looked over at Lilliana. "You need to bring in Andrew's parents and Sammy."

Lilliana nodded. "I just sent three black-and-whites to pick them up. If nothing else, we need to ask them a whole lot more questions than what they've given us so far," she clarified. "Kate, I can't have you taking part in the formal interviews."

Kate stared at her and then slowly nodded. "Right, I understand. … As much as I want to, as much as I want to hear them, I also know that it'll be ugly. So, better you than me. I'll watch from behind the glass."

Lilliana smiled, and this time her teeth showed. "Don't you worry," she declared. "If Ken's involved in the deaths of these kids, he will pay. And, if Ken really did have something to do with your mother's overdose, we'll get him on that too. And, if Ken withheld evidence on Timmy's disappearance, we'll add that to the growing list of charges against your stepfather. … In the meantime, we have some people to interview," she announced, standing up and turning to look at Rodney.

He nodded. "Let's go see how much Alana, Adam, and Sammy had to do with the deaths of their two kids." And with that they headed into the interviews.

# CHAPTER 20

BEFORE THE FORMAL interrogation began, Kate and Rodney walked into the interview room and faced Alana, the mother of Andrew. Kate smiled at her, sat across the table from her, and asked, "How're you doing?"

"I've been better," Alana replied, staring at her. "It's my son that we've lost, in case you've forgotten."

There was an edge to her voice, and that edge surprised Kate. She studied Alana for a moment and added, "Some other information has come to light, which is why we brought you in to talk."

"And yet you had to bring me into the station? You couldn't come to my house?" she asked. Her gaze narrowed as she stared at Kate and Rodney.

"Sometimes it's easier, and we get better answers when people are here," Kate replied.

At that, Alana's eyes widened. "Good God," she snapped. "I didn't have anything to do with my son's death, and I don't see how you could possibly even think that."

"It's not so much about that," Kate replied, "but there are other issues. Andrew did not die from being beaten, … at least, not this time," she added for clarity.

The mother winced. "I can't believe I stayed with that asshole. I can't believe I listened to his BS."

"I can't either," Kate agreed, "but that is only part of

what we need to ask you."

"What?" she asked, staring at her. "I'm serious. I didn't have anything to do with my son's death."

"Not intentionally, perhaps," Kate noted, "but it's more than that. Your son died of a drug overdose."

The woman stared at her in shock. "What?"

Kate nodded. "We've spoken to your neighbors, and apparently drugs were something that you guys had a problem with."

Alana stared at Kate. "I would never have given my son drugs," she cried out in shock, paling as she stared at them. "I'll do weed every once in a while, and that is legal here," she pointed out, "but it would only be to blow off some steam at the end of the day. I never did anything hard."

"And how about your husband?"

She winced. "Every once in a while, he would get into some of the other stuff," she admitted, "but I haven't seen any sign of that in quite a while."

"What about his brother Sammy?"

She immediately glared. "God, that piece of shit. All he does is drugs. I won't have him in the house if he's high. I won't have him around my son if he's drinking." And then she froze. "But I wasn't in town," she added, lifting her horrified gaze to Kate. "Please tell me that Andrew didn't die of drugs."

"I just said that he did," she murmured. "He did die from a drug overdose. Drugs that he ingested."

Alana started to visibly shake. "No, no, no, no, please, no," she wailed. "Please, no. Not again."

And she looked so sorrowfully at Kate, that Kate had to slowly nod and take a deep breath before she spoke again. "I'm sorry, but it seems, for whatever reason, whether

Andrew found them accidentally on the table or the floor or maybe it was given to him," Kate explained, "but Andrew did die from a drug overdose."

At that, the mother burst into tears, and Kate could only imagine what that felt like and knew nobody could say anything to make it better. At this instant, at this moment in time, this woman who'd thought she had absolutely nothing more to lose, was about to lose the last little bit of her own ability to even deal with life, as she now realized that the death of her child had been completely avoidable.

Kate waited until the woman calmed down and spoke again. "You should know that we have both your husband and his brother here at the station, and we'll talk to them next."

She just stared at her. "Oh my God," she whispered. "Can I talk to them too?"

Kate looked at her and gave her a slow headshake. "No, because, if you're anything like me, it wouldn't be talking you want to do."

Alana stared at her, tears were in her eyes. "And because it's something like this, what is the recourse for me? Do Sammy and Adam just get to walk away from this, free and clear?"

"I don't know about free and clear," Kate clarified, "but definitely not free from guilt and not free in the prison system."

"Oh my God," she whispered, wrapping her arms tightly around her chest. "Can I just go home now? If I can't see him, or scream at him, or do my best to kill him," she added, "I just need to get out of here." And, indeed, she was starting to hyperventilate.

Kate asked her, "Is there somebody I can call for you?"

She started to cry. "How could anybody ever want to have anything to do with us after this?" she whispered. "My own family told me to get rid of Adam, but no. … I was so sure he would get better, that he would change."

"Just your husband?" Kate asked.

"Him and my brother-in-law," she replied, with a vicious tone. "Christ, I should have left a long time ago."

Kate stood. "Look. If you have somebody we can call, we'll send you home with them. Otherwise I'll need you to stay here for a little bit." Kate looked over at Rodney, and he got up too. "We'll be back in a minute. Do you want a cup of tea or something?" Kate asked Alana.

She shook her head. "Absolutely nothing will ever make this okay." She stared at the two of them with a haunted gaze.

"You are right," Kate replied, "and the only thing I can do is get justice for your little boy." And, with that, she walked out.

She assigned a policewoman to step in and to keep an eye on the grieving woman. Then, with Rodney at her side, the two of them walked into the next interrogation room where the husband sat.

Adam immediately jumped to his feet. "Have you talked to my wife?" he asked. "I've been trying to get a hold of her, but she won't talk to me."

"We just talked to her in the other room," Kate said.

"She's here, now?" he asked, spinning around, as if she would come in with them. "Where? I need to see her. I need to apologize."

"You think an apology will fix this?" Rodney asked him in shock.

Adam frowned at Rodney and muttered, "No, of course

it won't fix it. I don't even know how to fix it."

"I'm not sure fixing this is a reasonable expectation," Kate stated, staring at him. "Your little boy is dead."

"I know, but I didn't do it."

"There is that," she noted, rolling her eyes. "What kind of drugs do you like to do?"

"Me? I don't do drugs," he declared.

She stared at him. "We've already spoken to your wife. Do you want take another stab at that?"

He flushed. "Okay, so, she probably told you that she likes to have a little bit of weed every once in a while."

"Yeah, she did tell us that," she confirmed, still staring at him. "And you?"

He frowned. "So, I have a little bit of weed with her every once in a while," he replied cautiously, obviously aware that something was going wrong.

Kate nodded. "And outside of the weed?"

"No," he snapped, then frowned. "Okay, so maybe, once in a while, I might have a little bit of something else, but … it's not a regular thing. It's just recreational use."

"How often, and do you have it around the house?"

"Sure, every once in a while, particularly if my wife's away," he pointed out. "She doesn't have any use for that kind of drug, and most of the time I don't either. Yet sometimes, when I'm with friends, you know?"

"Right," Kate said. "And what about your brother?"

"Yeah, he probably is a little more active in the drugs than I am," he muttered, "but, it's not as if he's a drug addict or anything."

"*No, of course not,*" Rodney quipped, sitting back and crossing his arms over his chest.

"And when you do partake in drugs, where would the

kid be?" Kate asked.

"Oh, nowhere around," he said. "That's always after he goes to bed."

"Right."

He seemed relieved, as if the answers he gave were the ones that they wanted to hear. Kate looked over at him. "We got the autopsy results back on your little boy."

Fear immediately crossed his face. "I didn't kill him. Honest to God, I did not kill him," he cried out. "I know I've been a little rough on him in the past, but I've been really working on it," he cried out.

She nodded. "He did not die from your physical abuse. Although the bruising was enough to make the coroner stop and assess the type of abuse that little boy went through," she began. "On the other hand, what he did die of ... was a drug overdose."

Adam sank back in shock. "A drug overdose? No, no, there must be some mistake," he muttered. "There's no drugs."

"There were drugs," Kate corrected, and she named the specific designer drug.

Adam immediately turned fifty shades of red.

She nodded. "Some drugs are like Russian roulette. You can take them once and think that you'll be fine every time, but it's like putting a loaded gun to your head, wondering if it'll be the one bullet that takes you out that day. But with children? ... They really don't have any resistance to drugs, and it takes very little to be an overdose for them."

"I would never give my son drugs," he cried out.

"No, you might not have. What about your brother?"

"No, God no," he stated, "never."

Such conviction filled his tone, she nodded. "And yet

would he have been quite so careful to ensure your son wasn't anywhere close when he did his drugs?" she asked. "Or would there have been an opportunity when Sammy may have just gotten up and left the drugs accessible, like on a table or somewhere close by?"

At first Adam's face turned fifty shades of purple, and then all of the color fled at once, as he understood what she was saying. "Oh my God."

She nodded. "There was enough in Andrew's stomach to kill four children," she explained. "You want to explain that?"

*I'VE BEEN THINKING*, whispered the voice in Simon's head.

He winced. "I'm sorry, Peter. I shouldn't be pushing you so hard."

*No,* he replied fretfully. *I'm trying, but I'm not getting very much. I keep thinking about what happened.*

"And did you come up with anything?" he asked curiously.

He took a moment before answering. *I just remembered wanting to play with something.*

"Something like a toy, an animal, a puppy?"

*A puppy,* he cried out. *Yes, I wanted to play with a puppy.*

"And who would have a puppy? Because you didn't have a puppy, did you?"

*No,* he said, his tone regretful. *I didn't have a puppy.*

"Do you know who did have a puppy?"

Again came silence, and he said, *I'm not sure. Not sure, don't want to say. Something about it makes me feel upset.* And, with that, he started to cry. Then suddenly he was gone again.

Simon swore as he stared off at the street around him. He didn't even realize that he'd started talking to the little boy right away, without even thinking about his surroundings. That was something he would have to be a little more careful with. The last thing he wanted was his reputation to go down the tube as somebody who stood around talking to himself. He pinched the bridge of his nose.

Wondering if any puppy was involved with Peter, Simon pulled out his phone and called Peter's aunt, Simon's stalking Realtor. When Ariel answered, both fear and curiosity filled her tone. "Did anybody around your nephew have a puppy?" he asked her.

"What are you talking about?" she asked in confusion.

"I'm asking," he repeated, "if anybody in that corner of your world had a puppy that Peter wanted to play with."

She hesitated, then said, "My brother-in-law wanted to get Peter a puppy but couldn't. He's allergic."

"How badly allergic?"

"I don't know," she replied. "Why? What has that got to do with anything?"

"I don't know, but I have to ask questions as they come up."

"Okay," she muttered. "I would really appreciate a little more information if you can give me any."

"So would I," he snapped, shaking his head. "So would I. Do you know if any of the neighbors had a puppy?"

"His parents got a puppy for Peter, but he couldn't handle it, … the allergies. So they had to return the puppy."

"And who had the puppy?"

"It went back to the original owner," she said, and then elaborated. "He was a friend from across the street."

"Ah, okay." And, with that, he had to stop and digest.

"Why?" Ariel asked sharply. "What has this … I …"

"I understand," Simon offered. "I often feel the same way. All I can say is, that was a question I needed answered." And, with that, he disconnected.

He knew she would try and call him back, so he just put his phone on Silent because he didn't want to deal with it. If he knew one thing, he knew when he didn't have any more answers to give people, and the only reason he was even asking questions, or talking to her at all, was because of Peter.

He glanced at this phone a moment later to see a call from Kate coming in. He took it off silent and answered.

"You always seem to know," Simon greeted her, with a note of amusement.

"What happened?" she snapped, her tone sharpening.

"Nothing bad," he said immediately. "I talked to Peter again."

"And?"

"And I was trying to get him to remember. As I mentioned to you, this whole *think* thing has him a little spun up and stressed out."

"Right," she agreed, "and did he come up with anything?"

"Just something about a puppy."

"A puppy," she repeated.

"Yes."

"I don't think there was mention of a puppy in the case files."

"Maybe not. I just phoned his aunt, the realtor who stalks me and who asked me if I could do anything to help. She remembers a puppy, but Peter was allergic, so they couldn't keep it. The mother had given in to the kid's demands, and it ended up that they had to give the puppy back."

"And where did the puppy come from?"

"Seems the original owner was somebody fairly close, a neighbor from across the street."

"Right, and all Peter remembers is wanting a puppy?"

"Wanting to play with a puppy," Simon clarified. "And I know that means nothing."

"No, it doesn't mean *nothing*," she pointed out. "We know that every detail helps."

"Did you have a reason for calling?" he asked her.

"Yeah, I got a weird feeling from you," she shared.

He smiled. "I'm fine."

"Are you sure?"

"Yes, I'm sure," he stated. "I've been worried about you though."

"I know," she muttered. "It seems everybody is."

"What about your stepfather? Any progress?"

"That's a work in progress. They're looking for him right now. Lilliana and Rodney are handling it. I'm looking after the cases with the kids, as much as they let me."

"Right, but—"

"I know. It's all likely related, which is why we're doing what we're doing," she explained. "I can only do what I can do and what Colby will allow me to do."

"Right," Simon replied. "I'm sure he understands how you feel."

"He does, but his hands are tied to a certain extent. As long as I continue to cooperate with the shrink appointments and the rest of the crap they want me to deal with, I'm allowed to be on the periphery of the cases. But as soon as they deem me to be unfit, then I'm off all of them."

"They won't do that," he stated with surety.

"You may say that," she replied, with a snort. "However, a lot of people could definitely say I'm not doing my best work, or I couldn't possibly do my best work because of all the emotional issues in my world."

"Maybe," he conceded, "but I also know that you will compartmentalize everything you can in order to continue to find out what's going on."

She laughed. "I'm glad you have such faith."

"I do have faith because I know you," he declared, "and honestly, as every day goes by, I think I know you more and more."

"I'm not sure whether that's good or bad right now."

"It's good," he stated, a note of amusement in his tone, hearing a smile in hers. "Don't ever doubt that."

"Maybe, but in the meantime," she said, "I don't know if I'll be over tonight. We're waiting for my stepfather to be picked up, and I want to be here when the interview happens."

"Of course," Simon noted. "I might stop by and bring you some food then."

"You're always so concerned that I'm not eating." She laughed. "You know, a lot of guys would be concerned that I was eating too much."

"Not likely," he muttered. "You burn through so many calories that it's amazing you're even functioning."

"I'm functioning," she said. "I just have to stay on top of everything."

"And, in order to do that, you need food."

"Fine," she muttered. "Deliver food if you want. I'll be here, hoping that things will come to an end tonight."

"You think so?"

"I hope so," she muttered, then chucked. "Yes, I'm pushing it, … but it definitely has that feeling."

"Good enough," Simon replied. "I'll see you a bit later, when I stop by the office then." And, with that, he ended the call.

He looked down at his phone and smiled. It was the first time she'd allowed him to deliver food. Now the questions were, how much should he deliver, and what kind of food should he bring?

Smiling at being given something to do that allowed him to help Kate, and, since he was at a dead end on all these other avenues, he headed back into work.

As he took another couple steps, Peter broke through with a wistful tone and shared, *I really liked that puppy.*

"I'm glad you had the puppy," Simon replied. "Sometimes animals can be our best friends."

*I really wanted that puppy,* he murmured.

Sensing something was going on here that could be important, Simon asked, "What happened with that puppy?"

And, with that, Peter disappeared. Up and gone, just like that.

Sighing in frustration, not knowing what was going on or whether it was an issue or not, Simon forged ahead into his work, hoping there would be no more interruptions. That way he could finish off his day, even as his mind was occupied by trying to figure out what to order in—in terms of dinner for Kate. By the time he'd finished and was headed back home again, he realized how late it was already.

He frowned and then decided that maybe a selection of pasta from Mama Rosa's would be the answer. Solid, filling, and, if more people were there in the station, working late, it would feed Kate and her team quite nicely because Mama's portions were always so generous. He quickly picked up the phone, talked to Mama, and explained what he wanted to do. She told him to come by in about twenty minutes.

That was another reason he went with her. She was always there, always available, and always willing to go the extra mile to make things happen. He had to appreciate that about a business owner.

When he stopped in right on time, he wasn't surprised to find three large boxes of food waiting for him.

"I can help you out to the car," she suggested immediately.

He smiled. "I won't say no. Otherwise this would take a couple trips."

"It's a good thing you're bringing this for Kate," Mama stated, giving him a brilliant smile. "I know she'll be too busy working. She's always too busy working,"

He smiled at her. "She is, indeed, which is why I'm delivering food," he shared. "Hopefully she will stop and take a few minutes to eat it."

Mama looked at him askance. "Surely she won't let it go to waste."

"Oh no," he clarified, "but, when things start to break in her line of work, things can get really wild."

Mama nodded. "We won't ever forget her and what she did for our family."

He nodded at that, knowing Kate would say she had only done her job, but, to these people, the family of a victim, it was going that extra mile. He quickly settled up the bill, realizing she hadn't charged a fraction of what this was actually worth, so he added a very hefty tip to help cover the loss. She didn't even look at the receipt, immediately handing Simon one of the boxes. Then, with Henri's help, they got everything out to the vehicle, and Simon immediately drove to the police station.

As he got inside, he saw Colby talking excitedly with somebody. He looked up as Simon walked by with one of the big boxes and said, "Kate's in an interview room at the moment."

He nodded. "She told me that it would probably be a late night, and, guessing she's probably not eaten all day, I brought in some food. Since the rest of you probably haven't eaten much either, I brought enough for everybody."

"For everybody?" Rodney asked, as he hopped to his feet, rubbing his tummy. "I swear to God my stomach feels as if my throat was cut."

He chuckled. "I'm sure you're not alone in that feeling," he noted, with a smile. "Let's see if we can rectify that a little bit."

And with that, he asked Colby, "Is there a place I can put all this stuff? I have two more boxes in the car."

Colby's eyebrows shot up. He eyed the first box and shrugged. "Let's put it all in the conference room that we're not using at the moment." Colby led the way to the room, where Simon could lay it all out. With that done, he and Rodney headed back out to Simon's car, grabbed the second and third boxes. Simon muttered, "I never even thought to get paper plates."

"It's all right," Rodney said. "We've got some."

"Good," Simon murmured. They both set down the boxes in the conference room. Simon stepped back and nodded. "That should keep you all fed for a little bit."

Rodney looked over at him. "You really do care about her, don't you?"

He faced Rodney and nodded. "I really do. She's like no

one I've ever met before. She's really special."

"Yeah, we've never seen anything like her around here before either," Rodney stated, with a laugh. "She's definitely a new experience for this office."

"On the other hand," Lilliana added, as she came in, her nose deciphering the contents of the containers, "Kate's been hell on wheels and has done a damn-fine job for the department. It took us a bit to get her integrated into the team, but we're there now."

Simon nodded. "Yeah, that team dynamics thing is always a challenge, but, once you're there, once everybody knows what's required, then trust begins to develop, so it just keeps getting better."

"That's the plan," she agreed, with a nod, "especially if you'll keep bringing food. I'm guessing, looking at the quantity, that it's for all of us, because I can't see Kate eating this much."

"It's for everybody," Simon confirmed. "I won't ever just feed one."

She laughed. "Kate does say that you enjoy feeding her."

"She never eats," he muttered, with a wave of his hand. "I figure half the time she just forgets, and the other half she's just too tired and can't be bothered."

"I understand that too," Lilliana replied. "We have lots of days where we just go home and crash."

He nodded. "I'm just trying to make those go-home-and-crash days a whole lot less stressful." Then he smiled and added, "I understand she's in the midst of an interview, so I won't stick around."

"Are you sure?" she asked, eyeing him. "She would probably like to see you."

"Maybe, but she might not like to see all this." Lilliana's

eyebrows shot up as she stared at him. Simon explained, "I think my largesse tends to embarrass her at times."

Lilliana snorted. "Kate's welcome to be embarrassed. I'm too damn hungry to care," she admitted, as she reached for a plate. "Honest to God …"

Just then, Kate walked out into the hallway, talking to somebody.

He turned, looked at her, and smiled. "Hey, dinner is here."

She stopped, blinking as if not quite comprehending. Just then her stomach growled as the aroma of the food reached her.

He burst out laughing. "Seems I'm right on time."

She groaned. "I am hungry, but they just picked up my stepfather."

"Good." Simon pointed to the food. "Time to grab a few bites before they get here. Besides, don't you want to let him stew for a bit?" When she hesitated, he raised an eyebrow and added, "It's from Mama's."

"Of course it is," she muttered, as she walked closer, her nose immediately sniffing the containers. "Good God." She stopped in shock at sight of all the food in the conference room. "Think you brought enough?"

"I'm not sure," he admitted. "How many people are we feeding?" he asked her curiously. "I never had a good understanding of how many are here."

She stared at him and shrugged. "We are short two at the moment. So me, Rodney, Lilliana, and Colby. That's just my team. I don't know how many others are around tonight. Yet it's your money, and you can spend it however you like."

"Exactly," he replied comfortably. "Now, would you

grab a plate and eat at least a little, before Ken arrives and you lose your appetite?"

"I hear you've met him," Lilliana noted.

"Yeah, I've met him twice now," Simon replied, with a nod. "The first time at the restaurant with Kate to get her to recant. Then the second time when he came to my apartment building to convince me to encourage Kate to recant her testimony. As you heard in the recording, Ken threatened both Kate and her mother... and me."

Kate froze, turned, and looked at him. "Does any of this affect you?"

"No," he stated, staring at her. "Why would it? Your stepfather is an asshole and a bully," he noted nonchalantly. "I've got nothing to do with that."

She gave him a bright smile. "Good. I would hate to think he could impact our relationship."

"Oh no, I can mess that up just fine on my own," Simon admitted cheerfully, "particularly if this Peter character doesn't stop contacting me."

He didn't realize his voice had carried so much, but, when he looked around, Rodney and Lilliana edged closer to them.

"What did you get?" Lilliana asked.

Simon shrugged. "Not a whole lot, nothing really useful. It's just ... I was trying to get Peter to remember more. So I told Peter that he needed to think, to spend a little bit of time trying to remember what happened to him, if he had any idea. I told him anything could help, and that brought me back to the note that Kate got, telling her to think, and that added pressure on the *think* part. Anyway Peter kept trying to *think*, yet complained how hard it was. He mostly checked in to say that he was still thinking, then he would disappear. This happened a few times, yet I never got enough to do something with," he explained.

"Then today he mentioned a puppy. He really wanted to play with a puppy, but he was allergic. I confirmed that with Peter's aunt. Still, the mother had broken down under the kid's insistence and had gotten a puppy from a neighbor or somebody close by. However, as expected, due to Peter's allergies, they had to get rid of the puppy, which is all Peter remembers."

"So, that memory was traumatic enough that it came through," Lilliana noted.

They all stared at Simon, and he shrugged. "Right, so useless then." Smelling the food, he put an arm around Kate, and they walked over to the table. He grabbed two plates, gave one to Kate, and shared, "I might as well eat while I'm here," he muttered. He served himself a big plate, made sure Kate did too, while the others stood around, talking.

"I guess we don't have anything on Peter yet, right?" Lilliana asked Kate.

Kate nodded. "He wasn't at the school at pickup time and there's no evidence he walked home from the neighbors' statements." Kate's tone was subdued. "Unfortunately it happens far too often."

Simon thought about it and nodded. "Especially if he wasn't close to his house, so nobody would have been on the lookout for him, maybe wouldn't even recognize him. So nobody would have noticed. It just would have been a case of turning around to wonder where Peter was, and, by then, it was already too late."

"Exactly," Lilliana confirmed. "I've been looking into it a little bit, and I put Reese on it to see if she could come up with anything. There were no other cases that we know of back then, two years ago. Peter just literally disappeared."

"And when you said there are no other cases ..." Simon began.

"There was nothing to connect him to any other case, at least not until we find the body and get DNA or something like that," she explained hesitantly, glancing at Kate, who was ignoring them, sitting off to the side, eating, yet half listening. "We don't have anything. Usually we have some eyewitness accounts, but don't even have those in the case of Peter."

"So, nobody saw anything ... as usual," Rodney added.

Lilliana nodded. "Exactly, which makes it even harder on everybody."

Simon sighed. "It always makes me wonder, even more so as I've learned from Kate, just how unaware people can be of what goes on around them."

"And yet it's not so much that they're unaware, as their attention gets pulled away, often by design by the predator," Rodney stepped in to add. "So, it's not that the eyewitnesses don't know. It's that they've been deliberately misdirected, and it's all over with so fast that nobody saw anything."

"Still sad," Simon murmured.

"As you should know," Lilliana noted.

"I do know," he agreed, "and it just seems to be a never-ending problem."

"It is a never-ending problem," Lilliana confirmed, "and, yes, before you ask, I did check into the police reports on all known pedophiles in the area, and they were checked. Everybody was interviewed, and nothing popped. There didn't appear to be anything to go on."

Kate shrugged, listening in to the conversation but not speaking up. She was eating though, so that was good.

"What would be required on something like that?" Simon asked. "I mean, just because these guys register as sex offenders, what does it mean when you say they were checked?"

"We don't talk to them," Lilliana replied, "because we're not part of that division. We may get pulled in, if it's connected to another case. However, in something like this, the police do a full search, looking for the boy. They'll contact every registered pedophile in the area. They'll talk to the neighbors. They'll do a full scout of the nearby area. They'll check street cameras, as well as cameras in the neighborhood. In this case, it was a small residential street, and they didn't end up with anything to go on. So it just becomes something that's always there, always in the background, but never really strong enough to follow up on, not until something changes."

She added, "To sideline a case is one of the hardest things for us, especially when we have another possible child abduction. However, until we have further information—which all too often is finding the body—we don't have a whole lot else we can go on."

Rodney nodded. "The sad fact is that, on any number of given days, we may have any number of killings and child abductions that are never solved. While all that is something we're constantly trying to improve on, it's damn hard if the family and the neighborhood aren't aware, and the child just disappears."

Lilliana muttered, "Very much like Kate's brother. One moment he was there, and the next he was gone."

Simon nodded. "And now Ken Reeves has mentioned Timmy getting into a vehicle."

"Which is now the second person to reference a vehicle,"

Rodney stated, turning to face Simon. "Wouldn't it be nice if Ken had told us whose vehicle it was all those years ago?"

"Ken told me it was a neighbor," Simon noted.

Lilliana nodded. "I checked Timmy's file on that. The cops back then spoke to the neighbors, but nothing came up. Apparently the closest neighbor went to pick up his own kids and went home. Period."

Simon just nodded at that.

Rodney sighed. "So, until something else turns up to the contrary, we have to believe him."

Lilliana clarified, "We don't have to believe the neighbor, but we do need a legitimate reason not to. If he's home with his kids, it's pretty hard for him to sit there with Timmy and lie about it. Plus, his kids were interviewed, and they didn't say anything about Kate's brother being there with them."

"Right," Rodney said, "and unlikely they would lie. Kids are far more likely to tell the truth."

Lilliana nodded. "That's another thing we could check. Those kids are adults now. Let me see if I can contact them and can double-check their references on that. It may have already been done, but I'm not sure I've seen a report saying it was completed." With that, Lilliana took her plate and disappeared into the bullpen.

"I guess this is constant for you guys, isn't it?" Simon asked Colby, now taking a seat beside Simon, ready to dig into the food.

"It is constant," Colby said, with a nod. "One day it's good. The next day may not be so good, but all we can do is keep working the cases. We do solve a lot of them, and, since Kate came on board, we've solved even more than our usual number. And since *you* have come on board," he added, with a smirk in Simon's direction, "I admit those numbers have stayed high."

"I wouldn't say that I was doing anything helpful," he muttered. "It seems, more often than not, what I offer is *less than* helpful."

"It certainly makes us go around in circles," Colby conceded. "And we can't ever use it for evidence, but, if it gives us a lead, a thread to follow, a direction to head in, that's a whole different story."

Simon nodded. "If I were to suggest something about Peter, I would say go back to where that puppy was."

"And do what?" Kate asked, turning to face him.

"I don't know. … All I can tell you is that the puppy is what's so concerning for Peter."

"The puppy or being with the puppy?" she asked.

"Both. I can't say any more than that because Peter didn't say any more than that."

# CHAPTER 21

KATE WATCHED FROM the doorway of a nearby office, as her stepfather was brought in to the station and taken right to an interview room. He looked at her and snorted. "Of course you hauled me in. What a joke. It's not as if I'll get a fair shake with you around."

She smiled and shrugged. "Got nothing to do with me. I'm not the one who had you brought in."

"No, of course not," he said in a mocking tone. "You always protect your friends, don't you?"

She eyed him for one long moment. "No, I can't say that I do." Then storming in right behind him and cussing him out was her mother. Kate winced. "Especially on days like today." She stepped into the hallway and watched as both were taken to different interview rooms. Colby stepped up beside her. "I know," she said. "I can't go in and talk to either of them."

"No, you can't," he agreed, "but I would suggest that maybe you watch from the adjoining room."

"I would very much like to watch," she said. "I can't stop thinking that maybe, just maybe, they aren't telling me something about my brother."

"It's possible," Colby replied. "Just remember I can't have you active in this one."

She nodded, then looked for Simon. He leaned against

the door jamb, still eating the food he'd brought in. "What about Simon? Can he come and listen?" she asked her boss.

Colby considered her and then nodded. "I don't see anything wrong with that."

"Good," Then she walked over to Simon. "Do you want to sit in and watch?"

Surprised, he nodded. "The actual interview?"

"Yeah, we'll be in the other room," she noted. "We'll see and hear, but they won't see or hear us."

"Perfect," Simon replied. "It'll give me a chance to see what Ken's saying."

With that, she led the way, realizing that his plate was now empty. Taking care of that for him, she then led him into another room.

"How do you think this will go?" Simon asked.

"No idea, and I'm not sure what Colby's planning on doing," she shared. "Again I'm not allowed into that aspect of it."

"And I'm sure that's hurting you."

"I don't know that it's hurting me," she clarified, shaking her head. "It's frustrating to not have all the info. Yet I'm still trying to deal with the whole idea that my parents—who I've been away from for all these years—are both right here, sitting in the box right now," she muttered. "You go through so much in life and think everything is good, that you've handled it and that you should be fine. Then, all of a sudden, you're not fine at all, and you're not sure why or how to handle it. So, I'm just doing what I can do. If I can't handle it, then I guess I won't. I'll just find something else to do while this is all happening," she murmured.

"You'll be fine," Simon reassured her. "So let's watch and see what happens."

"They'll be a little bit, getting organized and started," she explained. "Let's grab a coffee first."

"Do you want popcorn too?" he teased.

At that, she chuckled. "At times around here that seems like a hell of a good idea," she admitted, with a big smile.

"I'm not against it," Simon declared, "but I never thought to bring any."

"You brought a ton of food, so that will do," she said, looking at him. "I wasn't expecting you to feed everyone."

"Of course you weren't," he replied, with a smile, "and clearly neither were they."

"No, they wouldn't have been. However, you were right. Everybody appreciates it. We were all hungry."

"Good." He gave her a warm smile. "I'm glad that it will get eaten."

"Have you taken a look lately?" she asked. "I'm not sure how much is even left now from what you brought."

"It doesn't matter," he said. "As long as it is eaten, and you got fed, it's all good."

She just nodded. With coffee in hand, they walked into the empty room. "Sorry, we don't generally keep chairs in here."

"That's fine." Simon stood in front of the big window. "I always knew there was a space back here just like this."

"Yeah, there sure is. Most people think these viewing rooms are made up for the movies, but it really is a thing."

"Interesting. I've learned a lot hanging out with you," he said, wrapping an arm around her shoulders.

"Not necessarily the greatest things to learn though," she murmured.

"But not bad either," he added, with a smile. "It's knowledge, and all knowledge is helpful."

"I keep trying to say that to people, but it doesn't always come across the right way."

"You just keep being you and let everybody else adjust."

She frowned at him, then shrugged. "I'm as much *me* as anybody can probably handle."

He looked at her with a big grin on his face. "That wouldn't surprise me in the least."

Just then Rodney walked into the interview room, identified himself, and told her stepfather that the interview would be recorded. At that, her stepfather lunged across the table and was forcibly restrained, then reseated by the two uniformed policemen in the room. Rodney straightened up his clothes, then sat down, glaring at Ken. "I'll remember that," he stated. "Nice to know that's how you handle being interviewed."

"I don't need to be here at all," he snarled. "That bitch of a daughter of mine set this up."

Rodney studied him. "Why would she do that?"

"She wants me back in prison and out of her life. She's the one who sent me away in the first place."

"Funny, I thought the jury did that," Rodney noted.

"Based on her testimony," he snapped. "It's not my fucking fault she's just a little whining bitch, but no doubt you already know that."

Kate listened to him in disbelief. "Good God," she muttered, a bit unnerved. "No matter what the situation is, it's just not smart to go off and to run your mouth like that, not when you're being interviewed by the police," she muttered. "Jesus, it's like these suspects need coaching."

Simon turned to face her and asked, "Do you really want them to get coaching?"

"No, but he's just working against himself, when he

keeps opening his mouth and shoving his foot in."

"Good," Simon stated. "Let's hope he has a size twelve."

She smiled at that and then focused as her stepfather just let the poison flow from his mouth. She listened intently, hoping he would spill something that mattered, not just venting his frustration at having spent all those years in prison. But, at the end of the interview, all he ended up spouting was garbage.

It was the typical lament. *Poor me. I've had a raw deal. Nobody appreciates what I've done for the world and how good I am.* All a giant load of BS.

About twenty minutes later, Rodney stepped into the room where she and Simon were. "Well?" he asked her.

She shrugged. "Absolutely nothing was helpful in there, not anything concerning my brother. Now that he's spewed all that, you need to hit him up about the drugs comment that Simon recorded."

Rodney nodded. "By the way, we just got more forensics back. His vehicle was searched, and they definitely found drugs of the exact same kind in the trunk."

She frowned at him. "I suggest you go see what he has to say about that."

Rodney smiled. "Yeah, will do, but I want to let him stew for a bit. So I'll move over to your mom first." He looked at Kate hesitantly, and she nodded.

"Great idea. Go."

With a stiff nod, he disappeared, and she looked over at Simon. "We can go watch that as well."

She led Simon to the second room where they could see her mom sitting there, nervously chewing on her fingernails. Kate sighed. "She's done that for as long as I can remember."

Simon sighed. "No matter what's gone on in her life, I

don't imagine any of it's been easy for her."

"No, it sure hasn't," Kate agreed, crossing her arms over her chest. "But then there's my brother, and it hasn't exactly been easy on him either."

As soon as Rodney walked in, her mom looked over at him and said, "I don't want Kate in here."

"Kate won't be coming in here," Rodney confirmed immediately. "She has nothing to do with this."

Kate watched her mom physically relax. "Jesus, did you see that? Apparently I'm some hideous person to her."

"What you are is a reminder," Simon clarified. "A reminder that she can't handle the truth."

Kate nodded. "Yeah, I'm sure you're right."

Then she listened in stunned silence, hearing her mother completely meltdown over Ken and his coercions. Kate listened as her mother described how Ken had contacted her from the prison, insisting that she send a message to Kate. She didn't want anything to do with it, so she paid a kid to deliver it to the police department. She'd known Kate was here, had followed her career over the last several years, and was fully aware that Kate had become a cop, which had alienated her even further.

"Christ," Kate muttered, as she listened to that.

Realizing that her daughter was still trying to find her brother made Selene feel good, yet she felt Kate's actions were more about guilt. Kate listened in stunned fury as her mother went on about how it was Kate's fault that her brother went missing in the first place.

Rodney just let her talk most of the time. When she took a breath, he shared, "Your husband said Timmy got into a vehicle, potentially a neighbor's vehicle."

At that, she stopped and stared at Rodney. "What?"

"Your husband Ken said that Timmy got into a vehicle driven by a neighbor."

She stared at him for a long moment. "If that's the case, why in the hell didn't he say something back then?" And then she frowned. "I didn't even know he was there."

"He was there. It was few days before his trial," Rodney explained, "and he was out on bail."

"Yeah, I don't know how he paid for that either. Drugs most likely."

"So, he's busy with the drugs, *huh*?"

"It's the only way he ever got any money," Selene noted, "and then he would keep me hooked on the drugs so I would help him." She threw her arms down on the table, exposing the needle marks.

Selene had such a despondent look on her face and such a telling body language that Kate didn't have anything to say.

"And what about these drugs he's peddling now?"

"Yeah, they're deadly," she muttered, "and I don't want anything to do with them."

"And yet he's selling them?"

She nodded. "Yeah, but he's doing something to them first."

Kate sucked in her breath at that. "Oh good God."

Selene continued. "He's the one cutting some other crap into them. He told me that it would make them go farther, so he'd get more money out of it."

Rodney nodded. "Did you ever see him do it, cutting the drugs?"

"Yes, I … he did it at home for a while," she shared, looking around nervously. "I mean, until Kate came by. I told him that I would tell her and that I didn't want anything to do with it. And that's when he stuck a needle in my arm and told me to shut the fuck up," she shared. "He's always been very physically violent, so when he says shut up, I better shut up," she muttered.

"And is that why you shut up about your son all those years ago?"

She looked at him and said, "I had nothing to do with it. That was my boy who went missing," she whispered, staring at him.

"And what about Ken's trial?"

"I didn't go. Honestly, Kate did me a favor. He was abusive as hell."

"Did you believe her?"

She again stared at Rodney. "I don't know whether I believed her or not. I didn't care either way because, as long as she was telling that story, I was getting rid of him. And I really needed to get rid of him."

Hearing that, Kate sucked in her breath.

Rodney asked, "So, you didn't go to the trial then?"

"No, and I wasn't called as a witness."

"Do you know why?"

"I was deemed unreliable."

Kate winced at that. "Of course. Why am I not surprised," she muttered to herself.

Simon wrapped an arm around her, holding her close. She listened as her mother spouted more falsehoods about Kate being responsible for her brother's disappearance.

"How is it you figure that a seven-year-old child is responsible for the loss of somebody who was probably targeted by an adult? And why is it that you never seemed to think your ex-husband could have done it?"

She frowned at him. "No, Ken wouldn't have done that. He might have stayed quiet about it," she conceded, "but he wouldn't have done it," she declared. Then she dropped a bombshell. "Ken liked girls, young girls."

"You mean young girls, like Kate's age when she was seven?"

She stared at him and nodded. "Yeah, Kate's age of young girls."

"And you never put a stop to it?"

"*She* put a stop to it," Selene declared, a bit too forcefully. "She went and called the fucking cops, which was the last thing we needed at the time. But, like I told you, I don't hold it against her because it got rid of him, and I really needed to get rid of him."

"And what about protecting your daughter?"

She shook her head. "She protected herself. She was always good at that. The fucking cops never looked at her for her brother, even though I kept telling everybody to take a look at her."

"And what is it you think Kate did?"

"I don't know what she did. Conked him over the head and dropped him in the river for all I know."

Rodney sat back, struggling to keep a neutral expression on his face.

Kate understood how he felt. This was so not the kind of childhood Rodney would want for anybody, and to hear her mother say those things was difficult for them all.

Rodney continued the questioning for a little bit longer. "So, in terms of your ex and the drugs ..."

"What about it?" she asked. "I want to get as far away from that man as I can."

"But you've seen him adding something to the drugs?"

"Yes, I told you that," she snapped.

"And will you testify to that in court?"

"Hell no," she stated instantly. "No way, and your people will ensure that doesn't happen."

"Why is that?"

"Because if you try to make me, I'll go up there and testify about your bloody cop buddy doing something to her brother to get rid of him instead."

Kate didn't know when the shakes started, but, somewhere along the line, she realized Simon had his arms wrapped tightly around her, holding her and whispering, "It's okay. It's okay. She can't touch you anymore."

She looked up at him with tears in her eyes. "I was seven."

"I know," he whispered. "And this is her way of coping, because if she can keep blaming you, she doesn't take on the responsibility herself."

"I didn't do anything to him. I didn't."

Simon nodded, giving her a kiss on the forehead. "Honey, I know that. Everybody knows that. And we will find answers, somehow, somewhere. We'll figure it out, though it doesn't seem as if we'll get much for answers here."

"Except for the vehicle," she said. "I need to sort that out."

"And we will," he confirmed immediately, "just maybe not right now."

She faced him and let her breath out. "No, not right now. Dear God," she muttered. "Who knows how many people my stepfather has killed with his drug dealing."

"That's another thing," Simon noted. "If it's a homicide, it comes to you, right?"

"Yes, to our unit," she agreed, "but everything doesn't get flagged as a potential homicide. Overdoses and unattended deaths wouldn't normally get flagged, especially for known drug users. Now we'll have to run a check and see if there are any other potential cases," she explained, "and that'll be a whole different scenario."

"Understood, but the thing to remember is how this wasn't about you. In many ways, you've solved other problems and prevented other deaths."

She snorted. "I don't know about that, but I'll take any good news right now."

KATE HEADED TO her desk, seeing Colby was here with them.

He looked up and frowned when he saw her.

"I'm fine," Kate declared. "However, it appears that my stepfather is the one who's been mixing up these designer drugs that likely killed the little boy, the teenager, plus God-only-knows who else. What we don't know is where he got them from." She turned to Lilliana and said, "We need to find out from my stepfather if he recognizes the teen victim and the five-year-old's uncle."

Lilliana quickly printed copies of the photos and walked back into the interview room. She came out a few minutes later, her face grim. "Yeah, Ken's apparently been dealing with Sammy, the brother-in-law, for years, running a small operation from prison and now bigger since getting out— maybe even before he went in prison, although the brother-in-law would have been pretty young at that point. Anyway, Ken said Sammy knew the teenager. Told him that it would help him do better in school, all that BS they tell kids to get them started using. So, it wasn't suicide, but it was self-administered, ... thinking it would help him."

"But instead it ended his life," Kate muttered, shaking

her head.

"Yes," Lilliana agreed. "Ken doesn't seem to understand that two people are dead from it or that he has any culpability. He's just pissed that he might wind up back in prison on a drug-dealing charge."

"Yeah, he doesn't know the half of it. How about the other charges, considering the fact that this concoction he's been mixing up is a very potent killing machine?"

"It will be up to the DA to sort out the charges, but Ken won't see the light of day again," Lilliana vowed. "So, good job on that one."

"I'm sure my mother would agree, but she refuses to testify against him. She's probably still in there, spouting all kinds of poison."

Lilliana nodded. "I stopped in there for a few minutes to see if she knew either of them. She recognized Sammy, the brother-in-law. She apparently saw him when he came to pick up drugs just this last week."

Kate shook her head. "Christ. Talk about deaths that didn't need to be deaths."

"And yet nothing about your brother, except that your stepfather still says that Timmy got into a vehicle. He thought it was the neighbor's, but maybe it wasn't the neighbor's. He said it looked like the neighbor's. And, when we asked him what kind of vehicle, he said whatever vehicle that Larry dude was driving, it was that one."

Kate stopped and stared. "Larry? I've heard that name before, but I don't know where." She walked over to the case files, pulled it up, and said, "Larry was the neighbor that people said was driving the car, but he was home, with his own kids, having picked them up at school. He was driving a Ford Escort. And it was"—she flipped through the file—

"red, a red Ford Escort. So, maybe somebody else also drives a red Ford Escort. How many of those would have been at that school at that time?" Kate asked, staring at Lilliana.

"I don't know, but we can ask Reese to have her assistants pull those records. What do you want to do?" Lilliana asked.

Kate shook her head. "I kind of want to tear apart the neighborhood."

"We've already cleared Larry," Lilliana noted, "and we've talked to him since, and we've talked to the kids. Nothing. They didn't see that child at all."

"So, we have another vehicle to run down, but from many years ago."

"Right," Lilliana agreed, "but we can, and we will. Obviously we'll follow up to see if there is anything to be found. … The only thing I can tell you is that, after such a long time—"

"I know," Kate whispered. "I know exactly what that means. This might be over for Timmy, but it doesn't mean it's over for my mother and my stepfather," she muttered. "Make sure you charge them with whatever you can."

"In your mother's case, I don't think there'll be any charges," she suggested.

Kate hated the sense of relief that washed over her when she heard that. She looked over at Lilliana. "Any particular reason?"

"I think, with the stepfather and all, Selene may have been as much a victim as anybody."

"Maybe," She shook her head. "Whatever. I'll leave it up to the DA to make those determinations."

"Good," Lilliana said. "It looks as if we pretty well have these current deaths dealt with."

"Maybe, but not my brother."

Lilliana sighed and nodded. "No, that was your stepfather forcing your mother to drop off the message at the station, setting all this in motion."

"The same asshole who made things so miserable for—"

"That's because he knew what chain to yank," Lilliana reminded her. "And he's still trying for it now."

Rodney stepped into the bullpen. "He wants to make a deal, he says." Rodney looked at Kate. "He's trying to make a deal."

"Yeah, and what's the deal?" she asked, frowning.

"He says he has more information on what happened to your brother."

She took in a deep breath, then forced it out. "What do you think?"

"I think he's lying," Rodney declared. "I think he's finally realized that the charges this time will be a whole lot more serious than just selling drugs and that he probably won't ever get out of jail." He looked back at the room where Ken was sequestered. "That's a hell of a stepfather you had there."

"No," she argued, "he's a hell of an asshole. There's never been any fathering involved. My mom sure knew how to pick 'em."

"Makes you wonder why she married him."

"Yeah, well, sometimes I've wondered if she ever did or not. Was it a legal marriage, a common law situation, or just another one of the little things that they lied about?"

"I don't know if it matters to you either way."

"It does not," she confirmed. "He never adopted me, so it's not part of my world. As far as I'm concerned, he can just go back to prison and rot there."

Rodney nodded and turned to leave. "We're taking him

downstairs now and will escort him to the jail and get him booked in."

"Good. I want to be in the hallway when he passes through." Kate was already headed into the main hallway.

Rodney hesitated and added, "It might set him off."

She shrugged. "I'm not too bothered about that, are you?"

"No, not particularly," he said, "but I'm not sure that the boss man will like it."

She winced at that. "You're right. Colby wouldn't like it. Fine." But, just as she said that, the door to the interview room opened, and Ken was led out and walked right by her anyway.

She smiled at him and waved. "Have a nice life."

He lost it then and threw himself at her, his hands going around her neck in a quick movement that surprised everybody except Kate because she'd been waiting for this. In fact, she had been training for this for decades. She immediately picked him up backward, flipped him over her head, and slammed him to the ground. As he bounced back to his feet, Kate slammed her knee into his groin. Then, as he started to fall, she went in with an undercut that dropped him faster than anything.

Out cold.

She stepped back, looked down at him, and nodded. "You have no idea how happy I am that you decided to go after me."

Colby stood there, his hands on his hips.

Kate beamed with joy. "It was self-defense, completely self-defense."

Colby rolled his eyes and nodded. "Absolutely. I saw him attack you with my own eyes."

She looked over at the cops escorting Ken and asked them, "Think you can hang on to him this time?"

"Uh, yeah. Looks as if he might need medical attention," said one of the cops.

Colby snorted. "That's not happening. If nothing's broken, he's going right back to a jail cell. Get him out of here." And, with that, they quickly picked him up and took him away.

Kate sat down at her desk, feeling like a huge load was off her chest. "I know that nothing is sorted and that nothing is over," she said, "and I don't know why I feel so much better, but I do. That guy has been a boogeyman from my past since forever, and honestly discovering he was out had me rattled more than I realized," she admitted, with a shrug. "Just knowing that he's headed back to prison to stay this time is huge."

"Not to mention he won't be tainting the drugs and killing people with them," Lilliana added.

Kate nodded. "That'll be a rough one. I'm sure we'll find out many more have died from his drugs."

"What about Andrew's case against Adam and Sammy?" Lilliana asked Colby.

"The brother-in-law has just been brought into the interview room C," Colby noted, as he looked down at his watch and winced. "It'll be a late night."

"Yes, it'll be a late night, but we can wrap this one up too," Lilliana declared, and just then she walked to the holding cell to speak to the corrections officer stationed there. "Bring up both the parents too."

"I already let the mom go home," Kate shared. "I'll call her when this is over."

Sammy was brought into the same interview room her

stepfather had been in. And, with Lilliana at her side, Kate walked in and held up a picture of her stepfather. "Do you know him?"

He looked at it, winced, then nodded. "Yeah, he's a dealer."

"Yeah? He was taking the drugs you were buying and cutting them with something else that was killing people," she explained, staring him down. "The problem with that is, you left the drugs out, and your little nephew licked it up, didn't he?"

He closed his eyes, and the tears leaked out and trickled down his face. He nodded slowly. "Yes, God help me, … yes."

"And then what? You just put him in his bed?"

"I did. I did," And he started to sob. "I didn't know what he'd done, and I still don't know why he did that," he cried out. "I can't believe it. I'm not around little kids very much," he said between gulping back his tears. "It never occurred to me that he would touch it."

"He's a little kid, and it looks like sugar," Kate explained. "That is absolutely something a kid will touch."

He nodded, wiping the snot off his nose with his sleeve. "What'll happen now?"

She shrugged. "A child is dead, and somebody will be held accountable for that. Ultimately the DA looks at the information we collect and makes a decision on charges. Yet I don't understand one thing. You had the drugs there at your brother's house, but, when we tested you, we didn't find any in your system. How do you explain that?"

"No, I was just setting it up. Then honest to God, my girlfriend called, and we had a hell of a fight on the phone. When I turned back around, they were everywhere, and the kid was on the floor."

She nodded. "And that's why you're alive today," she declared. "We have another young man who also died from this, a young man you sold drugs to." She brought up the picture of the teen.

Sammy stared at the photo. "Jesus, what do you mean, *I* sold?"

She stopped him. "We already know you sold him the drugs."

He sank to the floor. "Oh my God, oh my God," he muttered. "My life is over."

She stared at him. "Nice of you to be worried about your life after not giving a shit about everybody else."

He stared at her. "But I didn't mean to kill him."

She shrugged. "No, maybe not, but he's still dead. And his mother took the rest of the drugs he had and deliberately overdosed because she couldn't stand the idea of living without her son. There are definitely consequences here. The DA will have the final say on the charges, and we'll go from there." Then she smiled at Lilliana. "Unless you want to lay it out so Sammy knows what to expect."

"Oh it's likely to be manslaughter, child abuse, child endangerment. There's possession and dealing, plus dealing a potentially lethal substance," Lilliana explained, looking over at Sammy.

He just stared at her, and his facial expression was void of any emotions. It was as if he had completely checked out of life.

Kate sighed. "Wait until your sister-in-law finds you."

He looked at her, wild-eyed. "Jesus, keep her away from me."

"Why?" she asked bitterly. "Doesn't she deserve to know

what happened to her son? The son you were supposed to be looking after? All you had to do was watch him for a few hours, without any drugs around."

"I know. I know. I just didn't think. I didn't realize he would get into it."

"Guess what?" Kate said, as she stood up. "Now you'll have plenty of time to think." And, with that, she got up and walked out.

FOR WHATEVER REASON, Simon wasn't quite sure, Kate insisted on going back to her place. Yet when Simon got her there, she sat down on the edge of her bed, silent, unmoving.

"Are you sure you want to stay here tonight?" he asked.

She nodded. "Yeah. I don't really know why, but, yes, I do."

"Fine." He didn't think much of the idea, but, if it was something she wanted or needed somehow, he wouldn't argue. She had a quick shower and crawled into bed, where he wrapped his arms around her, holding her close. It was obvious her mind was still focused, still tormented, by all the events of the day. "You did good," he whispered.

"We got somewhere, somehow," she conceded. "We have a vehicle to track down on my brother's case, which obviously won't be a quick fix now. My stepfather is well on his way back to prison, which I'm stoked about."

"Plus, you got a chance to punch his face in too," he added, with a chuckle.

She twisted to look up at him and smiled. "I did," she exclaimed, with a laugh. "I kind of hate to say it because I'm never really one who believes in violence, but, man, that felt good today."

"You did great," he added.

When the doorbell rang, he looked down at her and asked, "Are you expecting anything?"

"No, I'm sure not." She shook her head, slipped out of bed, and quickly pulled on a few pieces of clothing.

He watched as she pulled out her service revolver too. "Hey, hey, hey," he whispered.

She held up her fingers. "This time I don't need your warning."

He immediately saw pictures of her falling down, bullets riddling her body. He bolted from bed and raced to the door, catching her just as she went to open it. He slammed her to the ground, as the bullets traveled through the door and across the apartment. Then the shooter ran, his footsteps noisy.

# CHAPTER 22

S HE WAS UP and out the door, bolting down the hallway after the shooter in her PJs.

She lifted her handgun, steadied herself for a moment, then put a bullet in the guy's leg. When he dropped to the ground, she raced to him. Sure enough, it was Ken Reeves, her stepfather. "How the hell did you get out of jail?"

"They let me out on bail," he snapped. "I am not without resources."

"Not anymore," she declared, as she pulled out her phone and called for backup. Within minutes the place was swarming with cops, preparing to haul him away again.

She looked down at him. "That'll be the last time you ever get that chance."

He swore at her. "Don't be so sure," he snapped. "I'll be out and free in no time. Just wait and see."

"No, you won't," she argued, "and, if you do, you can bet on one thing."

"What's that?" he snapped, as they wheeled him away, handcuffed to a gurney.

"I'll be here waiting." When she finally walked back inside her apartment, she sagged against the wall and slipped down to the floor, where Simon immediately joined her.

"You okay?" he asked.

"I'm not sure I would call it okay. It just feels ..." Then

she smiled. "It feels like maybe it's over."

"Good," he said.

Her phone rang, and it was Lilliana.

"Are you okay?"

Kate snorted. "Not exactly sure. What time is it?"

"It's about six," Lilliana said. "I got the alert of what was happening and just came into work." Then she hesitated and asked, "Is Simon there with you?"

"Yeah, why?"

"Because something happened last night."

"What?"

Lilliana sighed. "I couldn't let it go, so I stopped off at Peter's family's house and asked where Peter might have gotten the idea that the puppy might still be around to play with, and they pointed out the neighbor who was the one they'd gotten it from. So, I called for backup, and we went to the neighbor's house. Unfortunately Peter was buried in the basement. Forensics is still there. But the old man, when I knocked on the door, he took one look at me, and he started to bawl.

"He swears it was an accident. The old bastard broke and kept repeating that it was an accident and that he didn't mean to do it, but he got angry when Peter was there, wanting to play with the puppy, wanting to take the puppy home. Anyway, he yelled at him, and Peter ran away, but he fell down the stairs and supposedly broke his neck. Not knowing what else to do, he buried him right there in his basement." The fatigue was evident in her tone. "So, I'm at the office now, but I'll go home soon and try to think of something good about today."

"Hey, at least the family will have closure, and considering that's something I don't have right now, I see it as a positive," Kate noted. "I mean, obviously it's not the outcome they wanted, but it is an outcome, and, speaking as family of a missing person, it's something I would dearly love to have."

"We'll get on that one when we get back to the office," Lilliana stated, "but, right now, I think we both need a few days off. These cases with kids are rough."

When Kate hung up, she turned to look at Simon. "So, it really was about the puppy." She smiled at him.

"But not the answer we hoped for."

"No, not the answer we hoped for, but as I told Lilliana, it is an answer, and answers are better than no answers, even if they aren't the answers we're hoping for."

He smiled and nodded. "I know it's winter, and it's cold, but—"

"The boat?" she asked, looking at him hopefully. "Could we even just move in for a few days, just pretend we're off sailing in crazy weather?"

"We can still probably take her out and do something," he suggested, with a smile. "It just might not be quite the same experience."

"It's fine," she replied. "I very much want to get out of here for a while."

"You'll have to deal with your door first. Are you insured?"

"Insured against someone shooting holes in my door? I can't imagine that'll go well with the insurance company." She groaned. "That door is not even safe anymore."

"No, it isn't, and I'm sure the neighbors are wondering when you'll move out."

"I would be happy to move into your boat, but I guess that's not an option."

He chuckled. "No, but I do know another option."

"Yeah, what's that?" she asked, as she glared around at her kitchen. Forensic technicians were still all over it, and everything was a disaster. "Jesus, what a mess." She turned to look at him, a question in her eyes. "What were you saying?"

"This should be obvious, but my place is an option."

She blinked. "Temporarily it is," she conceded. "And I would appreciate that."

He frowned and added, "I was thinking maybe more than temporarily."

She looked at him in surprise, then walked closer and wrapped her arms around him. "Are you asking me to move in with you?"

He cocked his head and asked her, "If I were to ask that, what kind of answer would I get?"

She raised her eyebrows. "I don't know because I haven't heard the question."

He rolled his eyes, cupped her face close to his, and whispered, "Would you be interested in moving in with me? We could always give it a trial and see how it works."

"I'm not the easiest person to live with," she pointed out.

He smiled. "I know."

"I get cranky, plus I'm messy, and I'm on the go all the time."

He smirked and nodded. "I know that too."

She frowned. "So, knowing all that, why would you want anything to do with me?"

He chuckled. "This isn't about our relationship. This is entirely about whether you would be interested in moving in with me."

She sighed and said, "I would love to move in with you,

but ..."

He frowned and stated, "I don't like the buts."

"I know you don't like the buts. Yet I'm just not sure it's a good place for me."

"And why is that? You're quite happy to be there on a regular basis." He stared at her, mischief in his eyes.

"Yes, I am," she agreed, "and I love everything about it. But it's kind of, ... you know, posh."

He snorted. "You do realize that most of my girlfriends wanted to move in precisely because it's posh."

"Yeah, well," she pointed out, "I'm not one of your girl-friends."

"No," he replied, as he pulled her up close. "I under-stand that you don't like this mushy stuff, but I'll tell you anyway. That's one of the reasons I really love you."

"Oh, yeah? What's that?" she asked, her eyes lighting with amusement. "Because I'm not posh and because I don't care about your money?"

"Partly," he agreed, "but also because you're you, and nothing ever changes with that." He leaned down, kissed her, and asked, "Now, do you think we can go someplace and get some sleep?"

"God, yes, please," she muttered, as she grabbed a bag and started packing a few items she would need for a longer stay elsewhere. "Your place?"

He burst out laughing and nodded. "My place it is, es-pecially considering you are off for the next few days and considering it's now"—he looked at his watch and shook his head—"Christmas Eve. Not that you've mentioned it ..."

"I haven't mentioned it because I haven't had two sec-onds," she stated, frowning at him, before taking one last look around her apartment. "We also more or less ignore everything seasonal. So, as long as you were ignoring it, I was okay to ignore it too."

"I just thought that maybe …" He hesitated, staring at her, then said reluctantly, "Maybe we could just spend Christmas on board the *Running Mate*."

She looked at him in delight. "That sounds perfect."

"You'll have to confirm that you aren't involved in another case."

She winced. "I did book some time off, but if something comes up …"

"Right. I understand." He nodded. "Let's just hope that it's all good and that we actually get Christmas off. I know we said that we weren't doing anything about gifts …"

"Don't," she declared, raising her eyebrows in alarm. "I have no idea what I could possibly give somebody who can go out and buy anything he could possibly want."

He laughed. "I wouldn't even know what to give you either," he admitted. "That's out of my realm of experience too."

"What about all your girlfriends?"

"They just wanted expensive jewelry," he noted, with a wave of his hand. "So that was easy."

She blinked, then smiled. "And I don't?" she teased.

He looked at her surprise and said, "No. Hell no. If I bought you diamonds, you would just frown at them and walk away with a shrug."

She burst out laughing. "You're right. So how about instead of Christmas gifts for each other, we do something for somebody else?"

"Like what?" he asked.

"Like maybe work at the shelter, a soup kitchen, maybe the animal shelter or something. We have so much. … So maybe our Christmas should be about giving to others."

He gave her a smile that started in his eyes and took over his whole face. He walked over, pulled her into his arms, and held her close, whispering, "Now that would be perfect. It's a date," he declared, then leaned in and kissed her.


This concludes Book 10 of Kate Morgan:
Simon Says… Think.
Read about Kate Morgan: Simon Says… Fight, Book 11

# Simon Says... Fight: Kate Morgan (Book #11)

Detective Kate Morgan is tasked with determining if a recently discovered body floating in the harbor is the result of a crime and, if not, to move on to one of the team's many other pending cases on their desks. However, nothing is ever simple in her world. So, when she finds several similar cases in the surrounding police districts, ... the scope of her hunt expands proportionally.

However, getting to the bottom of this one crosses into Simon's penchant for revitalizing old buildings in downtown Vancouver—or, in some cases, just giving those structures a whole lot of love.

As Simon warns her several times, he sees both himself and Kate participating in the final fight. Yet it's so much uglier than either of them can imagine.

Find Book 11 here!

To find out more visit Dale Mayer's website.

https://geni.us/DMSSSFight

# Sneak Peek from
# Simon Says... Fight



*First Week of the New Year ...*

KATE WALKED BACK into the office.

Rodney looked up at her and smiled. "You look better. Nothing like taking a week away to help reset your system."

"Yeah, it was a pretty rough for a bit."

"Ken really shot up your apartment, *huh?*"

She nodded. "Yeah, he didn't care. He waited until I got close to opening the door and started blasting. Simon tackled me from behind. As I was headed for the door, he had some vision about my body being riddled with bullets, and, the next thing I know, I'm flat on the ground, and my apartment is being razed with gunfire."

"Jesus," Rodney muttered, his eyes wide in shock. "I guess your stepfather figured that, as long as he was going down, he might as well have something to go down over."

"Maybe," she conceded, staring at him. "It still makes no sense to me. Anyway I very much want things to get back to normal, whatever normal is."

"Around here, *normal* can be all kinds of things, but it's never what we expect it to be," he said, with a smile. "I'm more than happy to have you and Lilliana back."

"Did she take off for the holidays too?"

"She was dragging by the time we got Peter's case dealt with, so she took some days to regroup."

Kate nodded. "Hopefully it'll be calm for a bit."

Rodney smiled. "I could go for calm. Calm for more than a bit would be nice."

"I agree, although evidence to blow my brother's case wide open would be nice."

"Sorry. Everything on Timmy's case was a false trail, which we figured, coming from Ken," Rodney noted.

She nodded. "How about *calm* for a long time?"

"I could get behind that," Rodney agreed. "Yet we've got this case …"

Just then Kate's phone rang. "Morning, Simon. What's up?"

There was an odd tone to his voice as he asked, "Do you guys ever have cases … where fighting is going on?"

"Fighting?" she repeated. "What do you mean by *fighting*? As in husband and wife, domestic kind of violence stuff?"

"No, no, as in an arena for boxers only, … more like underground street fighting."

"I'm sure underground street fighting is going on all the time, especially with people betting on it, but it's rarely something that comes to us. Why?"

"Because I just had one of those really unpleasant visions, with me in the ring, and everybody around was screaming, *Fight, fight, fight.*"

"*Uh-oh,*" she muttered, "often your visions don't mean anything even close to what we think they mean."

"I know," he said, "but I still got the feeling that something really ugly was going on, and it has to do with some fighting. The thing is, Kate, I don't think that any of the people in that ring were there because they wanted to be there. I think they were there because they had no choice. The other weird thing is that it seemed that the *fight, fight, fight* screaming was a recording."

She looked over at Rodney, who was frowning as he listened in on the conversation. "But ..."

Simon replied, "I know. You have nothing to go on, and I don't know that this has anything to do with you guys either."

"In a way, I do though," Rodney interrupted. "I was just going to tell Kate about one of the cases that came in. A body washed up downtown right off the pier where the aquabus lands," he shared. "The body was pummeled pretty good. We haven't got an autopsy on it yet, but one of the guys who pulled the body out of the river said the dead guy had been beaten from head to toe."

"What do we know about the victim?" Kate asked.

"No ID was on the body, and we still haven't figured out who he is, but the coroner did call this morning and said that he had a tentative ID. We're waiting for dental records because there might be teeth left," Rodney added. "The body's that bad. The family reported him missing approximately three days ago. Apparently he's a nice normal businessman, who goes to work every day, comes home to his kids, and all that good stuff. Then one day he just didn't come home, and nobody knew why, but now he's washed up in this condition, and we have no clues. However, maybe thanks to Simon's latest vision, we have an idea at least."

"Yeah, maybe," Kate muttered, staring at Rodney in shock. "Simon, you take care of yourself. Just because it was you in that ring—and often we think it isn't you—that doesn't mean that it can't be you."

"Same for you," Simon declared, "because, I swear to God, somehow I heard your voice in the middle of it." And, with that, he hung up.

Find Book 11 here!
To find out more visit Dale Mayer's website.
https://geni.us/DMSSSFight

# Author's Note

Thank you for reading Simon Says… Think: Kate Morgan, Book 10! If you enjoyed the book, please take a moment and leave a short review.

Dear reader,

I love to hear from readers, and you can contact me at my website: www.dalemayer.com or at my Facebook author page. To be informed of new releases and special offers, sign up for my newsletter or follow me on BookBub. And if you are interested in joining Dale Mayer's Reader Group, here is the Facebook sign up page.
http://geni.us/DaleMayerFBGroup

Cheers,
Dale Mayer

# About the Author

Dale Mayer is a *USA Today* best-selling author, best known for her SEALs military romances, her Psychic Visions series, and her Lovely Lethal Garden cozy series. Her contemporary romances are raw and full of passion and emotion (Broken But … Mending, Hathaway House series). Her thrillers will keep you guessing (Kate Morgan, By Death series), and her romantic comedies will keep you giggling (*It's a Dog's Life*, a stand-alone novella; and the Broken Protocols series, starring Charming Marvin, the cat).

Dale honors the stories that come to her—and some of them are crazy, break all the rules and cross multiple genres!

To go with her fiction, she also writes nonfiction in many different fields, with books available on résumé writing, companion gardening, and the US mortgage system. All her books are available in print and ebook format.

## Connect with Dale Mayer Online

*Dale's Website – www.dalemayer.com*
*Twitter – @DaleMayer*
*Facebook Page – geni.us/DaleMayerFBFanPage*
*Facebook Group – geni.us/DaleMayerFBGroup*
*BookBub – geni.us/DaleMayerBookbub*
*Instagram – geni.us/DaleMayerInstagram*
*Goodreads – geni.us/DaleMayerGoodreads*
*Newsletter – geni.us/DaleNews*